ALL GROWN UP

ALL GROWN UP

Catherine Evans

inkspot
PUBLISHING

First edition published in 2023 by Inkspot Publishing

www.inkspotpublishing.com

ISBN (Paperback): 978-1-7396305-5-3
ISBN (eBook): 978-1-7396305-9-1

Printed and bound in Great Britain by Clays Ltd, Elcograf S.p.A

Typeset using Atomik ePublisher from Easypress Technologies

Cover image: © Aila Bally

For Ricardo

In which the rose discovers that she is a weapon of war.

Victor Hugo, 1802 – 1885

FEBRUARY

TUESDAY

NEVEAH

Neveah lugs her overstuffed book bag up the stairs, wrinkling her nose at the smell of piss in the landings. Daft Punk is blaring from the flat. When the music's this loud, she knows her mum has company. A little crowd of mates, or one of her lame-ass boyfriends. Hard to decide which is worse. Her mum's friends like to party hard into the small hours, and when she's with the *boyfriends*, she doesn't keep things in the bedroom. Oh no. The whole flat's her boudoir. Neveah's sometimes too embarrassed to go to the loo, never mind poke her head out for a cup of tea.

Her mum's a waitress ('*Hostess*, darling') at Jack's Club, so most evenings Neveah has the flat to herself. She'd planned on having a quick supper and spending an hour on Giles's website, before devoting the rest of the evening to her studies. She'd forgotten it's her mum's night off. Her phone beeps. A current runs through her when she sees it's a text from Giles, all typed out correctly, with no abbreviations, as always.

I'd like to introduce you to an old friend who wants to create a website with his son. Can you join us for lunch tomorrow at around 1pm? Gxx

A moment later, a second text arrives, with a link to his mate's profile.

He's based in New York. He could be a great contact for you xx

God, she's lucky. Giles is so into her. He's set up his own consulting architectural practice and has paid her three grand upfront to create his website. Then he'll pay her a grand a month to maintain it and manage his social media. On top of all that, he's leading her to other clients. All thanks to Sweetman. She thinks about her schedule the next day. There's no way she can make lunch with Giles. Shit.

She lets herself into the flat.

Her mum, Marie, sashays over to her. 'Hi sweetheart,' she coos, as she leans in for a kiss. She's had a few, Neveah can tell. 'Good day?'

'Yeah, thanks. Hi, Archie.' She waves to a guy who is as bald as an egg skinning up on the side of the sofa. It's not a good surface. The coffee table in front would be far more practical. Archie's okay. He's a pisshead, but he keeps his hands to himself. And at least she knows him. Her mum brings all sorts home. As well as Archie and Marie, there are two women; a blonde sprawled over an armchair who looks familiar, and a good-looking black woman that Neveah's never seen before.

'You 'member Donna, don't you, sweetheart?' Marie says, waving her cigarette at the blonde, 'and this lovely lady here is Peaches. Peaches just joined Jack's as a hostess. This is my baby, Neveah. Vay for short. Isn't she gorgeous?' She pulls Neveah close and kisses her noisily on her cheek. 'Mwah mwah. My baby girl.'

'Aw, Mum,' says Neveah. She waves at the group. 'Hi, all.'

'Oh my Goooooood, Marie. She is, like, beautiful,' says Peaches. 'And I thought you said she was fifteen,' continues Peaches. 'No way is this little stunner only fifteen. You are a heartbreaker, girl.'

Neveah smiles politely. She takes her oversized navy coat off, revealing her school uniform. Peaches points at her and laughs. 'You look like you're in fancy dress, sweetheart!' She turns again to Marie.

'Can't believe she's still at school.' Then directly to Neveah: 'You gonna have a drink with us?'

'Nah, hope you don't mind, but I got work to do.'

'So polite, Marie. And a grafter too.'

'Yeah, she gets that from me,' says Marie, tinkling with laughter.

Marie's eyes are glassy. She's still waving that cigarette around like it's a wand, dropping ash everywhere. The three women are holding pink drinks.

'What's that you've got there?' Neveah asks.

'Peach Bellinis, darling,' says Peaches. 'S'how I got my name. Your mum's taken to them, haven't you, Marie? Archie here's real boring.' She sticks her nose in the air, affecting his accent: 'I'll stick to a good old G&T, thanks,' and cackles at her own wit.

Archie ignores her and carries on rolling.

Neveah escapes to the kitchen. She finds a lonely frankfurter in the fridge, the last of a packet of ten. She wolfs it down and chucks the plastic packaging on top of the overflowing bin, which is mouldering and stinks of old fag butts. She searches amongst the bottles and jars and is rewarded with a pot of no-brand strawberry yoghurt, which she peels open and spoons up while she continues her search. The Tesco economy brand pizzas she'd stashed in the freezer have vanished. She separates a couple of crusts of frozen bread and pops them in the toaster, before putting the kettle on. She wrestles with herself. Her mum sometimes gets annoyed if she doesn't offer a cuppa to anyone else. Other times, she gets laughed at for even suggesting it when there's booze aplenty. She just wants to eat some supper and get on with her work. Is that so much to ask? She can't help thinking of the home-cooked meals her step-mum, Sandra, produces night after night. Sandra has known Neveah since she was a baby and has always treated her as one of her own. Occasionally, Neveah has caught herself daydreaming that her mum was more like Sandra.

While she waits for the toast to brown, she tries her dad's phone. She hasn't heard from him in weeks. He never listens to voicemail, so she texts instead:

Dads! Call me, yeah?

She knows not to hold her breath. Her text joins an unbroken line of one-way messages with no response from him.

She checks out Giles's mate's LinkedIn profile. His name's Bruce Linneker. He's a partner of an asset management group, whatever that is, called Tremain Street Capital, which has offices in New York, London and Tokyo. Nice photo, she thinks. Quite good-looking, even if he is a million years old. Funny. She doesn't think of Giles that way anymore, and he must be the same age. She considers her timing dilemma for the next day. She has to hand in the English essay she'll finish tonight. She'll get her essay on Stalin back tomorrow. She can't think of anything she could have done to improve it, bar interviewing Uncle Joe himself. Maths at noon. Skiving any other subject is a doddle, but Sweaty Sumner has a preternatural ability to sniff out a lie and ruthlessly checks all alibis. She's wondering how the hell she can get out of school when Peaches spills noisily into the kitchen.

'Toooooooast ... I smell tooooooaast ...' Her eyes are bugged out and her arms are held aloft, like a zombie's. She collapses into giggles. 'Can you bung in a piece for me?'

'Er ... sure,' says Neveah. 'There's two bits there. Not sure if there's any butter though.'

Marie ambles in. 'I'm a bit peckish too. Archie? Donna? Want some toast?'

Neveah quells her irritation and resists the urge to tut. 'There's hardly any bread, and I can't find any butter.'

'Ah, Vay, be a darling and nip out. It'll only take five minutes.'

Neveah grabs her bag. 'Yeah, okay,' she says. 'No problem.' It is very, very important never to show any kind of temper in front of her mum's friends, as the shit that can rain down on her head for it is just biblical.

Marie makes a show of looking for her purse.

'It's okay, Mum. I've got some cash.'

'Thanks, sweetie. I'll pay you back.'

Marie hasn't given Neveah money since she was thirteen and isn't remotely curious about her daughter's constant solvency. Neveah shoves her arms into her coat and is about to exit the flat, bag over her shoulder, when she spins on her heels back to the kitchen. She might as well take the rubbish out, she thinks resentfully. Marie's had all bloody day to do it. She gathers up the corners of the filthy, leaking bin liner, trying not to spill fag ends and old teabags on to the floor while she ties them together. She holds it as far from her body as possible as she thuds down the stairs.

Before she marches to the corner shop, she decides she can bunk off lunch the next day and double English, which follows. She knows Sylvia Plath as if she'd written those poems herself. She'll hand in the essay at breaktime and invent a trip to the dentist's. Marie will sign a note for her. She taps out a text back to Giles.

Can't make lunch but can join for coffee 2ish. Text me location xx

She'll spend extra time on the website, so she can impress the hell out of Giles's mate.

It was going to be a long night.

WEDNESDAY

GILES

The large bedroom is dark, crypt-like. In the light, it's a tasteful mix of muted colours; purples, mauves, taupes and soft browns, but now it's bathed in gloom as it's early morning. So early that the dustmen have not yet been, and all is still except for movement on the bed. It's a man having sex with a woman. Nothing strange about that, but what is unusual about his current activity is that it's with his wife, in the bed that they've shared for close to twenty years.

The man, Giles Hawthorne, is approaching the pinnacle of this joint abandon, and is employing his usual tactic of thinking hard about the test match against Pakistan, to ensure that his wife, Christine, summits first. Once she's safely beyond the point of no return, he allows himself to surrender, and collapses on top of her. For a long while, neither of them speaks. Eventually, he raises himself onto his elbow and kisses her on the forehead. He lies on his back, drawing her close, and stares at the ceiling, which is gradually getting lighter. Where in the name of all the holies had that just come from? His wife, Christine, clings to him, and it's so quiet he can hear, as well as feel, her elevated heartbeat. This is the first time they've had sex with each other in seven years.

It's a breakthrough. Her extensive sessions with various psychotherapists and weekly attendance to a victim's support group must have finally worked. The years since her attack have been terrible. He'd watched, powerless, as she had disintegrated, and had completely withdrawn from normal life. When she emerged from hospital, she was a wreck and confined herself to the house. Now, seven years later, she still won't set foot beyond the garden gate unless someone is with her.

During those early days, she refused food. He did his best to coax her, preparing simple, nourishing meals; thick soups, shepherd's pie, spaghetti bolognese. She'd take in a spoonful, a bite, then would push the plate away.

'I can't face it,' she'd mumble, and would resume her constant stare into the middle distance, listless and lost, or she'd cry. She cried a lot. She tried to hold it together whenever their daughter, Serena, was with her, but the child was at school for hours at a time, and Giles arranged for her to spend some nights away with her grandparents or with Chrissie's sister. It was a relief to Giles when Serena was out of the house, as her bewilderment at the change in her mother was as painful to watch as Chrissie's breakdown itself. Week after agonising week it went on, and Chrissie became so thin she was always cold, and had to layer herself up even in mid-summer. Whenever he tried to comfort her, she flinched from him. It was heartbreaking.

'If you'd only eat something, darling.' He felt that if she took better care of her body, then her mind would begin to recover. He tried tempting her with her former favourites: cheese and pickle on toast, bacon sandwiches with onion and chilli, the gorgeously buttery pastries from the deli round the corner that she used to adore, but she took no notice of food, or would get tetchy that he could be preoccupied with something so trivial when it was plain she just wanted to destroy herself as slowly as possible.

He gave baby food a try: mashed banana, porridge, apple slices. Eventually, he became desperate. 'For the love of God, Chrissie, eat something! Do it for Serena, if for no one else.' Finally, it was only the prospect of being drip-fed in hospital that forced her to consume a few calories. She started with a cupful of soup. Then some cheese and crackers, followed by a buttered piece of bread and marmite, then a square of dark chocolate … and every waking moment since, certainly from Giles's perspective, she has not stopped eating.

'Could have been a lot worse,' his mate Bruce had said. 'Could have been booze or drugs. She'll come round, you'll see.'

And Giles, not wanting to be flippant, had refrained from saying, 'Yes, she has become round. Incredibly round.'

He's done his reading. His research. He understands that some rape victims want to build a barrier around themselves. They want to be invisible, to deflect attention, to make themselves as unattractive to a potential attacker as possible. And he recognised that she would not want sex for a while.

'For a good while,' her first shrink privately advised him. 'Wait until she's ready.'

'Of course I'll bloody well wait! What kind of monster do you take me for?'

The shrink raised her eyes to meet his. 'You'd be surprised what men expect from women.'

He learned to hold his arms in the air, as if facing an armed robber, and say, 'I'm coming in for a cuddle, Chrissie, that's all.' Otherwise, she shrank like a sea anemone. It was wholly understandable, he scolded himself. He would never rush her. He had all the patience in the world.

He had his first affair six months later with a structural engineer he'd met at a conference. They had furtive meetings in bars and hotels, sometimes they'd get together just for coffee and a chat. She had a stay-at-home husband who looked after their two children. On paper, it was the ideal arrangement, as each had as much to lose as the other. She broke it off after a few months. 'I feel too guilty,' she said. 'He trusts me. That makes it worse, somehow.'

The first affair is a bit like committing your first murder. Once you've done it, it's all too easy to do it again, and pretty soon the bodies begin to pile up. There followed a series of flings and one-night stands. He's careful. He goes for women who have no connection to Christine. Those who are bored, lonely, who need a boost to their self-esteem, who crave variety, a dash of romance or some good old-fashioned knee-trembling lust. It's not always him who does the running. They often come for him. This makes him feel less guilty.

He takes them to fancy restaurants, to bars, to decent hotels. He buys them presents and flowers. He likes these women, becomes fond of them, but he maintains a distance and he's always upfront. He tells them he'll never leave Christine. He sometimes tells them Christine's story, then feels grubby as it's the mother of all excuses for adultery. Even worse, it's like a cheap shortcut to intimacy. The tale can't be categorised as 'small talk.' And when he doesn't tell, they find out anyway, thanks to the power of Google.

He's the master of the dead-end relationship. The flash in the pan fling. He won't leave Christine. Not while she needs him. Not while she's battling to overcome her mental traumas. He loves her. He can't pile more misery on to her, let alone Serena, now fifteen and currently in the swirl of GCSEs.

And now he's seeing Neveah.

He becomes aware that Christine is crying. His arms tighten around her. 'Shh, darling. The first time's bound to be a shock.' He lifts her chin. In the stronger daylight, he sees that through her tears she's smiling.

'Oh, Giles. It's all going to be okay now.'

He holds her close and hopes she can't see his face. If Christine ever suspected his infidelities before, she'd never said a word. All the little liaisons he'd got himself involved in during the past seven years… he could have easily walked away from any of them. But he can't just wash his hands of Neveah. She's so adorable. So much fun to be with. She makes him feel half his age. The way she looks at him … as if she'd taken dedicated lessons in how to make a man feel good. Plus, it would be beyond tiresome to have to find someone else to do all that social media guff. She was doing a brilliant job. But Christ on a bike, if Chrissie found out about Neveah … he feels a tightening around his heart at the prospect. Christine's eyes are closed, and her hair is spread all over his upper body, covering her face. He can't see her smile, but he can sense it. He's got to dump Neveah, he thinks grimly. Nothing else for it. But then he pictures her lovely luminous young face, her laugh, those clever hands, that unbelievably cute dimple … he can't help noting the contrast between Christine's heft and Neveah's youthful slimness. He tries to banish the thought and feels shockingly disloyal when he can't. He focuses furiously on the batting stats of England against Australia to stop himself from getting hard again.

NEVEAH

Neveah checks her phone as soon as she's on the bus. Giles has sent the restaurant details. Still nothing from her dad. It hurts that he can't be bothered to even tap out a text every now and then. It would take him seconds and would mean the world to her.

She gets out a small notebook in which she has written out the full conjugation of dozens of French verbs. French is her weak subject. A *B* grade will wreck her planned clean sweep of *A* stars.

She's knackered. As well as new bin liners, she'd brought home milk, bread, butter, baked beans and a multi-pack of variety crisps, all of which had been devoured by Marie and her mates faster than if they'd been a pack of starving rats. She'd also bought a box of Cheerios, so there was something for breakfast. The corner shop feast gave the party a renewed kick, and they continued to drink for hours, playing their favourite tracks to each other, singing, dancing and noisily squabbling over the iPod. Neveah did her bit for Giles and tuned out the racket to write her English essay. God knows she's used to that.

She did all her work on a MacBook that Sandra had given her when she started secondary school. Sandra had always been way more ambitious for her than either of her own parents.

She got up to brush her teeth before bed. She'd been drinking cups of sugary instant coffee to keep herself alert, and her mouth felt coated in fur. Music still blaring, Marie had passed out on one of the sofas. Donna was gone. Archie was fast asleep, still upright on the sofa where he'd been sitting earlier, except Peaches was on her knees in front of him trying to coax his lifeless penis into action. Neveah had barked out a laugh, instantly covering her mouth with her hands to shut herself up. Peaches looked in Neveah's direction, but her gaze lacked focus. She showed no sign of embarrassment, but her lizard brain must have registered that she was wasting her time, so she got up and collapsed onto the sofa next to Archie, burrowing into him, her arm slung around his hairy stomach. Poor Archie hadn't stirred.

As the bus lumbers its way down Coldharbour Lane, Neveah thinks about how he must have felt on waking up with his trousers open, his todger sticking out with a drunken limpet stuck to him. She never found out, as by morning Archie was gone, leaving the two women to their slumbers. Rather than wake her mother, Neveah forged her signature on a note she'd confected to get herself off double English.

She can't help smiling at the memory of Peaches kneeling in front of Archie and how base and ridiculous they both appeared. She will never in a million years throw her dignity away like that, she thinks. An unwelcome voice in her head adds the word 'again'.

The bus is packed, so she loops her arm around a pole to keep herself steady while she holds her notebook with one hand, clutching her satchel with the other. She also has a rucksack on her back, containing her laptop and a change of clothes. She needs the laptop to show her work off to Giles and his mate. Fancy landing a client in New York. She has pictured herself in New York so many times. She's imagined herself in lots of places. The things she'll be able to do when she leaves school. She focuses on the French subjunctive. *Il faut que je le fasse.* It is necessary that I do it. It could be a motto for her life.

She glances up and sees a familiar blonde head among the throng of people. It's Fern. A memory hits her, of those buttery tresses flying through the air in the playground while jumping rope, Neveah holding one end, someone holding the other. *'Cinderella had a fella ...'* they'd chanted, but Neveah had been in another world, wondering what her life would be like if her hair had been that blonde, her skin that white, her eyes that blue.

Fern sees her and waves. Neveah waves back, hoping that'll be the end of it, but Fern threads her way through the crowded bus.

'Hey, Neveah,' she says, and gives her a hug. 'You okay?'

'Yeah, good. You?'

When Fern was ten, her mother landed herself a rich second husband, allowing her to indulge all her social ambitions. Fern, pale and hollow-eyed went home every day to extra maths, French tuition, music lessons, tutor after tutor recruited as part of her mother's desperate drive to get her into Tiffin Girls'. She even rented a place to be within the catchment area. Neveah could have told her for nothing that her efforts were doomed. Fern was quick-witted and funny, but academically, she was a dead zone. After the girls finished primary school, Neveah went to the local comp with the majority of the class, while Fern's tutors managed to shoehorn her into a selective private school.

'Yeah, I'm fine thanks. Mum's panicking about my exams.'

'And you're not?'

'You know what she's like.'

Neveah crumples the corner of her mouth in sympathy. 'You gotta learn to stick up for yourself.'

A glint enters the girl's eyes, and she smiles. 'I do all right.'

Neveah remembers when she and Fern were little, no more than eight, when Fern had skipped up to her mother and asked if she could have a sleepover with Neveah. Fern's mother looked nervously at Neveah, standing next to the furiously chain-smoking Marie, and said: 'We'll see, darling,' which even at that age, Neveah understood to mean not until hell and all its angels had frozen over.

'I went to one of your dad's gigs a couple of weeks ago with my boyfriend. He is soooo cool.'

'My dad or your boyfriend?' Neveah smiles. Her dad, Jackie, is the lead singer of a band.

'Both. You gotta meet him. Josh, I mean. He sells records at Camden Market with his dad. They got a vinyl stall. You'll really like him. His dad's cool too.'

Neveah wants to ask what Fern's mother makes of her talking wide Estuary and dating a market stallholder, but she doesn't want Fern to think she's having a dig.

'This is me,' says Fern, indicating the next stop. 'It was really cool to see you. I'll message you, yeah? Let's meet up.'

'Yeah. That'll be good,' says Neveah, and means it.

While the bus heaves passengers and sucks new ones in, Neveah watches Fern's blonde head bobbing off into the distance, gleaming in the winter sunshine like a beacon. Maybe she'd message Fern first. It had been good to see her. It wasn't her fault her mother was a snobby, racist, social-climbing, Grade A bitch. She looks down at her verbs again and tries to focus, then it strikes her that if she had a child, she wouldn't want Marie to look after it either.

GILES

Giles is at work, but he's taking a moment to surf Cartier's website. He's scrolling through trinket after trinket, imagining Neveah wearing each one, visualising the perfect gift. He can't take too long about it though, as he's got a number of calls to make and a meeting with a new client before he has lunch with his old friend, Bruce.

Christine's incredible comeback is darkened by the knowledge that he will have to end things with Neveah. He pushes the thought aside.

He takes a sip of coffee as he considers. A ring would be in very poor taste, obviously. He deliberates between a gold chain with two interlocking ovals riveted with diamonds, and a gold bracelet, which will gleam brightly against her beautiful skin. 'Yellow gold or rose gold: how far would you go for love?' he reads on the website.

It's a ridiculous question.

How much will you stake for lust? That would be more honest. As well as all the usual things a married man risks by having an affair, he's dicing with Christine's fragile recovery.

Christine wouldn't leave him, he rationalises. She couldn't. She can't even leave the house by herself. She wouldn't be able to cope without him. He recognises that banking on her dependency is actually quite loathsome.

He loves her. So why can't he ditch Neveah? Sooner or later, he's going to have to do it.

He decides on the bracelet. This will be a goodbye present, not a love token. As he enters his details, he's obliged to reveal his date of birth. He's often shocked by how far he has to scroll down to find the year that he first appeared on the planet. He has never been concerned by his age before, but suddenly the weight of all those years is oppressive, and they sit in the forefront of his mind when he thinks of Neveah. Men have always been drawn to younger women, as if their very youth and glow were properties that could be assimilated, sucked in like a vampire draws blood. He understands that these powerful feelings are a trick of the genes. He's read books about it. He opts to pick up the bracelet from Cartier on Old Bond Street. He can't have it delivered, obviously.

So. A goodbye gift then, he tells himself firmly. What he's doing is beyond stupid. She's twenty-two, for Christ's sake. When she reaches her thirties, the prime of her life, he'll be past retirement, approaching his dotage. He has to end it. It's a relationship that has no legs at all. But as soon as he talks any kind of sense into himself, he's overwhelmed by the impossibility of walking away from her. She intoxicates him. Only senility will erase the memory of their first kiss. His PA, Julie, had gone home and they were alone in his office; she on an armchair, and him on a sofa. The charge between them had been growing for weeks. They'd been talking about Yoast and SEO rankings, when she'd abruptly stopped speaking. She had stood up and slowly stalked the distance between them and sunk wordlessly into his lap. When he thinks of her, it's of a slow, knowing smile, that dimple, the feel of her in his arms. He's got to finish it. He'll do it soon, he promises himself, knowing it's a lie.

CHRISTINE

Christine is still a bundle of static. She feels like an athlete who has broken some kind of record. She accepts it's a flawed analogy, unless the athlete in question is a sumo wrestler. She stands on the scales. Three stone to go.

She understands that what happened that morning is the culmination of dozens of tiny changes that began a little over a year ago, a minuscule gathering of strength, a growth in her confidence, an ebb in her fear. It had started with her determination to exercise, to once and for all do something about her colossally excess weight.

Once she's alone in the house in the morning, she does at least an hour of work. She translates novels and non-fiction books from their original French or German into English. She works with three specialist agencies who offer her regular contracts. It doesn't pay well, but it's satisfying, and, occasionally, she's lucky enough to work on a book she loves and feels privileged to be part of the creative process. She translates not only the words but the sense of the author's meaning, and pays particular attention to characters, their class and educational backgrounds and likely speech patterns. All the while she's doing this, a part of her brain is gearing up for her physical workout.

She has stuck to the promise she made herself. Every day, when Giles is at work and Serena's at school, she begins with stretches, then she runs on the spot, does press-ups, star jumps, mountain climbers, burpees, squats, the plank. She needs to work on her form, she knows it's atrocious, but the air is pushed forcibly from her lungs and she goes red in the face as every muscle in her body screams, so it must be doing her some good. The groaning of the floorboards is almost as bad as her own gasping for breath. Thank God no one can see her. Once her routine is over, she gets herself ready for her run to the park, which she does Mondays, Wednesdays and Fridays without fail. She gulps half a glass of water and smears some salve on to her lips. Heavy breathing outside in the winter months can result in terrible chapping. On Tuesdays and Thursdays, she walks instead. No less of a game changer for someone who has locked herself up, Rapunzel-like, for so many years.

That morning, they'd all had breakfast together. She wondered if Serena could guess there was a change in the air, that powerful pheromones were flying about, but she gave no sign of it.

She tucks the key to the house in her bra and shuts the door behind her, then walks past the gate and begins to run when she is on the wide, tree-lined street beyond it. Every time she goes out, it's like a marvel to her, a gift. She's cautious, always watchful, but she's finally shaking herself free of the crippling anxiety that has kept her prisoner for so long. She remembers the first time she ventured further than the gate by herself. It all started with visualisation. She had lain on the sofa picturing every detail of the journey beyond the gate, conjuring up every house and every front garden, every tree on the pavement, every sign on the road. She'd gone beyond the gate countless times, but never on her own, not for years.

She focused on her body language; *Look confident*, she told herself. *Hold your head high. Relax. Look ahead, not at the ground.* And it worked. No one paid her the slightest attention. That first time, she walked the quarter mile to the gates of the park, gone for her run, then walked back home again, her heart thumping in her chest, and not only from exertion. Once she was back indoors, she picked up the phone to call Giles, then thought better of it, deciding to keep her adventure to herself. Better to go at her own pace. To manage expectations.

Each day, she starts slowly, then gradually picks up speed. Today is interval training. Short sprints alternating with a steady jogging pace. *I'm not a freak*, she thinks as she trots past a woman with two terriers. Christine's stomach wobbles as she runs, but it's hidden beneath her sweatshirt and the woman doesn't give her a second glance. Christine loves this feeling of invisibility, as reassuring as a safety blanket. A few of her fellow runners acknowledge her with a smile or a wave, as if she's part of a secret club. Most of them are listening to something, earphones in, clutching phones or iPods. Not her. She has to be aware of her surroundings and monitor the people around her, yet increasingly, she catches herself going for long minutes without thinking of lurking danger, but of mundane things, like what she'll cook for dinner, or she becomes wholly preoccupied with a tricky idiomatic phrase which has no easy translation into English. She'll worry at it from multiple angles and will suddenly find she's halfway across the park without the slightest sense of unease.

I'm perfectly normal, she tells herself. *I'm a runner. I'm a working woman, a wife and a mother, like thousands of others in this city. Okay, so I'm forty-seven, I've only recently managed to go out by myself, I've just lost my second virginity and I'm afraid of my own shadow. But apart from all that, there's nothing weird about me.* She smiles and breaks into a sprint as she crosses the road.

NEVEAH

Mrs Beck sweeps into Neveah's History class and hands back marked assignment papers on Operation Barbarossa.

'Katie … Soraya … Nice work, Mo-Q. Jason, I detected a bit of cutting and pasting. I hope you donate a quid or two to Wikipedia. Neveah. A fantastic piece of work. Really incredible. You've broken the mould. Mo-B …'

Blood runs to Neveah's head. In her peripheral vision, she feels the heat of Connor Johnson's stare. His little mate, Kerry Sellick giggles and falsettos: 'Weally incwedible. Bwoken de mould.'

Mrs Beck frowns. 'Settle down, Kerry.'

Kerry makes a face and looks towards Connor for approval, but he ignores her, and she flushes.

'Turn to page 121 in your textbooks please …'

In the next few minutes, Mrs Beck manages to take the entire class to Stalingrad. It seldom happens, but she engages them all with the horror of that wintry hell.

'The Russians made everybody fight. Men, women, children … anybody with a pulse who could pick up a gun had to fight. Guns were in such short supply that the Russians had to crawl behind each other in lines. Imagine wading into battle without a gun, only able to get your hands on one when the poor soul in front of you has been killed, knowing that there's someone behind you, on your side, eagerly waiting for you to die so they can get their hands on it.' Her hands are waving as she talks, and her voice is energised but tinged with solemnity, as if paying tribute to those masses, all long dead and forgotten. 'In the city, the fighting went on for months. People died in their droves.'

Neveah sees that Connor's eyes, so like his father's, are fixed on Mrs Beck and are glowing with a strange light. She experiences a flash of visceral hatred. He loves this kind of shit. Death on an industrial scale, a body count to dwarf the entire Bourne, James Bond and Terminator franchises put together. Like one of his stupid video games. There is only one person in the world she hates more than Connor. That's his father, Blue.

As is usual with Neveah, her research had taken her far further into the subject than required. Stalingrad, the Caucasus, Baku, the Volga, Sebastopol, Moscow, Murmansk, Kiev … she is enchanted with the beauty of these evocative names. In her head, she goes places, becomes other selves; in reality she's been out of London only twice, once with her dad to one of his gigs on the South Coast and years ago on a junior school trip to Cadbury World. Pathetic.

'Brighton and Fookin' Birming-gum,' Sweetman had laughed when they talked about it. It was all right for him. He goes to all kinds of places as his wife Laura works for BA. Neveah starts dreaming again of New York.

Mrs Beck is discussing Stalin. Neveah is thrown back a week to a hotel night with Giles. They had been lying on luxurious high thread count brushed cotton, naked except for soft white bathrobes, waiting for Room Service to arrive (rare steak and chips with a side of broccoli and almonds for him, club sandwich with chips and ketchup for her.)

'When did your family first come over?' Giles had asked her.

'To the UK? My granny and her husband were from Cork, and moved to London, but he didn't stick around after my mum was born. She brought Mum up in Tufnell Park on her own.'

'God, that must have been tough,' he'd said. 'She didn't want to go back to the mother country?'

'She's hard as nails, Granny North.'

'And your dad's family?'

'His grandad came over on the *Ormonde*. I wish I knew more, but Granny South doesn't like to talk about family history.'

'That's a shame.'

'Yeah, it is. There's loads of stuff on the Irish side. Medals, letters, photos, and they all like to talk, there are so many stories, but nothing on the Jamaican side. All Granny will say is that her dad didn't hang about in Liverpool, he made tracks for London as quick as he could. He married a nurse from Trinidad, and my Granny was born not long after.'

'And what's her story?'

'Her family wanted her to be a nurse too, but she couldn't stand the sight of blood, so she worked in the ticket office at Vauxhall Station for years. That's how she met my grandad. She sold him a travelcard and he asked her out on date. He died in a factory accident when my dad was a toddler.'

'God, how awful.'

'Yeah, it was. She never married again. She's got a nice little flat in Elephant and a decent pension with London Underground, but now she's retired it's like she's waiting for the Grim Reaper to show up.'

'Is she ill?'

'She's always moaning about this or that, but none of us can see there's anything wrong with her.'

'Maybe she's depressed.'

The truth of this had hit Neveah like a hammer. She'd been annoyed at not thinking this through properly for herself.

'What about your family?' she'd asked.

'Well, where would you like me to start?'

'Start at the most interesting point,' she'd smiled, and snuggled against him.

'My grandfather was with the RAF and trained Soviet pilots to fly Hurricanes.'

'That's funny. My great-grandad was with the RAF too.'

'Which one?'

'The Jamaican one.'

Giles had nodded. 'A lot of West Indians fought for the Allies during the war.'

'I wish more people knew about it. Most people think the war was purely a white thing.'

He was silent as he digested this. 'I've never really thought about it, but that's probably true. Try and get your Granny to talk. While you still have the chance.'

'We've all tried. She's like a clam. So tell me more about your grandad and the Soviets. Where was he posted?'

'Murmansk, on the Finnish border.'

'That's so cool. We're doing the Eastern Front and Stalin at –' she'd coughed to shut herself up.

'Doing it at what?'

'At college,' she'd said, unable to think of anything else to explain away the bomb she'd just dropped.

'College?'

'Yeah,' she'd said casually. 'I like to do evening classes when I can fit them in.'

'Bloody hell,' he'd said, looking at her in admiration. 'You must clone yourself.'

Another lie he'd swallowed whole.

'Anyway, it's really interesting,' she'd said, sounding lame, even to herself.

He stared at her and furrowed his brow. She held her breath, afraid that he'd finally put two and two together. Instead, he intoned:

'There once was an old bastard called Lenin,
Who did two or three million men in.
That's a lot to have done in
But where he did one in
That old bastard Stalin did ten in.'

And he'd roared laughing. She had smiled. And exhaled.

'Neveah?' says Mrs. Beck. 'Are you with us?'

Shit. 'Sorry, I was …'

'Come on, Neveah. Why was Stalingrad so important to both sides?'

She knows perfectly well, but her face is a mask and she says nothing.

Mrs Beck stares at her beseechingly. Mo-Q puts his hand up. 'Yes, Mo?'

'It was, like, symbolic, Miss. 'Cos the city was named after the boss.'

'Well, there was more to it than that, but yes, there was a lot of hubris at stake for both leaders. Back to you, Neveah. Can you tell us what losing Stalingrad meant to the Nazis?'

She can not only explain what it meant to the Germans, she could go into the ramifications for the whole course of twentieth century history.

She maintains her mask. She can't explain that while Connor's behind her, she can't say a word. She shouldn't care, but when she thinks of the things he knows about her, the things he's seen, she burns all over with a corrosive shame.

Mrs Beck throws her hands up in the air and shakes her head. 'Neveah, I read your essay.' She and Neveah's eyes lock. Kelly Sellick giggles. Mrs Beck looks around the room and blinks, as if remembering there are other children in the room.

'By the time Stalin died in 1953, he was responsible for the deaths of over forty million people, by starvation, execution, by using them in vast numbers as weapons, sacrificing them in whichever way he deemed necessary. Stalin himself said that the death of one man is a tragedy, but the death of millions is a statistic. That tells us something about the human psyche, don't you think? Doesn't that show ...' she pauses, in search of the perfect metaphor.

'That Stalin was a bit of a cunt?' Connor says and the class erupts.

'I'll not have that language in my class,' says Mrs Beck, but she's drowned out by giggles and guffaws.

Neveah doesn't laugh. She takes in Mrs. Beck's stricken face and feels really, really bad.

MARIE

Marie is woken up by the door buzzer. She's in bed. She'd picked herself off the sofa earlier, cold and stiff, swallowed a big glass of water, dragged herself to the loo then had taken herself to her bed, leaving Peaches sprawled out on the other sofa. She takes a look at the clock by her bedside. It's gone eleven. She feels rough. And old.

She drags herself up. Peaches is still comatose.

'Who is it?' she rasps.

'It's me, babe.'

Shit. It's Blue. She's in no state for him. She hesitates.

'Come on. I haven't got all bleedin' day, have I?'

She buzzes him in. She rushes to the bathroom to brush her teeth. She looks terrible and feels even worse. Her mascara has smudged halfway down her face. With the toothbrush hanging from her mouth, she rubs ineffectually at the smudges under her eyes, then flies to the bedroom and throws off her skanky clothes, covering herself with her red silk dressing gown. She's wearing socks, very unsexy, so she rips them off, only to find they've left deep grooves round her ankles. Her pedicure's all chipped, so she pulls on a pair of Uggs. She tears back to the bathroom, scrubs at her teeth then spits and rinses. She madly fluffs some volume into her bleached hair. God, her roots really need touching up. She wonders if she's got some time to splash her face, put some fresh mascara on … she doesn't actually have to open the door 'til she's good and ready … but no, she hears the door opening. Peaches' voice.

She leaves the bathroom and sashays towards them.

Blue takes the scene in. 'You girls had a late one, then?' He gives a rakish grin as he checks Marie out. 'God, you look like you've been shagged bandy already. You going to introduce me to your friend, darlin'?'

'This here's Peaches. She's new at the club.'

'Are you Blue?' Peaches simpers. 'Lovely to meet you. I've heard so much about you. God, this is so embarrassing.' She gestures down at herself and giggles. 'Still in yesterday's threads. I'm gonna have to do the walk of shame.'

'I wasn't expecting you now,' Marie stammers at Blue.

'Evidently not. I'm working 'round the corner so I thought I'd drop by,' says Blue. 'Looks like my luck's in. Two for the price of one.' His eyebrows do a double bounce.

Peaches giggles again. 'I gotta have a wazz,' she says, and makes her way to the bathroom. 'Any chance of a coffee before I head home, Marie?' she calls over her shoulder before she shuts the door.

'Get rid of her,' Blue hisses. 'Fast. I didn't come 'round for no little chitchat. 'Sides. She ain't exactly my colour preference. Not that I can afford to be that fussy these days,' he laughs.

'God, Blue. What are you like? You can't walk around saying things like that anymore. And don't forget who you're talking to. The mother of –'

He mimes a yawn. 'Yeah, whatever.'

'Well it's true. Neveah –'

He rolls his eyes. 'If anyone knows what colour she is, it's me. And all over too.'

'I can't believe you can be so bloody –'

'So bloody what?'

'Barefaced. Anyone else would be –' she pauses.

'Would be what?'

'Ashamed of themselves.'

'And why would I be ashamed? Beautiful little choc drop like her comin' on to me? I'm not made of stone you know.' A gleam enters his eye. 'I bet she's all grown up now.' He cups his hands to his chest. 'Filled out, I shouldn't wonder. No surprise you don't want me to see her.'

'You're disgusting,' she says. That was the thing about Blue. He always took things too far.

He laughs. 'I've asked Connor how she's turned out, but he won't say nothing. Says I should stick to birds my own age, the cheeky bugger.'

They hear the loo flushing and the tap running. He sits on the sofa and elaborately man-spreads while he puts his hands behind his head.

'And what am I gonna say to Peaches? I can't just kick her out.'

23

'You'll think of something. I don't have time to wallow in bed all day like some people. I've got work to do.' He looks her up and down. 'And don't think I'm shagging you, the state you're in.' He rubs his crotch. 'Soon as she's gone, you can get your laughing gear round this, my lovely.'

NEVEAH

Maths over, Neveah ducks into the girls' changing room. Hanging in her locker covered in a dry-cleaning bag is a dark red woollen jersey sheath dress. The plastic protects it from creasing and, she hopes, from the smell of Marie's constant chain-smoking. Neveah is always conscious of it on her clothes, in her hair … She'd been mortified once when Giles had asked her if she smoked. After that, she'd sealed the entire perimeter of her bedroom door with a heavy-duty strip of rubber draft excluder she'd bought from B&Q, and always kept the small window in her room slightly ajar, even in freezing weather. It drove Marie mad as she claimed to feel every gust of wind.

One more thing for them to argue about.

She loves the feel of the dress, which skims her body rather than clings to it. It's cut high on the neck and the hem sits just above her knees. She'd bought it at Selfridge's, where the floor manager, an elegant woman in her forties, had helped her choose something suitable.

'It's for a job interview. I need to look as smart and mature as possible.'

The woman eyed her up and down. 'I do have a few things. I'm thinking of one dress in particular, and you've got the height to carry it off.'

She picked out some items for Neveah to try on. She held the red dress up against her.

'It doesn't look like much on the hanger, but once it's on … I hope you don't mind me saying, but you've got gorgeous colouring. You should go for strong colours. Rich tones. Steer clear of pastels.'

Neveah noted that the woman had felt obliged to apologise, in case she took offence at a compliment. Of course she didn't mind. She wondered if she should say so. She decided it was better to ignore it and focus on the clothes.

Neveah has grown up amongst adults fanatical about clothes, and she's keenly aware of their transformative qualities. Marie's ability to morph from hungover skank into elegant vamp night after night before she goes to the club is little short of miraculous. Neveah's father, Jackie, is willing to spend hours combing the racks in markets and charity shops for the right article to complement a look, being obsessed with cut and detail. Both parents would spend their last brass farthing on clothes before just about anything, including food.

Neveah has also learned a lot from observing her step-mum, Sandra, whose working wardrobe consists of tailored dresses and trousers in sharp or dark colours which always fit perfectly, and never reveal too much.

Sandra had taught her from a young age how to do her hair. Marie used to tie it in tight bunches, to keep it from being 'an untameable mess', but Sandra had guided her on the right products to buy, and had shown her how to smooth it, braid it, train it, tease it. Right now, Neveah's hair is in long braids from scalp to tip, and she loves that she can leave it like this for weeks before the roots grow out.

She smooths her hands over the red jersey, enjoying the feel of the rich, soft fabric. In an ideal world, she could adapt her uniform, but her get-up for school is a study in scruffiness. Once white, her polyester mix shirt from Asda is greying and frayed at the seams, the buttons chipped or missing. The hem of her skirt has collapsed. Her school shoes are worn and scuffed. Her dark blue regulation jumper is massively oversized, with holes in the sleeve ends which she likes to push her thumbs through, keeping her hands warm while she's in class. Covering her hands has the added advantage of hiding her nails, raggedly bitten to the quick, as is the skin around her cuticles. Her nails are her Achilles heel, the chink in her armour. She has searched online for various methods to quit nibbling her fingers. None of them work.

She fishes her make-up bag from her rucksack. She has learned from a master. Marie has a vast cosmetic collection, and a talent for making the very best of herself, adept at working with texture and colour, at covering flaws and shadows and creating contours where none exist.

Neveah dots Golden Almond foundation on to both cheeks and her forehead, blending it in with her fingers, daubing her fine cheekbones with a subtle luminous sheen. She doesn't have time for eyeshadow, which feels too dressy for a day meeting anyway, but she skims her lashes lightly with mascara. She puts her bronze lip gloss in her pocket, ready for last-minute application.

She squirts her wrists and neck with a sandalwood and sea salt cologne which she'd got from Liberty's. 'I don't want anything over-powering,' she'd said to the lady at the perfume counter. 'Something clean. Nothing flowery or fruity.'

She's about to swap her tiny gold studs for a pair of plaited gold hoops but decides to do it only when she's out of the school grounds.

Her oversized coat covers the brightness of her dress and she saunters out of the gates and crosses the road right under everyone's noses, head held high, looking so entitled that no one questions her. She's about to turn towards the tube station when she hears someone calling her name. It's Mrs. Beck. She should keep walking, but she can't stop herself from turning around. Mrs Beck is marching fast towards her, breaking out into a run every few steps. She looks both ways then trots across the road to join Neveah. She pants like a walrus.

'Phew. Give me a minute,' she says. 'God, I'm so horribly unfit.'

'Miss, can we talk tomorrow? I've got to get to the dentist.' Neveah is irritated, as she hadn't bothered handing in the forged note, judging that she could get away with a straight bunk. She wanted to save the note for another time. If Mrs Beck checks with the school office, she's in for hassle.

'I want to have a very quick chat with you. It really won't take long.'

'What is it, Miss?' She feels self-conscious under the make-up.

'Neveah, your essays are excellent. It's not only the relevance of your arguments and the depth of your research. It's the beautifully logical way you arrange your ideas and the quality of your writing. In all my years of teaching, I've only come across two other pupils as bright as you.'

Neveah can feel a big *but* coming.

'But I wanted to ask why you continually refuse to participate in class? You could really raise the level of discussion. There are a couple of kids, Mo-Q, for example, who are really bright, but they need a kind of prod, someone to bounce ideas off, a kind of intellectual sparring partner, if you like.'

'Sorry, Miss, but isn't that kind of your job?'

Mrs Beck exhales sharply. 'If my job was just about stuffing facts into your head, my stress levels wouldn't be nearly so high. My role is to channel your intelligence, let you think for yourself. God knows you're good enough at that, but you hide that glorious intellect under a bushel.'

'Miss, I'm really sorry, but if I miss this appointment, I won't get another one for ages, and my tooth is killing me.'

'Yes, okay. Off you go, but promise me you'll think about what I've said.'

'I promise,' says Neveah, who marches off as quickly as she can without running, promises herself she'll breathe after thirty seconds, and begins a countdown in her head. *Thirty ... twenty-nine ... twenty-eight ...*

Mrs Beck calls her back.

Filled with anxiety and irritation, she responds: 'Yes, Miss?'

Mrs Beck bridges the distance between them. 'There's nothing wrong, is there? You know that if you have any difficulties, any at all, you can tell me.'

Neveah forces a smile. 'Thanks, Miss, but I'm fine.'

'I've noticed that you seem to react really badly to Connor and his little gang. They're not bullying you, are they?'

She almost laughs out loud. 'No, Miss.'

'Are you sure? It's just that – I have to ask. Are they being racist towards you? Because you know we won't tolerate –'

'Honest, Miss. They're' She's about to say that they're no trouble. She could add that a spot of bullying would be infinitely preferable to what actually happened to her, but she's in a hurry, and that can only lead to a bigger conversation. Is Connor racist? His dad is, so he probably is as well. Connor has never said or done anything racist towards her. He looks through her, as if she doesn't exist.

'They're what?'

'They're stupid kids, that's all. I've got to get moving, Miss.'

'All right, Neveah. Remember what I said.'

'I will, Miss. I promise.'

Neveah turns towards the tube station. She has a feeling that Mrs Beck is staring after her, so she doesn't dare turn around. That's all she needs. A teacher *taking an interest* and *showing her concern*. Why can't she be left alone? Neveah knows she's being unfair. Mrs Beck is a good teacher who's only doing her job. She's one of a small number over the years who have recognised Neveah's ability, encouraged her, spent extra time with her, let her take books home. She remembers her Reception teacher, Mrs Markham, who had responded so sensitively to her distress when Sandra had left Jackie, taking Cha-Cha, Neveah's half-sister, with her. The split between Sandra and Jackie had felt like the end of the world. Sandra had specifically asked for visitation rights to Neveah. 'I've known you since you were a baby,' she'd said in reassurance. 'You're Cha-Cha's sister. You're like my child.' Jackie hadn't objected, and Marie could hardly have cared less. Free childcare, as far as she was concerned.

She focuses on the meeting. She lifts her head high and composes her features. The feel of the soft jersey brushing against her skin as she strides across the park is working a kind of magic on her. She's adopting a different shape. She's growing taller, older, more elegant, wiser, more worldly. She's becoming her own avatar. She's shedding the petty concerns of school, homework, deadlines, dinner money, teachers, the politics and the gossip, the effort of doing what she needs to do, while escaping the notice of losers who are going nowhere and can cope with that as long as everyone around them goes nowhere too. She's learned how to navigate that world, how to be the grey girl.

Before she gets to the restaurant, she reminds herself of the points she has rehearsed. She'd checked out Bruce's company website, had a look at the stats and the traffic it was attracting. There were lots of features which could be improved. She knows it's a personal project he wants help with, but it wouldn't hurt to show she's done some homework. For the same reason, she'd googled 'asset management.' Investment, basically. Wall Street stuff.

'Don't undersell yourself,' Giles said to her on the phone that morning. 'He'll pay for quality. Don't forget to ask him lots of open-ended questions. He loves talking about himself.'

'He's a man, isn't he?' she'd responded, making him laugh.

She wonders if she'd pitched herself to Giles too cheaply. Maybe he would have been willing to pay a lot more. If you're really good at what you do, people pay up. It's a lesson worth remembering.

Before she enters the restaurant, she swaps her studs for the hoops. She's so fired up she almost forgets to change out of her cheapo school shoes into the elegant Patrick Coxes she's carrying inside her tote bag. She hastily switches them, and her transformation is complete. She lifts her wrist to her nose and takes in a deep breath of sandalwood and sea salt for luck, then swaggers into the restaurant with regal confidence, more prepared for battle than Boudicca herself.

GILES

Giles is thinking about Neveah's handling of the lunchtime meeting when Bruce calls him from the First Class lounge.

'Are you shagging her?' asks Bruce.

'No, of course not!' Giles splutters.

'How old is she?'

'Early twenties or thereabouts.' Of course, he knows she's twenty-two, but it wouldn't do to be too specific.

'Are you sure? I'd be willing to lay good odds that she's a lot younger.'

Giles feels a flash of alarm. 'Come on now. How many teenagers do you know who run their own business?'

'Anyone can set themselves up with a website and have a business card printed. You sure there's nothing between you?'

'It's not something I'm likely to be confused about. Why do you ask?'

'I don't know, I just have a feeling. I could be wrong,' he says.

Giles doesn't want to press him, knowing that will make him more suspicious.

'Did you see her hands?' Bruce continues, unprompted.

'You mean her nails?'

'Well yes, they were shocking enough. She had a ladder in her tights and when she got her laptop out, I saw she was hiding a pair of very scuffed shoes in her briefcase. Looked like school shoes to me.'

Unconsciously, Giles begins tapping his foot. 'You should have been a spook.'

'Probably. Anyway, I'm glad to hear you're not seeing her, as she's jailbait if ever I saw it.'

'No need to worry on that score.'

When the call ends, Giles goes over every moment of the meeting. Neveah had swanned into the restaurant with so much presence that Bruce turned around to look at her before she'd said a word.

'Neveah, so lovely to see you again,' Giles said, before shaking her hand and introducing her. She refused his offer of food, even though he and Bruce were still working on their mains. Instead, she ordered a sparkling water and a cup of coffee.

There was some chit-chat; about how Giles and Bruce had met at university, how they toured every year with the same cricket team, even though Bruce now lived in New York. Bruce asked her about her name.

'Where does it come from?'

'It's 'Heaven' spelled backwards. It was Mum's idea, but Dad registered my birth, and he got it slightly wrong. He can't spell to save his life.'

Bruce laughed. 'It's quite a popular name in the States, you know.'

'You're so lucky to live there. Of all the places in the world, I would absolutely love to go to New York.'

'Blimey, that's easy. All you need is a couple of hundred quid and a free weekend.' He looked at his watch. 'I have to go soon, so let me outline what I'm after.'

'Giles said you wanted to set a website up with your son.'

'Yes. We've written a book.'

'Wow. Congratulations,' Giles said. 'You're a dark horse. What's it about?'

'It's a memoir. About Sally. My wife died,' he had told Neveah.

'God, I'm so sorry,' she'd said.

'It was a couple of years ago now. Hugo was only sixteen at the time, and we both kept a diary after she died.'

'What happened? If you don't mind me asking,' she said.

'Car accident.' Giles noticed that Neveah's eyes had welled up. She controlled herself, which was just as well, as Bruce was not a touchy-feely kind of guy. 'Anyway, to sum up, I was writing almost daily, and it wasn't until a year or so later that I found out my son was doing the same. We compared notes, and realised that if we published what we'd written, it could help other people who are grieving.'

'That's so –' Neveah said, searching in vain for an adjective. 'That's really moving. Amazing that you're able to share stuff that's so personal.'

Giles couldn't have put it better himself. Knowing Bruce as he does, he's still astonished he would ever do such a thing.

'It's not a miseryfest. Well, maybe it is in places. The hardest part was sharing what I'd written with Hugo. He felt the same way about me. Showing it to others is easy by comparison.'

'Do you have a publisher?' asked Giles.

'Not yet. We haven't touted it round, but I've got a few contacts.'

'I don't know much about publishing,' Neveah said, 'but non-fiction authors are usually required to have a big social media following, especially if they're not household names.'

'Really?' Bruce said, sounding impressed for the first time.

'And it helps if you have a website. And if you're prepared to make appearances, give talks about your work. In bookshops and festivals. Stuff like that. What's the title?'

'Well, we're not sure yet. We have a few ideas. Can you help with the website?'

'Yeah, sure I can. Can I read the book first? I'd get a much better feel for what you need.'

'Absolutely. I can email it to you. No one else has read it.'

'I'm honoured, I really am. I can also help with social media. Do you or your son have any kind of presence?'

'Hugo does. He's better with tech than he is with people. I'm from the pre-Cambrian era. Like Giles.'

They had a brief discussion about site stats, SEO rankings, algorithms and Amazon categories, then Bruce had said his goodbyes.

'I think you've got that one in the bag,' Giles said as soon as Bruce had left. 'How do you know all that stuff about publishing?'

'I read an article about it last weekend in *Tech* magazine. A fluke, really.'

'Better to be lucky than good.'

'Yeah, I s'pose,' she laughed. 'I'm really sorry I can't stick around, G. I've got another meeting. You don't mind, do you?'

'Not at all. I have to settle the bill. I'll see you tomorrow, okay?'

That glorious dimple deepened as she smiled. She stood up and pulled him gently towards her by the tie. Brushed her lips against his mouth. 'I can hardly wait,' she breathed in his ear.

No teen could possibly have such unshakeable self-assurance.

Bruce really doesn't know what he's talking about, he decides.

NEVEAH

Neveah and Sharna are making their way to the swimming pool. Sharna's on a weight loss kick and has roped Neveah in. Neveah doesn't mind. She knows it won't last. Besides, she likes the pool.

'We'll swim for half an hour, yeah?' says Sharna. 'Then we can grab a MackyD?'

'I thought you wanted to shift a couple of pounds.'

'Oh, come on. We'll deserve it after burning all them calories. D'you wanna stay over tonight?'

'Yeah, sure.' Neveah never has to ask permission. She's a totally free agent. Marie works nights except for Tuesdays, and even then she's not fussed if Neveah isn't home.

'So you're not seeing Mister Loverman then?'

'Seeing him tomorrow.'

'D'you love him?' Sharna suddenly asks.

Neveah can't answer immediately. 'I like being with him, if that's what you mean.'

Sharna bobs her head from side to side, curls her lip and falsettos, 'I like being with him if that's what you mean.' She rolls her eyes. 'Ain't what I mean and you know it.'

'He's interesting. He talks about cool stuff.'

'Like what?'

'I dunno … like politics. History.'

'Fucking Snoozeville.'

'I *like* history. And I like that he's done things.'

'Girl, the dude's like a hundred. I hope he's done some things. There's gotta be more to it than that.'

'There is.' She pauses. 'He makes me laugh.'

'Well, fuck me,' Sharna grins. 'He must be good. He can make Miss Frostypants laugh.'

Neveah smiles and nudges her friend. Sharna persists. 'Come on. Seriously. I'm just dying to know what some old skinny white guy has that keeps you going back for more. Besides the dough, of course.'

Neveah rounds on her. 'You know it's not that!'

'Whoa. Easy tiger.'

'It's got fuck all to do with money. He pays me to work. He paid me before we even … did stuff. And he's not skinny.'

'Okay, okay. Chill, will ya? I just wanna get with what goes through your head.'

Neveah isn't sure she understands it herself. He engages her. He's given her a key to a whole new world. He's easy to be with. He's interested in her, not only her body. He gives her stuff to think about. She's happier, simply because he's in her life. And how has she repaid that? By lying to him all the time.

Sharna drops her voice to a stage whisper: 'Is he –'

'Is he what?'

'You know. Packin'? Is it, like, huge?'

'Shut up, Sharn,' says Neveah.

'Is he good in the sack?'

'Like I'd tell you.'

'Well who else are you going to tell?'

'Well obviously nobody.'

'So go on then. Spill.'

Neveah is silent. Does she like sex with Giles? It should be a simple question to answer, but it isn't. She doesn't want to tell Sharna, but Giles is definitely 'good in the sack'. He's a gentleman, he's good at making her feel special. Loved, even. She's good at the posing and the posturing and she knows how to appear keen without straying into porn territory. She loves the power she has over him, a power she senses that he willingly gives her. Altogether, she's fine about the sex. It doesn't feel dirty like it did with Blue. She shudders. Thank fuck her mum finally got it through her thick skull that Blue was a Grade A scumbag.

Neveah is aware that something deeper is going on. There's something she gets from Giles that no one else gives her. He's the only person who touches her. She can imagine Sharna's reaction if she tried to explain. 'Of course he touches you, you saddo. You're having sex, that's kind of how it works.' But he doesn't only touch her that way. He cuddles her. No one else does that. Both her grans used to cuddle her when she was little, and she's sure her mum must have, but now, no one gives her that simple affection. Her mum's all huggy kissy when she has an audience. As for her dad ... she and Jackie have a quick hug when they say hello or goodbye; a mask for the very slender bond between them. How can she explain this to Sharna, who lives with her mum and her dad and her brother and two little sisters, where the whole family cuddle each other all the time? When they're not fighting, she supposes. Bickering, rather. Neveah's seen fighting. She knows the difference.

She casts her mind back to the early days when she used to meet with Giles in his office to update him on the work she was doing. She started to really, really look forward to seeing him. She'd invent excuses to pop in. Yes, he was older, but there was something about him that drew her. He was still good-looking, despite his age. His creases and his crow's feet suited him. She liked his smile. He was always so considerate. He was always funny. Always interested in her. When she showed him things on the screen and he leaned in, she'd try not to let on that she was breathing him in. He smelled so clean. A hint of lime. The scent of a hot iron clung to his shirt. It was all she could do not to bury her face in his sleeve. She remembers trying to explain SEO techniques to him, while longing for him to put his arms around her. The thrill when he finally did ... God. She'll remember that moment for the rest of her life.

She has thought about her options, of course she has. Telling him the truth is unthinkable. 'Yeah, just one teensy thing, G. I'm actually fifteen. Which, er, makes you guilty of statutory rape. Technically speaking only, of course.' She shudders. She hasn't been able to stop herself from imagining a world where Giles has left his wife for a life with her. Once enough time had gone by, then she could tell him the truth. On holiday, maybe. Say they went to Tuscany, or somewhere like that. The sort of place where middle-class couples went all the time. Say he'd be toasting what he thought to be her thirtieth birthday, and she could give a tinkling laugh which would echo round the undulating hills, and she could say, 'Yeah, G, about my thirtieth ...' Stranger things have happened, haven't they?

Statutory rape. It's a horrifying thought.

Not for the first time, she wishes she'd never told Sharna about Giles. Shoulda kept her big gob shut. This secret may just be too juicy for Sharna to sit on.

'Sharn, you'll never tell anyone, will you?'

Sharna leans in, a conspirator's grin on her face. ''Course not. So, come on then. Tell me. What's he like?'

'I didn't mean that! I meant you'll never tell anyone about us, will you?'

'Oh, so it's us now, is it? Jeez Louise, Vay, can I point out to you that the guy is fucking married?'

Neveah wants to give a sassy answer, something like, 'That's his problem,' or 'I never said no vows,' but remains silent. She's thought about his wife, of course she has. She can't picture Christine at all. She feels something like awe for her. Fear, even. The thought of Christine makes her so uncomfortable that she'd rather not think about her at all.

CHRISTINE

Christine's mouth is zinging with the taste of mint and eucalyptus and she's had a bath. She's lying in bed reading while she waits for Giles to join her. Rather, she's holding a book in front of her, but she's not taking in a word. She's listening to Giles brush his teeth, anticipating the moment when they're in bed together. Such an ordinary, humdrum thing, a married couple going to bed, but she's been building up to it all day.

He undresses, tossing his clothes onto an armchair then sits on the side of the bed. He sets the alarm on his phone and turns off the notifications, and then places it on his bedside table, and crawls under the covers, yawning. He leans over and turns off his side light and rolls over to face her. He smiles gently and takes her in his arms, and she's half disappointed, half relieved when he says, 'Let's just cuddle tonight, Chrissie. Let's not rush things,' and he kisses her and is asleep within minutes. She lies awake in his arms for a long time.

THURSDAY

SANDRA

Sandra's wrapping up at work when she gets a text from Cha-Cha.

> Granny south not well. Gonna stay w her tonite.
> Luv u xx

Before she has a chance to respond, another pings up.

> Can get bus straight to skl tmrw

Hmmm. She's thought of everything.

What could be nicer than a teenage granddaughter showing concern for her aged Granny? Sandra is on red alert and calls Cha-Cha straight back.

'What's up with your Granny then?'

'Oh, you know. Same old. Her heart's feeling dicky, she says, and she can't sleep as per usual. The doctor gave her a load of sleeping tabs but you know what she's like, she won't take them. She was moaning that no one ever goes to see her, that we're all too busy, so I said I'd go over. You know. Sleep over for the night.' She sounds mighty casual.

'Is your dad in town right now?'

Officially, Jackie lives with his mother. As he's on the road so often, it does kind of make sense, although the truth is that Jackie has never grown up.

'He's touring,' she says vaguely. 'And Granny says that whenever he's in town he never stays over.'

'New woman, is it?'

'Yeah.' Cha-Cha giggles. She's proud that her dad's a "babe magnet". She has so much to learn.

'Will Neveah be there?'

It's not unusual for the two girls to sleep over at Granny South's, but Cha-Cha has never gone there alone.

'Look, Mum. I'm thirteen now. I'been getting to school by myself for like, two years. You keep telling me I need to take more responsibility. I can get home and pack up the stuff I need and can get to hers by seven. I can eat with her and do my homework after she's in bed.'

Granny South always retires by 8pm, 8.30 tops. It's always been a family joke, how much time a self-declared insomniac spends in bed.

'I'd feel a lot better if Neveah was there.'

'That is so unfair. Just 'cos she's older, don't mean –'

'*Doesn't* mean. All right, all right! Take it easy,' she says. Sandra resolves to call Granny South herself to double-check the arrangement. She has to let the girl make more of her own decisions, allow her more independence. Besides, she can't help a sneaking relief at the prospect of a peaceful evening alone with Leon, with Angelique tucked up in bed. She could pick up a bottle of wine on the way home, cook something nice ...

'Why don't you call Granny yourself?'

'I will. Listen, sweetheart. I'm proud of you, yeah? Looking after your Gran, I mean. You promise you'll do your homework and not just flop in front of the TV?'

Cha-Cha immediately brightens. 'Yeah, 'course I will.'

'All right, darling. I'll see you tomorrow then, yeah?'

'Okay, Mum! Love you!' She's in a rush to hang up, and Sandra lets her go.

She decides to call Granny South only when she's on the bus home. Calling her is not without its risks. The old lady is quite happy to chat at length, even with cold callers, about her bunions, her angina, her chilblains, the weather, the state of the nation. Sandra feels bad. Granny South has always been kind to her and was sad when she and Jackie broke up. 'He wouldn't know a good thing if it smacked him in the face.' She never failed to ask after Angelique, even though the little girl wasn't related to her. 'Tsk!' she said, when Sandra remarked on it once. 'Children are children; blessings, every one.' Nice sentiment, Sandra thinks, although she's not sure it's always true.

SERENA

Serena has told her mum that she and Georgie are going for hot chocolate on Baker Street after school, in case she decides to check Family Locator. She's being overcautious. Her mum's not on her case all the time. She's one of the lucky ones. Some of her friends are policed to within an inch of their lives, with barely a minute of the day to themselves.

It's raining, so she pulls the hood of her coat over her long fair hair and walks towards Baker Street, but not for hot chocolate. She's off to Wax4Life, to get rid of her mortifyingly wild bush. There's an expensive beauty salon off the main drag, but the one she's chosen is half the price. She's already splurged most of her money on a lacy black bra and matching thong. The pictures that Billy texts her are all of bald pubises. Not a spider's leg in sight. Those with hair have it shaved to impossibly narrow little landing strips, teeny little Hitler moustaches. Sometimes he sends her gifs of couples having sex. 'You gotta know what I like, babe.' She gets a dark thrill when they arrive. She plays them over and over when they ping into her inbox, but then deletes them within minutes. She'd shrivel with shame if anyone knew. She agonises that they may leave some kind of digital footprint on her phone.

She knows that real sex is not the same as porn. She's sat through the classes at school. 'Sex is one of the most beautiful and natural things in the world blah blah blah … between consenting partners

39

blah blah … pornography is choreographed and objectifies women blah blah … in real life, it's perfectly okay to say: 'Stop!' no matter how far down the process you've gone … loving sex is always about constantly checking that you have your partner's consent.' Well, duh.

But that was before she met Billy. Now, she doesn't want to let him down.

At Wax4Life, there's a small dark-haired Asian woman at the desk with a hygiene mask on.

'You got appointment?' she says, speech punctuated with glottal stops. 'You got cash? We no take card.'

She locks the door to the street and leads Serena into a side room which contains nothing but a massage bed and a metal trolley with two shelves, bearing various pots and potions, and a tiny sink. She takes the hygiene mask off when they're alone.

'You want bikini?'

'Yes, please.'

'What style you want? French? Brazil? Hollywood?'

'Um … what's the Hollywood?

The woman thrusts a laminated card at her with several pen and ink diagrams. French is a trim, a neatening round the edges. Brazilian leaves a pencil thin strip, and Hollywood-

'Hollywood is no hair. All hair off.' She gestures to her own genital area, then turns round and points to her butt. 'Even here. All hair off. You want?' She smiles kindly.

'No!' says Serena. 'I don't have any hair there.'

The woman laughs. 'We all got hair there,' she says with kindly authority. Maybe you go Brazil. Leave little hair here.' She gestures again to her pubic region.

'Yeah. Okay, thanks.'

'You want butt too?' Once more, she twists around to gesture to her own backside again.

'No thanks!'

The woman laughs again. 'Okay. Skirt up, or take off. Up to you.'

Serena opts to take it off. She doesn't know what to do with her knickers. Maybe she can pull them to the side. She hesitates. The woman gently chides, 'Knicker off! All off!' She obeys.

There's a giant blue paper roll next to the sink, and the woman tears off a long strip and lays it over the massage bed. It's nice to know she won't be lying in direct contact with the faceless strangers who have come in to be depilated, or whatever they call it. She lies down on the bed, naked from the waist down except for her socks. She fights a ridiculous urge to cover her pubis with her hands. Instead, she brings her knees up, but that leaves her bottom exposed.

The woman pays no attention, and hums to herself as she warms up a small pot of wax. She glances at Serena's nether regions and draws in her breath.

'You not have wax before!'

'Er, no. I haven't.'

'Better not have Brazil. Too much for first time. You too hairy. Hurt too much. Better have French. For first time.'

But Serena really wants the Brazilian. Billy will be completely turned off by anything less. The thought of him seeing her bush in all its untamed glory makes her shudder. The gallery of gifs runs through her mind. Bald as billiard balls. Little landing strips. 'I want the Brazilian. But not at the back.'

'Okay. But it hurt. You very hairy. It hurt a lot. Okay?'

'Okay.'

The woman instructs Serena to hold the skin at the side taut, and she applies the wax to the right side first. Deftly, she covers it with a strip then sharply yanks upward. Serena cries out, she can't help it. The pain is unbearable, and her eyes water. She isn't given a chance to recover, before more strips are applied and there is more pulling and an ocean of pain. The woman applies more wax right between Serena's legs. The wax is hot and the skin so tender that she flinches and yells, but, undaunted, her tormentor applies the strip to the wax and pulls again and dabs the wax over and over until she is satisfied. After what seems to be an eternity, she applies some cold cream that smells strongly of chemical cucumber to the outraged skin. Serena cries. She can't help it.

'You okay?' the woman smiles kindly. 'Other side now. You hold again, okay?'

Serena holds the skin taut, and the woman bears down on her with her wooden spatula. A moment before the hot wax is applied to her skin, she snaps her legs shut and draws her knees up to her chest. She doesn't care if her bum's on show.

'I can't! I'm sorry, I just can't!'

The woman chuckles fondly and wags a finger from side to side. 'You not do one side and not other side.' Sternly, she pulls Serena's legs down, grabs hold of her hand and pulls it, gently but firmly opening her fingers to hold the skin taut. 'You hold,' she instructs, as if lives depended on it. They go through the excruciating rigmarole again.

When it's over, Serena's whole pubis is on fire, and she reeks of synthetic cucumber.

'Now we do butt.'

'No. It's okay. No butt.'

'You very hairy there,' the woman laughs. 'I see it.'

Serena is torn. How can she never have noticed that her own bum has hair on it? If she doesn't know about it, then surely Billy won't ever find out? She looks down at herself. The skin is red and raised, mottled and blotched, like a poorly plucked chicken. All the blood in her body has rushed to the site and throbs with every pulse. She looks nothing like the gifs that Billy's so fond of. What if she has gone through this whole awful experience only to turn him off with a hairy arsehole?

Miserably, she nods at the woman, who pats her on the shoulder encouragingly. In resignation, she turns over and lies on her front like a martyred saint.

'Not like that!' says the woman. 'Like this!' and while still standing, she manages to demonstrate being on all fours, with her back arched and her butt well and truly in the air, the better to push her starfish up to the light.

'It soon over,' the woman smiles kindly and pats her other shoulder. Serena meekly does as she is told.

GILES

Giles lolls on the bed naked, scrolling through the cricket updates. He glances up at Neveah putting on make-up at the dressing table. They're in a small boutique hotel in Euston and are about to go out.

She's wrapped in a white towel, fresh out of a hot shower and smells of jasmine and grapefruit. She's sitting in front of the same mirror which had reflected their interwoven limbs, when the contrast between his lily whiteness ('It's okay, it is winter, G,' she'd laughed) and her youthful darkness had driven him almost demented with lust. Now, that beautiful rich brown skin is suffused with an underlying pink, thrown into stark relief by the blinding whiteness of the towel. Caravaggio would be drooling.

Bruce has no clue, he tells himself again. That kind of self-assurance can only come from experience. She's never told him about her previous sexual partners, and why should she? He would never dream of asking her. He reminds himself that it's not all about the sex. Maybe that's what all infatuated old gits say to themselves, he thinks.

She's hooked her phone up to the speakers via Bluetooth (she'd tippity-tapped a few instructions into her phone, and suddenly they had surround sound Spotify, something that would have resulted in hours of head scratching, ineffectual googling and swearing from him), and she's singing along softly to Sam Cooke... 'Yeah, my mum used to be a soul singer. It's how she met my dad,' and the colours and the music and the lingering feel of her touch and the taste of her skin... it can't last, it just can't. She is May and he's... well at least the fag end of October.

She looks at him in the mirror. 'What you thinkin' about, G?'

He gives a wry smile. 'How very lovely you are.'

NEVEAH

Neveah is seated across from Giles at a restaurant on Bruton Street. It's his choice. Modern French haute cuisine, her googling had revealed, with two Michelin stars. Neveah scans the menu with a poker face. What the fuck is a *girolle*? She reads through the litany of unfamiliar words … *langoustine, morel, polenta, jus, speck* … she is a machine which runs on toast, fired by simple carbohydrate all her life. Toast has kept her alive, and it's all she ever wants. Cheese makes it a meal, marmite a snack and jam dessert.

There's a glass of wine in front of her, a deep red which swirls in the glass like a beautiful oil when she picks it up. There is not much on this planet that she wouldn't give to swap it for Ribena. She yearns for the flavour of simply sugary blackcurrant, repelled by this bitter liquid that tastes of earth and metal and far gone fruit. She takes tiny sips which burn her throat.

'It's lovely here, G,' she smiles.

Giles leans forward. 'I wanted to bring you somewhere special. To say thank you.'

'You don't need to do that. You're paying me, remember? There's so much space in here,' she says. 'They could easily fit in a few extra tables.'

'They'd lose their USP.'

'Shouldn't it all be about the food?'

'The food's only a part of it. It's the atmosphere, the service, the pacing of the courses, the wine…' he leans forward and smiles. 'But for me, it's all about the company.'

'Smooth,' she laughs and takes another micro-sip. If she consumes tiny droplets at a time, evaporation might do some of the work for her.

'Have you seen anything you like?'

'Hmm. It all looks delicious.' She hits on the word 'sweetbread.' Yes, she could have that. It sounds simple and comforting. As for the mains, she knows that turbot is a fish, but she can't ask for it, as she doesn't know how to pronounce it. Turbot with a hard T or should she say turb-oh? Her French is bad, but her accent is worse. She could point at the menu when the waiter's in front of her. It comes with Cornish cockles and clams. The only seafood she has ever eaten is shrimp in Granny South's stir fry, drowned in soy sauce and garlic.

She cannot bear the idea of Giles, or even worse, the waiter, laughing at her.

'Do you fancy the tasting menu?' he asks.

Her brain whirs as she scans her choices. She could not eat an oyster, never mind an eel. She has no clue what *foie gras* is, and as for saying the words out loud … it's a bear trap that she would give anything to avoid.

'Maybe,' she says, stalling for time, then carefully says, 'You know, G, I had a really big lunch. I don't think I could eat half of the tasting menu. I might skip the starter too. Got to watch my figure,' she says. Women come out with this kind of bollocks all the time.

'Not on my watch. Why don't you go for the crab?'

The crab is served with a cappuccino of shellfish and champagne foam. She would not be surprised to see fucking mermaid on the menu.

'G, can you order me the sweetbread to start and the fish with the cockles and the clams? I must dash to the loo.'

He glances at the menu. 'You mean the turbot?' he says with a comfortingly hard T.

'That's it,' she says and escapes. To stall for time, she uses the loo. Then she splashes her face with cold water. She looks at herself. Sternly. Silently she instructs her reflection that whatever is put in front of her, she will eat, and she'll do so with a big smile on her face. Steeled, she returns to the table.

'I've got a present for you,' says Giles as she settles herself and picks up her wine glass. From his pocket, he produces a white box, sealed with red wax. It's Cartier. The closest Neveah has ever come to Cartier is Claire's Accessories.

'Oh G,' she says, overwhelmed, 'you really shouldn't have.' And she means it.

'You deserve it, my sweet.'

She lifts the lid to find a gold bracelet, which twinkles beneath the chandelier.

'Oh Giles, it's beautiful,' she says. 'That's the nicest thing anyone has ever given me.' Her eyes smart. She takes another sip of the loathsome wine.

Neveah's phone rings. It's her dad, Jackie. He calls her rarely, and of course, it has to be now. For a split second she considers busying him, but she may not hear from him again for weeks. 'Sorry G, I've got to take this,' she says, and leaves the table. He thinks she's a woman with a business to run, clients to manage. Her own power is intoxicating. She takes the call outside.

'Dads!'

'How you doing, sweetness? What you up to? You wanna see your ole Pop?'

'Yeah, 'course. I been texting you for weeks. Thought you'd been kidnapped by aliens or something.' She keeps it light. She's learnt over the years not to give him a hard time.

'I got a gig going on tonight. With the boys in Old Street. Place called the Havana.'

The 'boys' are his band, a jazz/reggae fusion.

'Dads …' She feels oddly coy telling him she's on a date. It's not as if he'd disapprove; he's really not that kind of parent. 'You couldn't tell me about it before?' It's a dumb question. He never gives advance notice. As far as he's concerned, she's preserved in aspic when he's not around. 'Is Cha-Cha coming?'

'You gotta be kidding me, right? You know Sandra …'

Yes, she knows Sandra. Zero chance of Sandra letting Cha-Cha out on a school night.

Sandra and Jackie have long since gone their separate ways. Now she's older, she understands why Sandra did what she did. 'It's hard having a woman when you're on the road,' she'd heard Jackie say to one of his 'boys'. 'They expect too much. They expect me to go to bed solo when I'm a long ways from home. That ain't easy, y'know? It's my soul,' he'd said, making a fist against his heart. 'It can't help longing for company, and it likes the female kind.' Then he'd smiled his slow, dimpled smile, and laughed. Women were drawn to him, and he couldn't resist them. Sandra and Marie were two amongst legions who had failed to tie him down.

Cha-Cha is Neveah's only known sibling. Perhaps she had others that even Jackie didn't know about. She thinks about this from time to time. She'd read an article in one of her mum's *Bella* magazines about a couple who met and fell in love, only to find out afterwards that they were brother and sister. It had made a huge impression on her. She promised herself that she would check out the provenance of any black or mixed-race boy she should ever be interested in, to eliminate Jackie as a possible parent. As far as she could tell, he'd slept with half of South London.

'Disgustin,' Marie's mum, Granny North, was fond of saying. Forty years of living in London had done nothing to blunt her Cork accent. 'What your mother ever saw in him –'

'Easy, Gran,' Neveah had said. 'He's my dad.'

'Aye, true enough.' She'd chucked Neveah under the chin. 'The morals of a feckin' tomcat, but he makes gorgeous girls. You and that sister o' yours… beautiful, the pair of youse. So true enough, he's given you a touch o'tar –'

'Granny,' Neveah had said wearily. 'You can't go round saying things like that.'

'Don't you be goin' all PC on me. Wi' or wit'out it, you're a looker, an' that's the truth. Your mother's not short o' looks herself. A good dollop o' Irish genes, see,' she'd said proudly.

She pulls herself back to the call. She's torn. If she doesn't drop Giles for her dad, Jackie may not bother calling her next time.

'Oh Dads, I'll see you at the weekend, yeah? I can fit in with whatever.'

'Come now, sweets. What's bigger than your old Dad?'

She reaches for the easy lie. 'I got a big test tomorrow. I –'

It's not Jackie's style to give her a hard time, but he manages it all the same. 'All right, I get it.'

She's stung. 'Dads, it's eight thirty on a week night. By the time I got to Old Street –' He doesn't know she's in Mayfair.

'Yeah, yeah… I get it. I'll see you next time, yeah?'

'So what are you doing later this week? Seriously, Dads, I wanna see you, I do. You going to be at Granny's? I can fit in with anything this weekend.'

'Not sure right now. I gotta go. I'll call you, all right? Take it easy, darling,' and he hangs up.

She takes a minute before she can go back to the table.

'Are you all right?' Giles asks.

'Yeah, I'm fine,' she says.

'Clearly you're not. What's going on?'

She decides to tell the truth. Makes a change, she thinks. 'It's my dad. He called to tell me he's in town and he's made me feel bad for not dropping everything to see him.'

'Where is he?'

'Playing a gig at some club in Old Street.'

'Do you want to go?'

'Do I want to see him? 'Course I do. I haven't seen him for weeks. But. Do I want to sit through a sweaty two-hour gig nursing up a Diet Coke fighting off leery old men only to have Dads disappear with some floozy as soon as he puts his guitar down? No, I bloody don't.' Giles takes her hand. 'Do I want to watch him and his mates getting stoned or getting lost in chat with a load of guitar anoraks? All Dads wants when he's finished playing is a beer and a spliff and a squeeze, and spending time with his daughters is pretty damn low on his list.' She wipes away the hot tears that spill from her eyes with the back of her hand. 'God, sorry, G. I don't know where all this is coming from.'

He reaches into his pocket for a handkerchief. It's blue linen, clean, folded. He hands it to her. She laughs through her tears. 'You're exactly the type of man who would have a clean hankie. No wonder I –' she stops herself.

'Hardly top of the list in a romantic hero.'

'It is to me,' she smiles. 'So did you order?'

'I did. Shall I cancel? It's not too late.'

'Nah. He can go –' She stops herself from saying *fuck himself.* 'He never tells us, never gives us a chance to plan.' She takes a big swig of her wine and narrowly avoids choking. 'He's always been like this. Me and my sister –'

'Your sister?'

'Yeah. I got a half-sister, Cha-Cha. Charlotte. She's also got a half-sister, Angelique. Angelique will probably get another half-sister one of these days. The line will go on and on, like them Russian dolls. Actually, that's not true. Sandra and Leon are pretty solid.'

'Sandra? Leon?'

'Sandra's Cha-Cha's mum. My step-mum. She's all right. Leon's her husband, Angelique's dad. So far, so EastEnders.'

'How old is Cha-Cha?'

'She's thirteen.'

'Oh, so a fair bit younger.'

'Uh-huh,' she says noncommittally, sipping more wine. Her mind buzzes, as she takes stock of the traps she has set for herself.

'Are you close?'

'Yeah, but she thinks I nag her all the time. Sandra's always trying to keep her in line. She worries about her seeing Dads. Don't blame her, really. Cha's only thirteen but she looks a lot older and she's a man magnet. She's a flirt, loves attention, and Dads doesn't exactly keep a close eye on her. The only time we get to see him is when he's playing, so Sandra only lets Cha come if I'm there as well.'

The food arrives.

'Sweetbread for Mademoiselle,' says the waiter. Neveah stares in dismay at the pink ectoplasm she's been presented with. It sits in a red syrup which shines like a gelatinous pool of blood. The entire horror show is garnished with small green leaves and a few slices of… fuck. Radishes. She doesn't dare to breathe.

'Mmmm. That looks delicious,' says Giles. He has something cheesy in front of him, something that looks like one of Granny North's cheese scones. It spills generously from a ramekin, looking like a jaunty little chef's hat, and is surrounded by a tempting white sauce, spoilt only by more malevolent radishes. They must have a job lot in the back. The entire arrangement is dusted with a sprinkling of red powder.

'What's that you've got there?'

'It's a crab soufflé.'

Ugh.

'What's that red stuff?'

'Espellette pepper. Gives it a little kick.'

'Looks yum.' Shit. Swapping plates is not an option. She can't even eat a Chilli Dorito.

'Go on, my sweet. Tuck in.'

She picks up her fork. She'll put one piece of blubbery pink after another into her mouth until it's gone. How hard can it be? She can ignore the radishes. Giles waits for her to start. She picks up her cutlery, then notices that he only has his fork in his hand. Maybe she should do the same? Put her knife down? She breaks up the ectoplasm with the side of her fork. Through the metal, she divines that it's soft, like rotted ham. She remembers the pep talk she'd given herself in the cloakroom. No matter how long the next ten minutes may seem to last, they will soon be over, and she will survive this horrendous experience, and the ectoplasm will not. Simple as that.

SERENA

Serena is lying on her bed with her homework scattered about her. Her mother nags her about using her desk instead. 'Much better for your back,' but she prefers to stretch out on the bed, writing propped up on an elbow or leaning against the bedrest, cushioned by a mountain of pillows. She has the radio on. 'How you can concentrate with that racket on ...?'

It's not the music that stops her from concentrating. She wants to call Billy. Her fingers are tingling with the desire to text him, but she doesn't want to appear too keen.

Her nether regions are still throbbing. She has applied more cream to soothe the area, but her newly naked pubis is inflamed with raised bumps, like the skin of a red and mottled raw chicken. She prays that it calms down by tomorrow. The woman at Wax4Life had also suggested she get her eyebrows threaded. She'd drawn her finger across her own brows and said:

'Here. I make neat, no? You very –'

'Yes, I know. Hairy,' Serena had said in resignation.

Her mum had noticed immediately. 'Oh darling, I wish you'd told me. I'd have taken you to –'

'Does it look that bad?'

'No, not at all,' Chrissie had said hastily, 'just painful, that's all. It'll settle down in a day or two. You can calm it down with a dab of foundation until then. Why did you suddenly decide to do it?'

'Dunno,' she'd said miserably. 'I got fed up with looking like a werewolf.'

'That's ridiculous, darling. You had – you've got lovely eyebrows. I probably wouldn't have chosen to have as much off, that's all. Anyway, the genie's out of the bottle now,' she'd warned. 'Now you've started, you'll have to carry on.'

She wonders how her mother would react to the Brazilian. The girls in the gifs must submit to that kind of torture all the time. They weren't red and mottled. They looked smooth, tanned, natural, as if no hair had ever sprouted there in the first place. She winces when she recalls the agony. To add insult to injury, her throat is burning. She hates smoking but has been practicing with Georgia so she can look cool when she's with Billy and his mates on Friday. Georgia's been smoking since she was thirteen. She's got a load of older siblings and all of them are dedicated nicotine fiends.

She's too wired to focus on river erosion and oxbow lakes. She picks up her files and dumps them on the floor. She'll get up early and do it in the morning. She turns her main light off, making sure her night light is on before she settles herself for sleep.

She thinks about Billy. Her parents wouldn't approve. If she's honest with herself, she'd be embarrassed to introduce him to them. He's not educated. He smokes, he drinks, he takes drugs. She's never seen him do it, but he speaks casually of 'scoring some weed,' 'rolling a spliff', 'dropping acid' and 'taking E's.' Mainly, she's afraid Billy will realise what a dork she is. She's never done any of that stuff, not that she's ever wanted to. She knows that the truly cool kids do whatever they want, that they don't succumb to peer pressure. They know when to dig their heels in. That's exactly the trouble. It's not easy gauging when to yield and when to stand your ground. She's afraid that whatever Billy asks her to do, she'll go along with, and then he'll despise her. She shivers when she remembers the feel of his touch, the smell of his skin. He's bristly, and when they first kissed, he'd rubbed the skin around her mouth raw.

Her phone pings. He's sent her a gif of a guy going down on a girl. She stares at it, fascinated, then deletes it. There is no way she can endure his bristles scraping against her newly raw tenderness. She clamps her legs shut at the mere thought.

She can't stop thinking about him. She wants him. For a long time, she'd worried she might be frigid, but now she knows she can't be, as the gifs he sends her turn her on. They make her want to have sex, which is a good thing. It must be.

They've never done it, not yet. Friday is D-day. His mate Deacon is having a party, as his old man's away. 'Deak's sorted it. We've got a whole room to ourselves, babe.'

Billy has slept with a load of girls, apparently. He likes girls who are 'totally up for it' and has dismissed some of his exes as being 'a lousy lay,' or plain 'shit in bed'.

'How can a girl be shit in bed?' his mate Andy had asked him. Serena had been dying to ask the same question.

'You know. She just lay there, like a slab of meat. Wanted me to do all the work.'

Andy said, 'Me, I'm so grateful for a piece o' gash I don't care, so long as the owner's breathin'.'

They'd all laughed, including Serena. It *was* funny, until she'd set to thinking. What 'work' will she be required to do? Was it something you learned, or did it come naturally, like dancing? Now she's seen some of the gifs she has more of a clue. She wants to get it over and done with, so the next time she'll know what to expect, and can relax and enjoy it.

Having sex at a party poses its own set of problems. Will the room be private? What if someone walks in on them? What if she needs the bathroom?

She hopes she won't choke on his dick. Her gag reflex kicks in even when she brushes her back teeth too vigorously. The girls on the gifs look as if they're loving it. That's the secret to being good in bed, probably. To look as if you're having a whale of a time, no matter what is done to you.

'I've never waited so long for a girl before,' Billy had whispered to her when they'd last met up. 'You're special, babe. Worth it, you are.'

She hasn't told him she's a virgin. He must know, mustn't he? She hasn't spelled it out. He may think it's lame. On the other hand, she doesn't want him to get the idea she's a slut.

'You should just tell him,' Georgia said. 'Everyone's got to start somewhere.'

There are so many moving parts to worry about. Even if she'd wanted to leap on him the moment they met, they haven't had the opportunity. He lives with his mum. She's old-fashioned, and Serena hasn't met her yet. It's out of the question that she brings him here. Christine never leaves the house. He laughed when she told him. 'What? Never? She's been indoors for seven years?'

It's all she's ever known, her mother not leaving the house. It was only gradually that she began to realise that other mothers left their houses all the time – to go to work, to the shops, to take their kids to school, to get a breath of fresh air, a change of scene. There were a million reasons to get outside, but her mum never did, not on her own. 'That is so fucking weird,' Billy had said, and she wished she'd never told him.

Then there's the problem of protection. Maybe he'll expect her to be on the pill? She isn't, and there's no way she can go on it before tomorrow. Georgia's been on it for at least a year. Her mother got her the prescription to help get rid of her acne. 'You have to start on the first day of your period,' her friend told her.

Hers isn't due for another couple of weeks. Right in the middle of her cycle, isn't that her most fertile time? Should she say something, ask him to bring condoms? She would shrivel up and die rather than buy them herself. And even if she turned up with a three pack, wouldn't he think her a Grade A slag?

'That is so dumb, thinking like that,' Georgia said. 'This is the twenty-first century. Hasn't he been banging on about having sex with you for weeks?'

She's right. Having sex at Deacon's party thrills and terrifies her. Deak and Billy work together at the cycle shop. Billy's been working there for six years. She can't believe that someone of his age and experience could possibly be interested in a schoolgirl with spots and braces. 'You're beautiful, babe,' he'd said, and kissed her.

She's told her mum that she's staying at Georgia's. Her mum has already texted Georgia's mum to check that it's okay. Georgie is coming to the party with her. She's the youngest of five, and her parents are pretty relaxed about what they get up to. They all do their own thing, go out to parties, to sleepovers, and her folks aren't bothered, as long as they come home eventually.

Serena's mum knocks on the door. The night light's quite bright, so she can't know Serena was trying to sleep. She comes in, looking grim-faced.

'What are these?' she says. She's holding up a packet of cigarettes.

Shit.

NEVEAH

The uber drops Neveah outside the Havana in Old Street, where Jackie's band, Moore Town, are doing their set. She's been furiously chewing gum in the car, to get rid of the taste of the eye-poppingly extortionate dinner she's just shared with Giles. The remembered feel of the sweetbread lingers and makes her want to gag. The turbot was just as bad. 'The taste of the sea,' the menu had promised. Instead it was like a blast of Billingsgate right in your face. She would have paid the bill twice over to swap it for a fish finger.

'Let me get this,' Giles had said.

'No, I told you,' she insisted, reaching for it. 'It's my treat. For all you've done. For being such an ultra-cool client. For introducing me to Bruce. For not giving me a hard time 'bout seeing my dad. Not many blokes would be happy with me disappearing in the middle of a romantic night out.'

'I'm not happy,' he said drily, as he picked up her hand and kissed it.

These are the things she can't explain to Sharna.

'Sure I can't come with you?' he said.

'Seriously, G … I can't even be thinking about introducing you to my dad, not yet.'

'He won't know we're involved. I am your client, after all.' Thinking about it now, she almost laughs out loud at how Jackie would respond if she introduced anyone as 'her client.'

It's not only her dad she's worried about. Sweetman doesn't miss a thing. Someone's bound to mention school or say something that could give her away. She can't take the risk. She's glad Giles is safely tucked up in the hotel.

'But I'll see you there later, won't I?' she'd said. They don't manage to spend a whole night together very often. He has to catch a 9 o'clock train from Euston to Manchester in the morning to visit a client. She told him she has an early morning meeting, but of course she has to go to school. Her uniform is in the girls' changing rooms. Her coat hides her disguises.

'I'll probably be asleep when you come in,' he warned. 'I'll try and wait up for you, but I can barely keep my eyes open past eleven. That's what happens when you date a geriatric. I'll leave a key for you at reception.'

She laughed. 'I'll slip in beside you. I'll be like a ninja. You won't even notice I'm there.'

'Believe me, sweetheart. I'll notice,' he said, and kissed her.

When the bill arrived, it gave her a brain freeze. Giles again tried to pay, but she'd stupidly insisted. 'I can claim it on expenses, G…' The wine by itself … it baffles her that people pay to drink that bilge. She's furious with herself. What was she trying to prove?

She wraps her thin coat tightly around herself as the wind is blowing right through her. The guy at the door asks for her ID. She's got a fake one which he barely glances at before nodding her through. Her shoes stick to the red carpet bolted on to the stairs leading down to the basement. The sound of the music is muffled as she follows a narrow corridor past the cloakrooms, then as she pushes her way through a pair of swing doors leading into the darkened club, it ramps up into a wall of sound as she enters a cavernous room full of people, breathing in heat, booze, electricity and sweat, mingled with aftershave, hairspray and perfume.

Jackie's in his stride, singing *Skin to Skin*, which he wrote for Marie when he still loved her, and he keens in an unstrained falsetto while 'his boys' do their thing: Sweetman on drums, Bingo on bass and Stevie on guitar. Jackie plays guitar too, but Stevie's lead. Sweetman sings harmony, his deep bass a counterpoint to the falsetto. Bingo's wearing his customary sunglasses. The others josh him for it. 'Think you're Bono, bruv?' but he pays them no mind.

She leans against a pillar to listen. She can't understand why they've never hit the big time with this song. They're signed to a label and they have a manager, but it's always jam tomorrow.

They have a small but dedicated grassroots fan base, and they eke out a living playing support to bigger and better-known bands, appearing at music festivals dotted around the country, sometimes abroad if they can get their expenses covered, but mostly they play in clubs like this one, earning a few hundred a time which they split between them, squabbling over phone bills, petrol money, printing costs and other expenses. Bingo can be relied on to recall, even after several weeks, who paid for the last round of drinks and how much four boxed sandwiches at Leigh Delamere Services set him back and pro rata how much. The others moan about it, but he stands his ground, and they all eventually pay up. Jackie never gets involved in the wrangling. He squares things with the others when they demand it, but he cheerfully gets away with not paying his share when he can. Getting away with things is what Jackie does.

She loves watching Sweetman when he's drumming, keeping time while backing Jackie. His short dreads have cast a dramatic shadow on the curtain behind him, and he has beads of sweat on his brow. He's wearing one of his tight Hawaiian shirts. He's not fat, but he's stocky, well-padded, and his head, his body and his feet all move in time to the music while he leans into the microphone, his belly pulsing back and forth as if it's an independent organism.

For a long time, she'd had a mini crush on Sweetman. No way would she ever have acted on it. He thinks of her as a daughter. Even if he didn't think of her that way, he would never cross that line. Too loyal to Jackie, and he and his wife, Laura, are solid. Laura's been good to her.

Laura and Sweetman have always had an open door for Neveah. He's the only member of the band that has an outside income, creating websites and managing social media for sole traders and businesses, including other musicians and bands. At age twelve she started helping him when he had too much work on, and within a few weeks, she was working for him on weekends. 'You're a natural, girl. Promise it's not eating into your homework time?' She's learned a lot from him. 'It's better than flipping burgers or flogging weed, let me tell you. It pays way better than music, sad to say.' They talk shop a lot; they're both passionate geeks.

It's Sweetman who referred her to Giles.

'Some guy rang. Wants a website. I got too much on. You think you can handle it? He sounds posh.'

She'd gone for it, and it had changed her whole life.

Bingo and Steve scorn his day job, calling him a sellout, even though he has never failed to turn up to a gig, and it's thanks to his social media work that they get most of their opportunities. 'Yeah, but if you spent your days on the band and not just nights, we coulda made it by now.' He rolls his eyes and laughs. 'Coulda. Woulda. Shoulda. It's kismet, innit?' He loves the tech as much as he loves the music, so he bridges both worlds. He's tried to explain to the others, but it's 'like talking a different language' as he told Neveah. 'I can't raise a family on gig money. Let them dream about the big time, but some of us gotta stay real.'

Jackie would never vote to kick him out, so Sweetman stays. He's not worried. He knows Jackie well. Jackie would happily give a kidney to avoid any kind of confrontation.

Sweetman sees her. She smiles and waves. He fixes his eyes on hers, widens them and swings his gaze in an arc towards a couple dancing as if the tables around them don't exist. She follows his gaze, but it's too dark to see them clearly. A white guy dancing with a black woman, that's as much as she can make out. They're under a strobe, which highlights the woman's red dress and her wildly teased long hair. She's got some moves on her, Neveah thinks, even though she's clearly drunk. Sweetman looks at her again and gestures with his head once more in their direction without breaking time. He's trying to tell her something. She decides to get a drink, then edge closer to find out.

The club's busy. This is good, as Bingo often wangles a percentage of the bar takings. She orders a Diet Coke. Some dark, flavoured fizz is squirted into a glass overfilled with ice cubes, for which she is charged a fiver. 'A slice of lemon too, please,' she shouts above the music.

'We're out,' the barman says.

'What about those?' She can see a few whole lemons lurking behind a stack of greenery.

'Only for mojitos, love.'

The vast profit margin attached to the watery aspartame surely merits a lemon slice, but she doesn't argue. She takes her glass and eyes the tables, looking for an unobtrusive place to perch until the set is over. She doesn't fancy the kind of company that lurks in these clubs, but whether she likes it or not, she's never left alone for long. She heads for a quiet corner near the dancing pair. They're really going for it. The woman in red laughs as she is suddenly and violently spun round, clasped by the waist and then bent over backwards by her partner, almost knocking Neveah and her drink over.

'Watch it,' she says. She doesn't fancy wasting another fiver.

'I beg your pardon,' the man says. He's wearing a white trilby and an ice cream suit. Who does he think he is? James Bond? He has a moustache. That's enough for Neveah to dismiss him completely. If he's famous, he's no one she recognises.

The woman turns and waves glassily in her direction.

'Cha-Cha!' says Neveah. 'What the bloody hell are you doing here?'

'Nice to see you too, sis.'

'Your sister?' says the man, raising his eyebrow. 'This evening just got a whole lot more interesting.'

Neveah is about to let loose, to tell the scumbag that Cha-Cha's only thirteen, but she shuts herself up. She'll get them both kicked out.

'Have you been drinking?' she hisses at her sister. It's a pointless question. The scumbag laughs.

'Has she? She's got a thirst, haven't you, little one?' He has his arm around Cha-Cha's waist, as if he's propping her up. 'Can I get you something too?'

'She really can't hack it,' Neveah says. 'I'd better put her in a cab.'

'Oh go on, Vay,' says Cha-Cha. 'Lerrim buy you a …' she hiccups, 'a drink.'

'I've got one. It's a soft drink,' she enunciates, as if she's talking to a toddler. 'Maybe you should try it sometime.'

'That's not very festive, is it?' says Suit. Neveah can see him more clearly now. That moustache makes him look like a paedo. He has a pinched look around his eyes.

'Seriously, I should get her home,' says Neveah.

'I don't wanna go home, Vay,' says Cha-Cha, hiccupping again.

'Your mum's gonna kill you,' she says. 'How did you get her to let you out?'

'I'm not a cat, you know.'

Suit laughs. The song has ended. Jackie launches into 'Alone Now'. Anyone listening would think he knows how it feels.

The man in the ice cream suit looks at one girl then the other. 'Sure I can't get you ladies a drink?'

Neveah really, really wants to tell him to piss off.

'Double voddy for me with orange,' giggles Cha-Cha, looking lovely, even if she's wasted. Her eyes are wide and her cheeks shine with exertion and booze. I bet she'd get a slice of lemon, thinks Neveah sourly.

'I don't think so,' says Neveah, sounding like their Granny, even to herself. 'I've got a Diet Coke.'

Cha-Cha turns her attention to the band, swaying from side to side, her arms in the air singing, *Alooooone Now. Can't you see I'm Alooooone Now.'* She builds up to the crescendo: *'Never been alone before... so afraid and still so raw ... Alooone Now ... Never been alone before ...'*

'Can you get her an orange without the vodka?' she whispers to Suit. 'She'll never notice.' He scuttles off to the bar.

'Seriously, Cha ... you gotta go home. You are wasted. How'd you even get out?'

'I blagged a stay with Granny South tonight. She's not been well, you know?'

'What's wrong with her?'

'The usual. Mum thinks it's really sweet that I'm being such a good granddaughter,' she bursts into laughter, abruptly silenced by another hiccup. 'All I had to do was wait for the old girl to go to bed. You know what she's like.' Neveah does know. 'It's even worse now she's sick.'

'What if she wakes up and finds you gone?'

'I thoughta that.' Cha-Cha is clearly proud of her own cleverness. 'I left a note for her saying you needed to see me. I can bunk at yours, can't I?' Cha-Cha has stayed with Neveah before. To be fair to Marie, her open door policy even stretches to her ex's children.

'No. You can't. I'm not going home tonight.'

'Whaddya mean you're not going home? Where you going?'

'I'm staying with a friend.'

'Sharna won't mind if ...'

'Not Sharna. It's ... complicated.' There is no way she can take Cha-Cha back to the hotel. And she can't let Giles down. Not again.

'Well, where'm I gonna stay?'

'You shoulda thought of that before! Why didn't you call me first?'

'Why didn't *you* call *me*? You didn't even tell me Dads was gonna be here tonight,' she pouts accusingly.

'He called me literally one hour ago. You know what he's like. I didn't bother telling you 'cos I thought there was no way your mum would let you out on a school night. How did you even know Dads was gonna be here?'

'Saw it in *Time Out*, didn't I?'

Cha-Cha gets unsteadily to her feet and turns toward the band to join in the chorus. Neveah catches Sweetman's eye. He winks at her, clearly relieved that she's taking charge of her younger sister. Jackie's unconcerned, even though his thirteen-year-old daughter is getting smashed and throwing herself at some ancient old geezer right in front of him.

'What's gonna be's gonna be,' is his byword. No wonder Sandra goes ape about Cha-Cha spending time with him unsupervised. Cha-Cha can sneak into Granny South's the same way she sneaked out, Neveah decides. And if she gets caught, that's her problem. She glares at her sister but softens as she watches her singing along to the band. Cha-Cha loves Jackie, same as her, and gets precious little of him. Same as her. She stands and takes her sister's hand and lifts it in the air in a salute to their father onstage, who beams down at his two lovely daughters. *'Alooooone Now ...'* she sings. Cha-Cha turns towards her, delighted, and ramps up the volume. The two of them croon up at him together, *'Never been alone before ...'*

CHRISTINE

Christine is sitting on the sofa, too wired to go to bed. She's drinking herbal tea to calm herself down. She can't get hold of Giles. God, she wishes he were home. The cigarettes were one thing, but this ... she thought she knew her daughter.

'I can't believe you've been snooping in my things!' Serena had shrieked when Christine held up the packet, going from nought to a hundred in an instant. The two of them seldom have a cross word for each other, so it was a shock for Serena to launch into banshee mode.

'You left them in the pocket of your skirt. Which you put in the laundry basket. I hardly call that snooping. Haven't we warned you? Don't they constantly lecture you at school? Look at the disgusting picture on the packet, for crying out loud.' The pack bears a rank picture of a smoker's blackened teeth and diseased gums.

'I'm looking after them for a friend.'

Christine laughed. 'Can't you think of something more original?'

'For fuck's sake! Do you even know what it's like to be me? To have a mother who's so off the scale weird that she never leaves the house?'

'Serena, I –'

'If I smoke, it's so I can fit in. So I can feel normal. Do you even know that? Do you even care? Other people get on with their lives. Other people get over things.' Then she burst into uncontrollable sobbing.

Christine knew Serena wasn't upset about what she was pretending to be upset about. 'I do leave the house. All the time.'

'Yes, but never alone.'

'Are you sure this is the only thing bothering you?'

'Yes of course I'm sure!'

'I have a feeling you're stressed out about something else. I've felt it for days, weeks even. You know you can talk to me, darling. To us, I mean. But before we get off point, you know I can't have you smoking. It's a stupid, disgusting, ridiculously dangerous, addictive and expensive habit. How long has it been going on?'

'Not long. I hate it, Mum. Honestly, it's horrible.'

'Everyone hates it at first. You do know that, don't you? When I –'

'Yes I know!' Serena violently interrupted. 'When you were young, you smoked like a two-stroke engine. You've told me before. I get it!'

'Calm down, Serena. Your dad will be home tomorrow. We'll spend the evening together, the three of us, and –'

'I'm going to Georgie's tomorrow, remember?'

'I don't think so. I know Georgie smokes. I'm not stupid. The older crew in her family puff away like dragons. I naively thought you were smart enough to stop yourself from going down that dead-end track. We need to talk to your dad, and the sooner the better.'

'Just because you don't ever go out, you want to turn me into some kind of hermit freak!'

'Don't be so melodramatic.'

'Mum, please don't stop me from going,' Serena begged.

'I have to tell your father. I can't cope with this on my own.'

'You can't cope with anything on your own!'

'You have no right whatsoever to pass judgment on me.'

'I'm sorry, Mum. Please, I just really want to go to Georgie's tomorrow. I promise I won't smoke any more. I hate it. Please don't tell Dad. I swear I won't touch a cigarette again.'

'What do you and Georgia have planned that's so important to you?'

'Only a pizza and a movie, that's all. I've been looking forward to it all week. It's true that Georgie smokes, but she doesn't do it a lot, and I swear I'll never, ever light up again. I'm sorry I had a go at you about going out. I know what happened to you, and –' The rest of her sentence was drowned out by sobs.

'Shhh, Serena. Look, darling, I have to tell you something.'

'What?'

'I have started going out by myself.'

'What, seriously?'

'It started a few months back. I began to go for walks on my own. Now I go running in the park. Almost every day.'

Serena's eyes shone through her tears. 'Mum, that's brilliant. I'm so proud of you.' She leaned forward and gave her mother a hug. 'Why didn't you say anything?'

'I didn't want to give you and your dad false hope. I still worry every time I set foot outside, but it's getting easier all the time.'

'That is so cool, Mum. And you haven't said anything to Dad? You should tell him.'

'Well, now I've told you, I supposed I'd better.'

'Mum?'

'Yes, darling?'

'Please let me go to Georgie's tomorrow. And please don't tell Dad.'

Christine sighed heavily, then looked her daughter squarely in the eye, and waited for her silence to count before speaking. 'Don't make me regret keeping this from him.'

'Oh thank you, thank you, Mum! I promise I won't,' and she leaned in for a proper hug. 'Twelve seconds, remember.' Someone had told Serena that a hug that lasts for a minimum of twelve seconds made a meaningfully beneficial impact on hormone and stress levels.

'Speaking of Dad …' said Serena, and she picked up her phone. She frowned.

'Anything wrong?'

'No, not really, just that I've been looking at Dad's location all evening and it looks like he's still in Euston.'

'That can't be right. He took the train to Manchester tonight as he has such an early meeting tomorrow. Why are you looking at his location, anyway?'

'I thought it would be fun to watch the red dot move towards Manchester.'

'Oh yes. I see what you mean. And it's stuck in Euston, you say? Let me see.' She took Serena's phone. 'I hope he hasn't left his phone behind in some café at the station. Maybe the trains are up the spout. I'll call him.' She was just about to do so, when the red circle that marked his location suddenly disappeared.

'That means he's turned locator off. Or someone else has.'

'You mean someone's nicked the phone?'

'Maybe. Or his battery has run out.'

Christine was about to hand the phone back when a text announced itself with a ping.

CU tmrw night sex 💣

Serena squealed and tried to grab the phone, but Christine was too quick for her and jerked her arm away. Another text arrived within nanoseconds, a gif of a woman's naked torso with an enormous penis pistoning in and out of her. Then a third:

Cant wait babe bxx

NEVEAH

Suit comes back with a drink for both of them, despite Neveah's refusal. He and Cha-Cha are dancing again. While they're preoccupied, Neveah takes a tentative sip of Cha-Cha's orange. She winces. The bastard has completely ignored her. Not only is there vodka in the glass, but it's a double shot. Vodka is supposed to have no taste, no smell. She doesn't understand how Cha-Cha even gets it down her. It has a slice of lemon in it.

Suit's return has put a stop to the sisters' moment of togetherness. Neveah is sitting at the table watching the two of them on the dance floor, cavorting like they're possessed. Then Jackie starts singing *Moore Town Ladies*, a slower, more sensual number, and Suit grabs his opportunity to go in. He holds Cha-Cha close, and she leans into him, her head against his shoulder, as if they're lovers. It makes Neveah want to throw up. She knows if she tries to do anything, Cha-Cha will make a scene. Her sister hates being told what to do – who likes it? – but if she could only see herself ... She gets up and taps Cha-Cha on the shoulder, whispering fiercely in her ear.

'Sis, seriously, you gotta stop this guy hitting on you.'

Cha-Cha's eyes are glazed. 'Huh? What?'

'We're only dancing,' says Suit.

'Listen up, mate. She's, like –' she stops herself from saying 'only thirteen, you disgusting perv.' Instead, she says, 'She can hardly stand. And I don't think it's appropriate ...' God, she never thought she'd ever hear herself saying that word, '... that you're pouring drinks down her neck. Look at her! She's wasted.'

He looks down at Cha-Cha, who gives him a lazy smile. 'You're all right,' she says. 'Don't mind her. She always bossin' me about.' She saunters unsteadily to the table and downs her double vodka and orange in one.

Neveah feels a rush of blood to her cheeks. 'Cha! You are being so –' she thrashes around for a word and can only find 'irresponsible,' another word she swore she'd never hear herself say, so instead she says: 'fucking stupid!'

'Lea' me alone!'

Cha-Cha pulls Suit away from Neveah and very deliberately, she steals her arms around his neck and pushes herself against him. Suit looks at Neveah nervously.

Neveah advances on the pair. 'Right. That's it. Listen, whatever your name is. She is only –' Before she has a chance to say anything else, Cha-Cha clamps her mouth shut with both hands and stumbles for the loo. Neveah goes after her.

No sooner is the bathroom door open than Cha-Cha hurls an evening's worth of vodka and orange plus whatever indistinguishable mess that was once her last meal all over the bathroom floor.

'Oh, just brilliant. Well done, Cha. You couldn't even make the bloody bog. Feeling grown up now? Feeling good about yourself?'

Whatever Cha-Cha is feeling, it certainly can't be described as good. She lurches into a cubicle, and sinks to her knees, oblivious to the filthy floor, not minding her lovely dress. Her hair falls forward as she is sick again. Neveah huffs, but she gathers up her sister's hair to keep it from the torrent of vomit. Gathering up her hair exposes the label of Cha-Cha's dress. Valentino. Fuck! How is Cha-Cha in Valentino? Cha-Cha is sick over and over, until there simply can't be anything left. Yet still she heaves. With her free hand, Neveah pulls a hairband out of her pocket and ties Cha-Cha's hair up into a pile on the top of her head.

She looks around for something to clean up the mess. One cubicle has no loo paper in it at all, and the other, the one currently being christened by Cha-Cha, has only a few squares, hanging by a thread

66

off a bare roll. That miserable scrap is so inadequate for the task that there's no point wasting it, as Cha-Cha will need it to clean herself up. There's a thin blue hand towel, damp and dirty, and it's been sewn on to the rail. She has a small packet of Kleenex tissues in her bag, but there is no way they're going to do the job either.

She's torn. Cha-Cha has made a proper mess of the floor. Once she's finished vomming, she can bundle her upstairs and get her into a taxi. Assuming a taxi will bloody take her, the state she's in. On the other hand, someone may come in, and in this neon strip lighting whoever enters may correctly see exactly what the two of them are: underage girls playing at grown-ups. Clubs have lost licences for a lot less. She wants to turn her back on the whole shit show. She wants to get back to Giles.

Fuck. She cannot believe that her sister has so royally messed up her evening. And Dads has let her get smashed right under his nose.

'Listen, Cha, I'm shutting the door on you. Stay here, okay? I gotta get some stuff from the bar.

She opens the door and is once more enveloped by darkness and the sound of the band. Suit is waiting outside.

'Is she okay?'

'Nah, she's sick as a dog. I told you to get her a straight orange. What did you think would happen? That if you got her pissed enough you'd have a chance?'

'I'm sorry,' he says. 'I really am. She seemed to be having a nice time.'

Neveah snorts in disgust. 'You're old enough to … Never mind that. Can you go into the men's and see if there's any paper? There's none in there, and we're going to need a lot. See if you can rip off the hand towel too.'

He disappears inside. He comes back with a whole roll of loo paper and the twin of the sad blue towel sewn to the rail in the Ladies' room. It's a lot cleaner and drier too. Maybe blokes just don't wash their hands.

'Thanks,' says Neveah grudgingly.

Back inside the Ladies', she says: 'You okay, Cha?'

No reply. Another monumental heave. Neveah drops the blue towel onto the floor and gathers up as much of the puke into it as she can. She drops the disgusting bundle into a swing bin. She cleans up the remainder with some of the loo roll, gagging as she does so.

She washes her hands for the third time as Cha-Cha groans and emerges, ashen-faced.

'You okay?'

Cha-Cha nods. 'Yeah. Sorry, Vay.'

'I'll call you an Uber.'

'No way! I wanna see Dads. He's nearly finished, isn't he?'

'You. Cannot. Be. Serious.'

'I just wanna say hello. Come on, Vay. I hardly ever get to see him. You see him all the time.'

'That is so not true. Seriously, you don't want to see anyone the state you're in.'

Then it strikes Neveah that Jackie should take a good look at Cha-Cha exactly as she is. Right now.

'Come on then. They'll be winding up soon.' And he can take her home, she thinks. Then she will be free to go and join Giles. God, she is tired.

'Wait, Vay,' says Cha-Cha, inspecting herself in the mirror. She wipes her mouth with a square of bog roll. 'Can I borrow your lippy?'

'You gotta be kidding me.' Neveah rolls her eyes, but she fishes it out of her bag and hands it over. 'Keep it. It's yours now.'

'Ah, thanks. I'll be out in a minute.'

When Neveah steps out of the bathroom, Suit is waiting outside. 'Fucking hell. You still here?'

'How's she doing?'

'Much better, no thanks to you.'

'Listen, er … Neveah, isn't it? I really am terribly sorry.'

Neveah doesn't know whether to pity or despise him.

'She was on a mission,' she says. 'Do me and the world a favour and don't buy her another drink. No matter how much she begs.'

She walks towards the music. Jackie and the boys are finishing their last number. He doesn't move. She turns and says: 'And don't hang around the girls' bogs. It ain't a good look.'

He smiles ruefully. 'I suppose not. I just feel responsible, that's all.'

'So you should. She won't be sticking around long. I'm gonna get our dad to take her home.'

'Your dad?'

'Yeah. He's the singer.'

His eyes widen. 'Wow. You mean Jackie Sansom? I'm quite a fan.'

She doesn't like the matey tone he's adopting. 'Look. I gotta go.'

A big bloke in a tight dinner jacket is onstage thanking each member of the band. Perfect. They're finished. As soon as the applause dies down, she'll hand Cha-Cha over to Jackie. About time he took some responsibility for his youngest (to her knowledge) child. Jackie can take her back to Granny South's. Then she, Neveah, can get back to Giles. God, I hope he's not waiting up for me, she thinks to herself. She'll steal into the bed, wrap her arms around him. She smiles to herself.

Sweetman hugs her. 'You a sight for sore eyes, girl. Who's that creep sniffing round Cha? You shown him the door, yeah?'

'Nah, he's still around somewhere, but he knows the score now.'

He laughs. 'Good.'

'My girl Vay-vay!' says Jackie with his arms outstretched. 'Give your ole pop a kiss, sweetness. Where's Cha-Cha?'

She tells him and they all laugh.

'Talking to God on the big white telephone,' observes Bingo, his teeth shining in the strobe light. Now the band is no longer playing, Neveah's ears are ringing. The silence is suddenly filled with recorded music, The Bueno Vista Social Club.

'Dads, you better take her home, yeah?' says Neveah, raising her voice to be heard. 'She can't be on no tube solo.'

His face clouds over. 'I can't, sweetness. Imagine me taking her down Lewisham this time of the night. Sandra, she will proper kill me.'

'She's staying with Granny South tonight.'

'Still can't be taking her, Vay-vay. That's gotta be your job,' he looks sheepish. 'Truth is, sweetness, I got a date tonight. Darling, meet Livvy. Where is she?' He looks around.

'Dads. You can drop her home first, then go on to your date. You watched her down one drink after another tonight, being pawed by some disgusting –'

'Take it easy, sweetness,' says Jackie.

'You shoulda put a stop to it.'

He drops his voice, even though the music's loud enough to block out what he's saying. 'You know it ain't my way to stop anyone from doing what they wanna do,' he says.

'Dads! She's thirteen!' she says desperately. 'You're her father!'

Sweetman is looking at Neveah and Jackie, taking in every word, despite the background noise. It's not his style to tell another man how to live his life. Sweetman's little girl is only seven, but when the time comes, Neveah is sure he'll protect her from the scumbags around her. Why won't Dads do that for her and Cha?

'I got school tomorrow. So's she. We're both here to see you, staying up way too late on a school night, and for what? So you can leave us to get home solo while you run off with some piece.'

'Listen up, girl,' says Sweetman gently. 'I can take you both home.'

She furiously backtracks. She can't explain why she'd want to be dropped in Euston. 'Cheers, Sweetman. Just get Cha home, yeah? I'll be all right.'

'Nah, you're fine. I'll take you both.'

Jackie looks from his daughter to his friend, not saying a word, allowing his present problem to be neatly solved between the two of them.

A very slender blonde caked in make-up materialises and slips her arm around Jackie's waist. She leans against him and turns his face towards her, so she can plant a long and lingering kiss on his lips. If she were a cat, she'd be pissing on him. 'You were brilliant, Jacks.' She looks shyly at Neveah. 'Ah Jackie, this your daughter? She's sooooo beautiful. Hi, I'm Livvy,' she says, grinning nervously.

'God, don't you look like your dad? 'Cept more feminine, obvs.' She laughs.

Neveah is not in the mood to meet one of Jackie's girlfriends, but Livvy doesn't notice the waves of temper radiating from her. She slinks towards Neveah and wraps her arms around her neck.

'Ah, it is so amazing to finally meet you. I've heard so much about you. Your dad talks about you and your sister, like, aaaaaaalll the time.'

'God, that must be boring,' Neveah says, and takes a step back.

'Don't be silly! I love hearing about you girls. Been wanting to meet you for, like, ages. Where's your little sister? Gaah, is she as lovely as you?' She leans forward and strokes Neveah's cheek.

Neveah flinches. 'I better go see how she's doing,' she says, and turns to stalk her way through the tables back to the bathroom.

'Cha-Cha, Dads is –' she says as she opens the door, but the two cubicles are empty and there's no one in front of the mirror. Neveah climbs the stairs in annoyance and pokes her head out on to the street, in case she stepped outside for a breath of air. She's nowhere to be seen. She looks for the doorman to ask him, but he's not at his post. She goes back inside, walking past the loos again, looking in every direction to scan every inch of the club.

Sweetman takes in her panic and frowns. 'You okay, girl?'

'It's Cha-Cha,' she says. 'She's gone.'

GILES

Giles can't sleep. He's lying in semi-darkness in the hotel. He's left Neveah's sidelight on so she can see her way around when she finally gets in. *All by Myself*, he thinks, allowing Celine Dion to warble in his head, accompanied only by his guilt and his longing.

He wonders if he should switch his phone back on. He'd turned it off earlier when he'd suddenly remembered that his location was available to Christine and Serena, signalling his duplicity like a beacon. He's supposed to be in Manchester tonight. Installing Family Locator was his sodding idea after all – he'd suggested that they all load it up on their phones months before he'd even met Neveah. He's never had to use it. He knows where Christine is all the time, and Serena has never given him a reason to worry. He remembers reading somewhere that most affairs are exposed by technology. And stupidity, obviously.

Presumably they ignore the app as much as he does. They have absolutely no reason to check up on him. They're probably both fast asleep. Despite his deep sense of unease, he switches his phone back on. In case Neveah needs him. He continues to lie sleepless in the dark.

No sooner has his phone booted up than messages begin to flood in.

Three missed calls from Neveah. One from Christine. He's about to check the messages when his phone rings. It's Neveah. Before he's had time to open his mouth, she says; 'It's my sister. She's gone missing. I'm not gonna come tonight. I've got to find her.'

He sits up. 'Whoa, whoa, what do you mean she's gone missing?'

'She was dancing with some creep and now she's disappeared with him. She's only thirteen! I was supposed to be looking after her. I don't know what I'm gonna do. I got to get off the phone in case she calls.'

'You're in the Havana, aren't you? Old Street?'

'Yeah, but –'

'I'm on my way.'

'No! Giles, seriously, don't.'

'I'm coming,' he says, and hangs up, while swinging his legs out of bed.

SANDRA

Sandra is woken up by the sound of her phone ringing. She fumbles for it, and it drops to the floor. When she picks it up, she sees in the darkness that it's Neveah calling.

'Neveah? What's going on?' she clamps the phone between her ear and her shoulder as she reaches for her dressing gown.

'It's Cha-Cha,' the girl says. Her panic is audible despite the background din. 'She's gone missing.'

All Grown Up

'She's with her Granny tonight,' says Sandra, but as soon as the words are out of her mouth, she knows they're not true. 'Where are you?'

'I'm at the Havana. It's a club on Old Street. Dads and the band were playing. Cha-Cha was here, and now she's disappeared. She was dancing with some old geezer. He's not here anymore neither. I'm scared she left with him.'

'Did you see her go?'

'No. She was in the loo. She– she was taking a long time. Then when I went back to check on her, she was nowhere.'

Sandra's heart contracts. She's filled with fear and fury and a blind desire to lash out, which she forces herself to suppress. 'Old Street, you say?'

Neveah gives her the address.

'I don't know how long it'll take me to get there. Is your dad there?'

'Yeah. Sweetman too. We're all looking, calling around.'

'Have you tried her phone?'

'Of course! It's switched off. It's going straight to voicemail.'

'Maybe she's on her way back to Granny's,' says Sandra. Wishful thinking. 'Do the people in the club know who the guy is?'

'I'll ask.'

'Can you describe him?'

'Yeah, sure I can. Just get here quick as you can.'

Sandra pulls on some clothes.

'What's going on?' mumbles Leon.

She tells him. 'I'll take the car.'

'Babe, you can't. You had half a bottle of wine, remember? Besides, you're too wired to drive. I'll call you a cab, yeah?'

'Tell them to be quick.'

She brushes her teeth and finds her shoes.

'You got your bag and your keys? Is your phone charged up? I can give it more juice while we're waiting for the cab.'

'It's fine. 97%,' she says.

Within four minutes, she hears an engine outside. 'That's them. Thank God.'

'Okay. Take care. Call me, yeah? Let me know what's going on.'

As she runs down the stairs, Angelique cries out for her. She can't stop, not for a moment. It's her other baby that needs her now.

NEVEAH

'Did you see the guy who was in here earlier, the one in the light suit? He had a hat on,' Neveah asks the barman. She raises her voice and leans forward so he can hear her above the music.

'Nah. Don't know him.'

'Can you ask the guy in the back room? Only he's gone off with my sister, and I'm really worried about her.'

If the man was wearing a T-shirt with *I don't give a flying fuck* emblazoned on it, it would be hard for him to appear more indifferent.

'Please,' says Neveah. 'It's really important.'

With a barely concealed eye roll, the guy goes to find his colleague.

Sweetman comes over. 'Have you asked him?' he says. She nods. 'Thing is, girl, if she's gone off with that geezer, we have got zero chance of figuring out where she is. We have to wait 'til she comes crawling home tomorrow.'

'These guys might know him. We can't just let her swan off with some random stranger. He could be anybody!'

'Likely he'll just get his leg over. If he still can.'

Neveah flinches.

'Sorry, Vay, but we gotta face facts. She ain't the first and she definitely won't be the last that did something stupid with someone who means nothing to her 'cos she's drunk and has shit for brains.' Despite the harsh words, she can see he's exasperated. Upset. More affected than Jackie is.

The barman sticks his thumb over his shoulder to his colleague behind him, who approaches Neveah and Sweetman.

'You looking for Simon? The guy in the suit?' he says.

'Yes!' Neveah says, hope surging through her chest.

'He comes in here all the time, but I don't know where he lives.'

'D'you know anything about him? Do you have a number for him?'

'Sorry. We don't keep a register, you know.'

'Is there anyone still here that he hangs out with who could tell us? Please, it's really important.'

'Look, sorry, but no. I just serve the drinks round here. I don't give the customers the third degree. His name's Simon, he's a music buff and he likes to think he's a natty dresser, but that's all I can tell you. He likes the ladies, but don't we all? He's not a perv, if that's what you're worried about.'

Jackie comes over with Livvy. 'What did he say, sweetness?'

Neveah tells him. 'Do you think we should call the police?' she asks.

The effect on Jackie and Livvy is electric. Livvy says, 'Fuck! Don't get the pigs involved.' Jackie says: 'No way, Vay-vay. We'd be stepping into a world of trouble. She only thirteen.'

Sweetman says, 'Seriously, Neveah, what can they do? They won't know any more than we do. That she's flounced off with a guy called Simon in a James Bond suit, and they've been swallowed up by a tiny place called London. They could be anywhere. She woulda shown some kind of fake ID to get into this place and she was throwing herself at him all night. She's another little girl chucking herself into the world sooner than what's good for her.' He looks at Jackie. 'Sorry man, but you shoulda been looking out for her.'

Neveah wants to defend her dad, but she knows Sweetman's right.

Livvy sticks her oar in. 'You got no right to speak to him like that.'

'Maybe not, but he ain't saying nothing. That's 'cos he knows it's the truth.'

Neveah sees over Sweetman's shoulder that Giles has arrived. He's wearing a collared shirt, tailored trousers and a blazer. He sticks out like a hangnail. She's dismayed that he's turned up. Her mind goes into overdrive.

'Neveah,' he says, and stands awkwardly, not knowing what to do with himself. It's the first time she's seen him anything other than self-assured.

'Giles,' she says, sounding alien, even to herself. 'This is my dad, Jackie. His girlfriend, Livvy, and this is Sweetman.' Sweetman and Giles have never met, only spoken on the phone. 'Giles and I work together.'

Sweetman throws a shrewd look her way. Thankfully, he doesn't ask questions.

'So what's happened?' Giles asks.

'Cha-Cha's gone off with a bloke she was dancing with. She was drunk. Like, so drunk she was sick. I turned my back for two minutes so she could clean herself up and she disappeared. The barman doesn't know where the guy lives. He can only tell me he's a regular, and that he's 'not a perv'.'

'Like he'd fucking know,' interjects Sweetman.

'We were debating whether to call the police,' says Neveah, looking around at the other three adults.

'Are you sure she's gone off with him? Maybe she just went home,' says Giles.

'I've called her and called her, but she's not picking up, and now it's going to voicemail.'

'You called your Granny, yeah?' says Jackie.

'Of course I have. She wasn't picking up. I'll try her again.'

Granny doesn't have a mobile. Neveah can picture the old lady emerging tortoise-like from her room. She'll be well pissed off, but that can't be helped. Neveah's fear is diluted with irritation. Cha-Cha is a brainless little fuckwit. Jackie is an irresponsible father. Sandra is a dumbass for believing Cha-Cha's lame story about staying with Granny because she's such a good and considerate granddaughter, and Granny South is beyond naïve thinking that Cha-Cha was going to meekly take herself to bed. Yet who's the one picking up the pieces as per fucking usual?

'There's no answer. But that doesn't mean she isn't there. She's just slow, that's all. I'll try again in a minute.' Neveah is suddenly conscious that she's lowered her voice and poshed up her speech because Giles is there.

She waits for a minute, then tries the line again.

'Who this?' Granny says, sounding concerned rather than tetchy.

'Granny, it's me. Is Cha-Cha there?'

'No. She's out with you, en't she?'

'Can you check she hasn't come in?'

'She en't in. I know it.'

'Please, Granny. Can you check her bed?'

The old lady tuts but does as she's asked. After an age, she comes back to the phone.

'Not here. What's goin' on?'

Neveah takes a deep breath and tells her.

'Oh Lord,' sighs the old lady. 'What will we be telling Sandra?'

Neveah wants to scream down the phone: 'You mean what will I be telling Sandra? It's always up to me to clean up everybody else's mess.' Instead, she says, 'I've called Sandra already. If Cha comes in, will you call me, yeah? We'll keep looking for her.'

How can they look for her, she thinks, feeling desolate. Sweetman's right. She rings off and looks up at the circle of adults. 'She hasn't come back.'

Sweetman says, 'Maybe she just ain't there yet.'

'It's only the Elephant she's getting back to. She's going to Granny's, not back to Sandra's.'

As if on cue, Sandra sweeps in, and stalks towards the group, her long black coat billowing behind her, giving her the look of a tall avenging angel.

'Oh, Lawd,' breathes Jackie.

Sandra's eyes flash fury towards him. No one bothers to introduce Giles or Livvy to her. 'Any news?' she says to Neveah.

Neveah shakes her head. 'I called Granny a minute ago. She's not home yet.'

Sandra gives Jackie a basilisk stare. 'You should be ashamed of yourself, bringing your girls to a place like this. How could you let Cha disappear with a complete stranger? I always knew you were a deadbeat dad, but even I never thought you could sink so low. She's just a child, Jackie. A child!'

77

'But I was singin'. I couldn't be watchin' out for her.'

'She shouldn't have been here in the first place.'

'Don't you speak to him like that!' says Livvy, stepping in front of Jackie. 'She's your daughter too, you know. Her being here is just as much your fault as his.'

Sandra doesn't even bother to acknowledge her.

'S'all right, sweetness,' says Jackie to Livvy in alarm. He pats her arm, clearly desperate for her to shut up.

'Women like you make me sick,' says Livvy. 'Blaming everyone else for everything and not taking no responsibility for anything yourself.' Despite the fraught situation, Neveah notices that Livvy says 'everyfink' and misses out the T in 'responsibility'. Giles's presence is turning her into the grammar police. She feels as if she's observing them all, including herself, from outside her own body.

Giles is taking the whole of the little drama in. Mercifully, he keeps his mouth shut.

Sandra keeps her eye on Jackie. Livvy is clearly not worth troubling herself with. She enunciates her every word. 'Cha-Cha is only thirteen. Past eight o'clock at night, she should be nowhere else but at home, and not in some dive full of booze and sexual predators.'

'But Neveah was lookin' out for her. I never have to worry when my girl Vay be here.'

'She's fifteen years old, Jackie. She shouldn't be here either. Anyway,' she says, widening her eyes and shaking her head. 'I don't know why I'm even bothering to argue the toss with you.' She gets her phone out. 'I'm calling the police.'

CHA-CHA

Cha-Cha's on the bus to Granny South's. The journey should take twenty minutes, but the traffic, even at this time of night, is mental. This city is proper mad. She's exhausted, slumped against the window, trying hard to keep herself awake. Her cheap high-heeled shoes are killing her and she has a horrible taste in her mouth. She wishes she had some water. Or a stick of gum. She has her coat wrapped tightly around her, but there's a draft blowing right through the bus, and the thin material isn't doing a particularly good job of keeping it off her, especially as her legs are bare.

She wishes she could go home. She wants her mum. She wants to be petted and cuddled and put to bed. She wants to be allowed to sleep in under her lovely warm duvet in her warm room for a very long time. But that ain't gonna happen, she thinks darkly. If she went home to her mum, she'd get a serious tongue-lashing. Her mum would be horrified at the state she's in. And the rage that'll be directed her way when she sees she's stolen her best dress and trashed it. Cha-Cha feels a stab of fear. Her mum had splashed a fortune on it for a wedding last year. Someone at work, not family. Typical that she'd make a huge effort for someone at work. It had been specially taken in to fit her. While Cha-Cha had been packing up her things to go to Granny South's, everyone was out, and she couldn't resist sneaking into Sandra and Leon's room to try it on. It fitted her like it was made for her, not her mum. And her mum wasn't likely to wear it again in a hurry. It was rotting away in the wardrobe, among Sandra's boring old work suits and jackets, just waiting for a chance to be unleashed on the world. Once she'd tried it on, she couldn't wear anything else to Jackie's gig. It looked the business on her. She wonders if the stains will come out. She'll bung it in the washing machine at Granny South's tonight before she goes to sleep. She yawns, not bothering to cover her mouth.

She thinks about the bloke she'd been dancing with. Neveah's so dumb to worry about her. As if she'd get with someone like him. He'd been nice though. A laugh. He'd treated her like a proper grown-up. Bought her drinks and everything. She feels a swell of pride. He wouldn't have done that if he didn't fancy her. Neveah's such a misery-guts. Cha-Cha's mortified she let herself down by puking.

Neveah's worried about her. She knows because she'd had several missed calls and a slew of texts. Not only from her, but from Sweetman and Jackie too. In a fury, she switched off her phone. If Neveah's worried, then it serves her right. Let her fucking well fret. It serves them all right. She'd seen them laughing at her. Her cheeks burn at the memory. Neveah must have blabbed about her being sick. Bitch. Neveah acts all grown-up and posh and superior, but she's only two years older. She didn't have anyone buying *her* drinks, there's no fucking surprise.

The driver stops to let someone out, then the doors close and he sets off again. She panics that she's missed her stop so she presses the red button repeatedly and calls out to him. He slams on his brakes and growls something at her, which she doesn't hear over the hiss of the opening doors. She mutters an ungracious thanks and lurches into the night. She takes a look around to orientate herself and realises she's got off a stop too soon. She'll have to walk. Her shoes are so painful that she takes them off and pads barefoot on the wet pavement towards her Granny's flat, flinging curses into the rain.

GILES

Sick isn't quite the right way to describe how Giles feels. Something in his chest plummets to his stomach, leaving a painful, buzzing hollowness in its place. His first refuge is that he misheard the magnificently angry black woman giving Jackie a hard time, but he can't give that a moment's credence, as every word she uttered was as clear as a bell. She's Neveah's stepmother, and ought to know exactly how old Neveah is.

Neveah is gazing at him in horror, and takes a step towards him, then stops herself. The music in the club abruptly stops, and the lights come on.

He hears a hubbub of raised voices; Jackie and Livvy are trying to dissuade Sandra from calling the cops.

With uncanny timing, his phone rings. It's Christine.

He answers. Even as he does so, he realises that he will have ample cause to regret it.

'Giles, it's me. There's something going on with Serena. She got this awful thing on her phone.' Giles is barely listening, his eyes are fixed on Neveah. 'Sorry, ignore me, I'm not making sense. I'll tell you when I see you, but,' there's a pause. 'We're worried about you. Where are you?'

His mind switches abruptly to Christine. Her voice is charged with urgency. She asked him where he is. He has an overwhelming urge to lie. There are several stories he could spin. Like a chess player calculating move and counter-move, he rapidly considers the consequences of each possible falsehood.

He looks up at the circle of unfamiliar people who have all turned their attention to him and Neveah, eyeing him with suspicion. He's an idiot. Neveah had been right to try and keep him from the club.

He closes his eyes and quells the urge to utter anything other than the strict truth to Christine. He's enough of a student of history to know that it's the cover-up that gets you, not the crime. 'I'm still in London.'

'What's going on? I thought you were in Manchester?' She's not accusing, she's concerned, confused, worried.

He sighs. 'It's a long story. I'm coming home now, Chrissie.'

'Thank God. Come as quickly as you can.'

Neveah's eyes well up. He has never seen her cry. He wants to comfort her, but the girl standing in front of him is not the one he knows.

FRIDAY

SERENA

Serena is eating Weetabix in the kitchen. Her mum's still in her dressing gown. No change there, then. She's chugged so many cups of thick black coffee that the place smells like a Columbian factory.

Her mum is pale, distracted, and looks as if she hasn't slept. Her eyes are rimmed with red, as if she's been crying. As the time approaches for her to leave for school, Serena can't stand it a moment longer, and says: 'Mum, please don't tell Dad about the gif.'

'The what?'

'You know, the video that came through on my phone.'

'It's too late, sweetheart. I've already told him.'

Serena's insides twist with humiliation and hot tears spring to her eyes. 'You're not serious, are you, Mum?'

'I told him when he came home last night.'

'I thought he was in Manchester.'

'Yes, so did I. Anyway, he came home instead. He left to catch his train before you got up. He'll be back this evening.'

Serena tries to picture her father's face when her mother told him. She cringes in mortification. 'What did he say?'

'We can discuss it when he's home tonight.'

'But I'll be at Georgie's!'

Her mum turns towards her. She doesn't even sound angry. She speaks as if she's a long way underwater. 'No, darling, you won't. You're coming home.'

Serena knows better than to argue. She's on the back foot and doesn't like it. She dumps her bowl in the sink, as heavily as she can get away with.

'Into the dishwasher please, darling,' says Christine, as if she's on autopilot. She takes a sip of her coffee and stares out of the window.

Serena is so filled with fury that she picks up the bowl and wants to smash it against the edge of the counter, but of course, she reins herself in and does as she's told.

She picks up her satchel and PE kit, which are at the foot of the stairs, and is about to march out of the house when she has a thought. She runs upstairs and quickly throws a few things into a bag. Whatever she does when school's out this evening, it will not involve coming home. She's got eight hours to think of something.

SWEETMAN

Sweetman comes downstairs in his dressing gown, a ratty blue towelling robe he's had since his student days. Laura has threatened to chuck it out and buy him a new one, but he won't part with it.

He takes a look around. She has cleared the kitchen counter, tidied all traces of the kids' breakfast, and the washing machine is churning with a soapy dark load, a basket of whites awaiting its turn. All of these things are normally up to him, as every morning she's in a rush to get the kids out of the door to school and she jumps on the tube straight to work after walking them there, but on Fridays she works from home.

He can hear her tapping away on her keyboard. He fills the kettle and switches it on, before putting a couple of pieces of bread in the toaster. It's the multi-grain stuff that he likes. He pokes his head round the door to the living room. She's got her laptop out and a few papers spread around the table. The winter sun's streaming in through the window behind her, giving her blonde head a halo.

'Hi babe, you okay?' she says.

'Yup. Just put the kettle on. D'you fancy something?'

'A cup of builder's please. You were late home last night. How was it?'

'The gig was cool. Nice crowd. But we had a bit of drama with Jackie's girls.' He perches on the arm of the sofa and tells her what happened. '... so Sandra was about to call the cops when Jackie's mum called to say she'd just arrived home.'

'Thank God nothing happened to her. That's something at least. I bet Cha's in the doghouse now.'

'You can say that again. Thing is, the whole thing really set me to thinking. The guy was out of order –'

'Revolting old creep.'

'Yeah, but you shoulda seen her. She was in some swanky dress, wearing heels and make-up ... I mean, if I didn't know, I would have sworn she was, I dunno, late teens, twenties even. Jackie dodged a bullet last night. If she'd come to harm, it would have been right under his nose, and he did jack to stop it. He could see the guy buying her one drink after another, and she was totally getting off on the whole trip ... you know, she's out, she's in a club, she's being treated like a grown-up –'

'Maybe, but it's obvious she's only a kid. As soon as they open their mouths they kind of give the game away. I mean, Cha's not the world's greatest conversationalist.'

Sweetman laughs. 'Ah, so that's it, is it? The guy just wanted to have an interesting chat!' He butts his forehead with the palm of his hand.

'Ha. Ha. You know perfectly well what I mean.'

'Imagine if she'd gone home with him and he'd got his leg over. He'd get banged up.'

'Yes, and it would serve him right.'

'What, so you're saying that any bloke that picks up a girl in a club shouldn't make a move until he's seen her birth certificate? In the original?'

'I'm just saying that blokes see what they want to see, and they ignore the blindingly obvious. Especially if it contradicts the way it suits them to interpret the world.'

He snorts and goes back into the kitchen. He comes back a few minutes later carrying a tray bearing two steaming cups and a plate of buttered toast. She takes one of the cups and pinches a piece of his toast.

'Oi. I'm a growing boy,' he says mildly.

She pats his belly and smiles.

'So let's say that you're right –' he continues.

'Wow. You have been thinking about this.'

'Well, yeah. I have. We're going to be struggling with this kind of thing sooner than we'd like.'

'Petra's only seven. And she's not going to be in a nightclub at the age of thirteen.'

'Sandra thought Cha was with her gran. You can't second guess everything.'

'Hmmm.'

'But let's say this bloke should have been able to magically divine somehow that Cha-Cha was only thirteen. By the intellectual pitch of her conversation or whatever. But what about Neveah?'

'What about her?'

'She wasn't there to pick anyone up or get drunk. She was just there to see her dad.'

'So …' Laura lengthens the word and leaves it hanging.

'So what if a bloke chatted her up and managed to get her home? If she went with anyone, there's no way for them to know she's just a kid. But they'd still be guilty of a crime.'

'And a good thing, too. The law's there to protect these girls if they won't protect themselves. Blokes who chase young girls in clubs deserve everything they get. Anyway, Neveah would never let herself be chatted up by some old greebo. It's one of life's little ironies. The dumb ones get themselves into dumb situations, and the clever ones that have the brains to get themselves out of the dumb situations, don't get into them in the first place.'

Sweetman considers this. 'Maybe. There was this other guy there last night. He turned up while we were all running around like headless chickens looking for Cha. He was a suit. You know, a corporate type. Vay introduced him to us. Said she worked with him. I put him on to her a few months back. It must be him. There aren't many blokes called Giles in this world.'

'And?' Laura knows all about Neveah's little empire.

'She changed when he turned up. Her voice, the way she spoke … everything.'

'We all do that. You wouldn't eff and blind around your clients, would you? What was he doing there, anyway?'

'I never got a chance to ask. We were all too busy worrying about Cha. But seriously, Laur, I'd bet good money that they're shagging each other.'

'God. Are you being serious? And he's how old?'

'Like around fifty.'

It's her turn to consider. 'Should we talk to her?'

'I dunno,' he says glumly. 'On the one hand, I kind of think it's none of our business. She's a smart girl, and she's entitled to make her own decisions. On the other, though …'

'She's just a kid.'

'Exactly. And it was me who threw her his way.'

JACKIE

'Gaaah, Jackie, I feel rough. What did you put in that spliff?' Livvy rasps.

They're still in their clothes from the night before, lying on the floor of her studio. That's what she calls it, but Jackie knows a bedsit when he sees one. They're wrapped in a throw she dragged from the sofa. She extricates herself from his arms and crawls over on all fours to the window and pulls the curtains apart to allow light to flood in. Jackie's eyes had been opening slowly, but now they shut like clams. He's aching everywhere. His belt is undone, digging painfully into his side. He has a vague memory of trying to get it on before passing out. At his feet are a couple of empty wine bottles and a third which is well on its way, next to a cereal bowl full of fag butts and dead joints, an empty Rizla packet and a lighter, along with a cellophane wrap containing his gear, which is open and likely all dried up by now. He promises himself he'll wrap it up in a minute. Once he's summoned enough energy to get vertical. By some miracle nothing got kicked over in the night.

Livvy groans as she gets to her feet to pull the old sash window open. Freezing air blasts in, cutting the heavy staleness of the room, blowing some of the ash from the bowl onto the scratchy beige carpet. Jackie remains still and takes in deep breaths far down into his lungs. It feels healing. He wants a shower, but at Livvy's you have to stand in the bath and drizzle water over yourself with a leaking hand-held extension, then soap down in the freezing cold before rinsing off. It's not appealing at the best of times. Her bathroom wall is tiled in cream and a murky light green, which someone at some distant point in time, say the mid-fifties, must have decided was a winning combination. Whatever colour the tiles, the bathroom is damp and grubby, falling far short of his mother's stratospherically high standards of cleanliness. He loves Livvy's hair, which falls in an elegant blonde wave to her waist, but only when it's attached to her head. When it clings to walls and bathroom fittings, and when it clogs up sinks and shower drains, it's positively disgusting.

He's not overly keen on Livvy's place full stop, but he's not in a position to offer an alternative. He can't bring women to his mother's place. Not to stay overnight. Not 'til they have a ring on their finger are they welcome to sleep there, and he's determined never to get himself caught like that again.

He likes it when he's on the road. Sometimes he gets his own room, and when he shares with Sweetman, he takes himself off to the women's places. It's like a fresh adventure each time. Student digs, bedsits, flats, terraced houses, once a gorgeous pad in the countryside with stables and a swimming pool, with an older but seriously foxy brunette whose husband worked in London during the week, kids safely tucked away in boarding school. She'd called him a taxi early in the morning: 'I need you out before the house-keeper comes in, darling.' And she'd pushed him against the wall and gone down on him before it arrived. The memory alone gives him the horn.

Now, Livvy always angles to come with him. It hampers his freedom, and the others grumble as she throws the sleeping arrangements out.

"S'like Yoko Ono all over again,' Bingo moaned. 'You gotta learn how to say no.'

'Haven't you got to work, sweetness?' he asks her nervously each time.

'Nah. I work when I want. I'm mobile, in' I?'

She's a manicurist. 'Nah, I'm, like, a nail technician,' she corrects, whenever anyone mislabels her. Her mobile rings at odd times. She visits her clients at home, often at outlandish hours, and she's always paid in cash. Her own nails are currently a deep iridescent dragonfly green, with a pineapple etched on to each one. They are supernaturally long. So long that Bingo had asked her how she managed to wipe her arse. Everyone had laughed, including Livvy, but Jackie could tell she was pissed off.

Sweetman's wife Laura has only ever travelled with the band on a couple of occasions that Jackie can remember, and only when she could get her mother to babysit. She doesn't trust anyone else longer than an evening. Bingo is resolutely single. He's decent looking, and he's sharp, funny even, and he has a good patter with the ladies, does his fair share of pulling, but any time a woman threatens to extend her tenure beyond a night or two, he snuffs her candle out, usually with a well-timed and devastating put-down.

'Can't be doing with it,' he told Jackie when they'd talked about it once. 'Having a woman hanging round all the time … costs time and trouble and money.' Steve's girlfriend has a steady office job, which claims her during the week, and weekends she likes to go riding.

'So it's just you stuck with that limpet,' Bingo had said, 'which means we's stuck with her too.'

Jackie's never experienced this particular problem before. All his other girlfriends have toed the line, but Livvy's a force of nature.

'Look, an extra room in a poxy Travelodge or whatever, it's just another coupla quid. And I don't mind crashing. S'long as I'm with you. You and me are like, together, babes.' She'd slinked up to him and stolen an arm around his neck. She'd looked up at him with wide and seductive eyes, her mouth in a pout. With her free hand, she'd cupped his balls and given them a gentle squeeze. 'Your mates better get used to it. 'Cos I ain't going nowhere.'

'Gaaah, it's freezing out there,' says Livvy, and slams the window shut. 'I'm gonna run a bath, babes. You wanna jump in with me? Then we can grab some nosh, yeah?'

Jackie raises himself to his elbows. 'I got nothing clean to wear, sweetness. I'd better get back to –'

'To Mumsy Wumsy?' she says, sticking her bottom lip out and wobbling her head from side to side. 'You know, Jackie, I been thinking.' He holds his breath. 'I only have to give a month's notice on this place. Don't you think we should, like, shack up? I mean, in a couple of weeks it'll be, like, three months since we been together. This place costs a fortune for what it is. We could, like, get something much better if we pooled our money.'

Jackie's wide awake now. He gets to his feet and knocks the wine bottle over. It spills all over his gear.

'Ah Jackie, what are you like?' says Livvy wearily, as she reaches for a grubby old tea towel from the kitchen. He picks the cellophane wrapper up carefully, trying not to let any of his stuff fall out. He'll have a go at drying it out. A wine-infused spliff ... might be nice.

She chatters while she cleans up the mess, then she steps into the bathroom and starts running the bath water. 'I mean, I've even met Neveah now. She's so lovely. Terrible nails though. I'll soon sort them out. She really liked me, I could tell. Shame Cha-Cha did a runner. I was, like, so gagging to meet her. She'll love me. I'm like, brilliant with kids. Her mum's proper scary. What you ever saw in a loudmouth cow like her defeats me. I wanted to deck her, spouting off like that. You shouldn't stand for it, Jackie. It's bang out of order. You know, your problem is you let everyone walk all over you.'

Jackie follows her into the bathroom and is disconcerted to see her on the loo. She's strewn her clothes all over the floor, and she's naked, peeing noisily, completely unembarrassed and rubbing her arms vigorously against the cold. He mutters an apology and beats a hasty retreat. Jackie likes his women to keep their bodily functions to themselves.

She laughs. 'Gaaah, Jackie, what are you like? It's nothing you haven't seen before now, is it? I mean, you should be able to, like, draw a map of my muff by now. Anyway, I was just saying, if we got our own place, we could even have the girls to stay over. That would be lovely, don't you think? I'm sure little Cha-Cha would jump at the chance to get away from that mean ole mum of hers. She'd be much happier with us. I can't wait to meet her.'

Jackie knows better than to say anything. Set to transmit and not receive, this one. He hears the loo flushing and the sound of the water rippling as she gets into the bath. Then she runs the hot water on full again, and a thick steam fills the room, so he feels less embarrassed about using the loo himself. He would prefer to be alone, but his need is pressing and sometimes she stays in the bath for hours, topping up the hot water every now and again. He angles himself so his back is to her.

'Gone all shy now, have you? You're such a one, you really are,' she laughs again. She sweeps her hair up into a pink plastic claw. 'Sure you don't wanna jump in? It's lovely in here.'

'Nah, sweets. I'm gonna head out. Make tracks.'

It's his turn to flush the loo, then he washes his hands. 'Gaaah, look at you, Jackie. Mumsy Wumsy would be proud. Speaking of, don't you think it's time you, y'know, introduced me?'

Jackie clears his throat. 'Soon, sweetness,' he says, and bends down to drink from the tap, but changes his mind when he gets a closer look. He'll buy a bottle of water at the tube station. 'My old Ma … well, she's proper old-fashioned.'

'Aaah. That's nice. I like that. But let's deffo sort out another time with Neveah and soon, yeah? Tell her I'll do her nails for her. They are totally munched. I can build up a nice gel on them. Then she'll stop all that nibbling. Who was that bloke with her?'

'Hmm?' says Jackie.

'You know, the tall bloke. The posh looking one.' Jackie was wondering himself. 'What was his name again?'

'Name's Giles,' says Jackie.

'Is he, you know …'

'What, sweetness?'

'Are they, like, together? He's older than you, I reckon. I mean, she's not even legal yet.'

Jackie had asked himself the same question. He prefers not to dwell on it. Of course he has always known that his daughters would sooner or later grow up and start having sex. That's the way the world turns. But the thought of Neveah with a guy like that makes him deeply uncomfortable. He thinks again about what Sweetman said. That he didn't look out for his girls. That he didn't spend time with them. Why would Neveah need a Daddy figure if she had a perfectly good father already?

Jackie's working on a new song, inspired by Livvy's hair. The hair on her head, that is, rather than the stuff that falls out onto the furniture and fittings. He knows the colour comes out of a bottle, but it's still sexy as all hell, and it always smells so good. This is some achievement considering she smokes like a steam engine. He loves seeing her walk around naked, with her blonde mane slinking around her slenderness, like a pale pre-Raphaelite. Although he has to admit those lovely ladies in the paintings don't have any tattoos; Livvy has a dolphin on her ankle, a rose on her shoulder and a yin and yang on her coccyx. He loves winding skeins of her tresses around his dark skin when they're naked together. He especially loves it when she's on top, and she lets her hair fall over his face. He reminds himself of these intensely erotic moments when she's being especially clingy and irritating or when her constant stream of consciousness starts to grate. If she ever had a filter, she lost it years ago.

The songs come to him first in snatches, and once he starts giving them time and space, they grow in his head, and become like an itch that needs scratching. He allows the song to flood his brain, knowing that it won't leave him alone, that he won't think of anything else all the way home. He's been told that poets are similarly affected. Song-writing is not his only talent. He is also really good at pushing deeply uncomfortable thoughts to the recesses of his mind.

CHRISTINE

Christine has bunked off her daily run. She had tried going back to bed once Serena had left for school, but sleep did not come. Her nerves are in shreds and her mind is in overdrive.

Giles had come home in the small hours, and the two of them had talked almost all night. If you could call that talking. He talked and she had raged and cried. Serena hadn't stirred. And it was obvious from the brief exchange in the kitchen with Serena at breakfast that she had no idea her father had even returned last night. She envies that ability to sleep. She hasn't slept like that for seven years.

She can't believe Giles has gone ahead with his trip to Manchester, but she supposes the alternative, the two of them in the house alone together re-hashing everything, jointly overdosing on caffeine would have been beyond ghastly. She needs time to think. She *has* time to think, but she's not using it well.

We're all just animals, she thinks glumly. She ponders that her sexual revival, dormant for so long, was probably entirely due to the pheromones Giles has been pumping out; he's been wafting them around in his super-stud wake, all because he's been shagging some girl in her mid-teens. The same age as Serena. The fact that she has had a physical response to it all is simply disgusting.

'You have to believe me,' he said, sounding desperate. 'She turned up to my office a couple of times a week for months, carrying a brief-case, a newspaper. Wearing glasses. High heels. Make-up.'

'For fuck's sake, Giles, girls wear make-up from the age of twelve,' she yelled. 'Even I wore make-up at twelve, and that was in the bloody Dark Ages. How could you be so fucking stupid?'

'Sometimes she turned up at my office with a set of car keys looped over her thumb.' He had screwed up his eyes and let out an anguished cry.

Propelled by some masochistic force, she held out her hand for his phone. 'Let me see her picture.'

He stared at her, then dug into his jacket pocket. His hands shook as he tapped in the code, then handed it to her.

The first picture in his photo gallery is of a young girl smiling shyly at the camera over the rim of a wine glass. Very pretty. Mixed-race. Christine's heart had twisted at those lovely brown eyes, lit up by a luminous smile. She had swiped the screen to the right, only to see another picture of the same girl reclining on a bed, wrapped in a white towel. The kind of thick, soft, blazingly white towel you only find in hotels.

Giles made a half-hearted move to stop her from looking further, but had wilted, visibly defeated. The second picture is still alive in Christine's head. The girl was laughing, holding her arm out to the camera. Foreshortening had made her hand as big as her face in the frame, it was a joking attempt to ward off the man holding the camera, that being her, Christine's, own bloody husband. Christine can even imagine her squealing 'Oh don't,' or 'Nooo!' but it's clear she didn't mind, her smile says so … and why would she? Christine reckons if she looked like that, she'd be preening for the camera night and day. The light had highlighted the curve of one cheekbone and the smooth skin of her shoulder. She looked young, of course she did, but she could be anywhere between thirteen and thirty.

The pain is lacerating, but each time she thinks of it, from whatever angle, a fresh pang strikes her.

It wasn't the girl's youth or beauty that had struck her. What had hit her was that she looked so happy. Happy to be larking about with Giles. Happy to be with him. Shit, just happy to be. How can he possibly want to come home after that?

'God, Giles, the girl is just a child. It's revolting that you've had sex with her.'

'But you have to believe me,' he kept saying, like a stuck record. 'When I see Serena and her friends, they look like children to me.'

'That's because they are.'

'Yes, I know. That's what I'm trying to tell you. Neveah's not like that.'

'That's her name?'

The pain competes with her fury. How could he be so blind? To be so willingly led by his dick, like so many other tosspot twats before him. A child. When you know her age, the photos take on another dimension, like an optical illusion. Christine's rage at Giles is competing with rage at herself. She has been utterly blind to what has been going on under her own nose for months.

She casts her mind back a couple of years, when it had occurred to her that Giles may have been having an affair. He'd been staying out late, organising weirdly timed business trips, getting up unfeasibly early in the morning, making excuses which rang a little hollow, all the usual clichés. Then, one day he'd called her and told her to pack a bag each for her and Serena. He'd booked a couple of rooms in an independent hotel with a pool and a spa in the Lake District for a long weekend. He'd taken a couple of days off work and they'd pulled Serena from school.

Giles had been so attentive to them both. Instead of insisting that they get up at the crack of dawn and yomp for miles each day, he was happy doing what they wanted, which was to wander round the local town, spending time in the art galleries and independent shops. He doesn't mind book shops, but any other kind bores him half to death. That was how she'd known it was all over. Maybe it was his way of telling her. She'd stopped worrying about it.

And now? She'd been so busy focusing on her running, her weight loss, her newfound independence that she's been blind to anything else. She's been like a child, preparing for a big reveal that is impressive to no one but her: 'Hey, look at me, folks. I can go out by myself! I can exercise. I can make the choice to eat for one person rather than three.' Pathetic. What did she expect? A medal? And all the time she's had tunnel vision, oblivious to her husband tomcatting with a teenager and her daughter being groomed by some sick paedophile.

She is suddenly gripped with a powerful desire for fat and sugar. She puts her shoes and coat on and grabs her bag. She'll go to Waitrose on the Gloucester Road. She's going to buy a family pack of crisps. Salt and vinegar. Maybe prawn cocktail. Why not both? Pork scratchings! She'll get some doughnuts while she's at it. And some chocolate. A huge Galaxy bar. Turkish Delight. She hasn't touched a frosted corn-flake in months, and she fucking loves them. She's going to browse the shelves and buy whatever the fuck she feels like. Then she's going to bring her haul home and gorge on the lot. She'll have plenty of time to hide the evidence. She'll go back on the straight and narrow tomorrow. She reaches for her keys and is about to step outside when she remembers to take a couple of carrier bags with her. Just because her world is imploding doesn't give her the right to wreck the planet.

BILLY

The shop has been busy, and Billy hasn't had a moment to himself since the Amazon package arrived, but there's an unexpected lull, so he gets it out of his backpack and opens it on the counter while he's munching a sandwich. It's a mini spy camera, a wireless portable nanny cam with two-way audio and night vision, that can record in the dark. It has a smart motion detector and advanced invisible infra-red night vision up to fifty feet. He'll only need it to work at a fraction of that distance. The packaging promises that the camera will provide clear images via Wi-Fi even in total darkness to a mobile phone or a computer, and that it will be completely unnoticeable, as it has no lights to betray its presence. Not bad for forty quid. James Bond couldn't expect any better.

He won't tell Serena. It will freak her out. She's a bundle of nerves already. Depending on how it goes, he'll play it back to her afterwards. It'll be something ultra horny they can share. She'll thank him one day. It's not everyone who has a recording of their first time.

He starts to read the instructions. Technology doesn't come natu-rally to him. Give him all the constituent pieces of any bike, on the other hand, and he can put them together blindfolded.

Andy emerges from the stock room behind Billy and peers over his shoulder. 'Mmm. What's Mummy made for you today?' Billy's eating a BLT. His mum, Elaine, makes him a packed lunch every day. The others rib him for it, but he knows they're pig sick jealous. His sandwiches are always made exactly as he likes them, and she always includes fruit and a bag of crisps.

Andy takes a look at the contents of the Amazon package. 'Is that a spy cam?' He's a proper techno geek. He reaches across Billy and picks up the box. 'This is a good piece of kit.'

'You couldn't help me set it up, could you? At Deak's later, I mean.'

Andy looks at him, a smile spreading across his face. 'You're not, are you?'

Billy meets his gaze and gives a modest shrug.

'You dirty bastard,' Andy says and laughs. 'Better make sure the battery's charged up. Sometimes they take hours.'

'Shit!' says Billy. 'Come on, give us a hand. Help me put it together.'

'Chill out, dude,' says Andy, and he slots the battery into its charging station and plugs it in. 'Even if it's not fully loaded by the time we knock off, you'll get at least a few hours out of it. And let's face it, mate. You'll only need it for a few seconds.'

'Shut up, wanker,' says Billy, swatting his friend on the arm, and the two of them laugh.

MARIE

Marie's slapping on make-up, in a rush as her boss has asked her to be at the club early tonight. She's fine with that. She could do with the extra cash. Her phone rings. It's a mobile number, not one she recognises.

'Hello, is that Marie? It's Sandra here.'

'Oh, yeah. Sandra. How are you? What's going on?'

Marie doesn't have a particular axe to grind with Sandra. Jackie had gone through a number of women before he'd met Sandra. Fair play to her, Sandra had hung on to him longer than most. Even managed to get him up the aisle. Wonders will never cease, she'd thought at the time, and not without bitterness. She and Sandra had each come away with a lasting memento from their respective entanglements with Jackie, which is more than can be said for any of the others. A daughter apiece. They've had brief contact in the past about getting the girls together, always instigated by Sandra, but it must be at least a year since they last spoke.

'I don't know if Neveah told you what happened last night.'

'Nah, 'cos I haven't seen her since … ooh, must be Tuesday, when I was last off. I work nights, you see.'

Sandra sketches out the events of the previous evening. '… So you know what Jackie's like. Not willing to do the right thing by his daughters, but he won't let anyone else take care of them either. He was trying to stop me from calling the police. Lucky Granny S called before I did, to say that Cha-Cha had turned up. Safe, if not sound.'

'Oh yeah, okay, good,' says Marie, wondering what any of this has to do with her.

'I'm a touch annoyed with Granny S, to tell you the truth. I know Jackie's her son and in her eyes he can do no wrong, etcetera, etcetera, but seriously. She should know that parenting teenage girls is not one of his natural talents. Letting Cha-Cha out with him when she'd promised to keep an eye on her, well. You can imagine how I felt about the whole thing. Anyway, the reason I'm calling is because – well, I've been thinking about it a lot, and I came to the conclusion –' A conclusion would be good, thinks Marie, as she looks at her watch. '– that I really should talk to you. You see, there was a guy at the club last night with Neveah. A guy by the name of Giles. Giles Hawthorne.'

'What about him?'

'Well, there's something going on between them. He's much older than her. Like, seriously older. He's middle-aged, like forties, fifties. I just think you ought to know, that's all. If Cha was involved in a situation like that, I'd want someone to tell me.'

Marie's peeved. She's bridling and she can't put her finger on why. She has a vague sense of irritation, that someone else is telling her how to behave as a mother. Sandra's implying that Marie doesn't know what's going on in her own daughter's life.

She wants to ask questions, but that would be tantamount to admitting that it's true. Nonetheless, she can't help herself. 'What do you mean by *something going on between them*?'

'I tried to ask her, but she wouldn't say. They had some kind of argument before he left and when he did, she was really upset. I didn't hear what it was about. She said she was just exhausted, and emotional from all the worry about her sister, but I could tell it was because of him. Still, you know what she's like when she doesn't feel like talking.'

Marie knows only too well. Unbidden, a picture of Blue and Neveah together springs into her head. That was more than two years ago now, but still. There are some things that can never be unseen.

'Well, thanks for telling me. I'll have a word with her.'

'Don't be too hard on her, will you? It's not easy for her having such a rubbish father.' Sandra's tone is conspiratorial. 'Of all people, I know you'll understand. No wonder she's latched on to a Daddy figure. It's a classic, isn't it?'

'I think I know how to deal with my own daughter.'

'I didn't mean –'

'Look, I have to go. I gotta be at the club around now. Thanks for ringing, yeah?'

GILES

Giles is on the train back to Euston Station. He must have made all the right noises at the meeting, as the client seemed happy enough. Not for the first time, he's grateful for his ability to compartmentalise.

He remembers the terrible time after Christine's attack. While she was in hospital, he had looked after Serena, who was only eight at the time. He'd done all the myriad mundane things children need doing for them and had continued doing them even after Christine was back home, as she was too depressed to manage anything other than lie on the sofa and cry. All human beings, he supposes, are capable of blocking out horror, even temporarily, simply because the world depends on people getting on with things, no matter what is happening around them.

He's drained. He and Christine had not slept the night before. The memory of her stricken face swims in front of him. Her pain. Her revulsion at what he's done. And there's a voice in his head asking him what the fuck did he expect?

'Giles, you could end up on a sex offender's register. What will that do to us? To our family? What about Serena? How's she going to cope with having a dad who's a statutory rapist?'

Rapist. It's a ghastly word. She'd spat it at him in fury.

The memory of Christine's crying is still torturing his inner ear and makes his throat constrict.

He forces himself to concentrate on the document he's composing on his laptop. It's a contemporaneous note, which he will lodge with his solicitor to be produced in case of future reprisals. He has no idea if it will protect him, but he's a practical man, and he needs to do whatever he can to look after his family.

The letter is a dry account of his first meeting with Neveah; her pitch for his business, and the development of their relationship during subsequent meetings, during which she had only reinforced his impression of her maturity and business acumen, and the date on which their relationship changed from professionalism to romance. To sex, he thinks brutally. What they – what *he* had done could not be seen through the false lens of romance. Not anymore. He lists each occasion over the past few months since they first met – he has them all recorded in his electronic diary – and it's all he can do to stop himself from crying. Or punching himself very hard in the face. The memory of each occasion has released a flood of visual and tactile feelings, all tainted now.

He's also haunted by the memory of Neveah's face in the night club. The feelings he has for her haven't disappeared. They're trapped, like a leaden lump inside him, with nowhere to go. What feelings? he thinks savagely. She's a child.

A child, yes. A person, too. A person with a character and a soul. A fierce self-loathing rises up inside him.

To add insult to injury, some depraved filth-bucket has been sending porn to Serena's phone. It's horrifying to think of his daughter associated with porn. He shudders. Serena has never given him any anxiety. She's happy. She does all right at school, she's got friends, plenty of outside interests, she's good company at home. It's a cliché to say that his daughter's a joy, but she is. She's never moody or difficult. She's a laugh. The fact that she's living some kind of secret life that doesn't involve him and Christine is deeply distressing. It would be one thing for her to find a boyfriend, some nice young lad around her own age. They wouldn't object to that at all. It's only natural. But what kind of monster sends images like that to a young girl? He can't believe she would even begin to encourage it. Perhaps she's being targeted by someone. She can't help what people send her. But the message accompanying it suggests she's complicit. He reminds himself, as if he could even begin to forget, that he's been having sex with a girl the same age as his daughter. He and Christine will have to insulate Serena from this, try to keep their internal drama away from her. When he thinks about what he and Christine have survived together … perhaps this will finally break them.

He takes his phone from his pocket. It's been on silent all day. He sees that Neveah has called a few more times. She hasn't texted or left a message. He can't call her. He can't think of a single thing to say to her that will help either of them. He pulls up his favourite picture, the one of her wrapped in a white towel. Before he gives himself time to consider, he deletes it. He does the same to the others.

SERENA

Serena and Georgie are in Starbucks. Serena is expected home at around six and will have to leave for the tube any minute if she wants to be on time. She's been egging herself on all day, talking herself into not going home, but it's hard to visualise going through with it. She's never been openly defiant. She's never had to be. That's the trouble with having altogether reasonable and understanding parents. It means that you don't get any practice at being a rebel. But going home and letting Billy down is unthinkable. He'll despise her for it.

'I can't believe my mum told my dad. The bitch!' she says, not for the first time that day.

'Oh, come on. What would you have done if you were in her shoes?'

'Whose side are you on?'

'Yours, you know that. Look on the bright side. It could have been a lot worse. It's only a gif. It could have been you on that video. I read about this girl who –'

'Yeah, I know, you told me, remember? But seriously, what am I going to say to him? I won't even be able to look him in the face.'

'When in doubt, lie.'

'What do you mean?'

'Just tell them it was a wrong number. That it was sent to you by mistake. I'm sure you'll think of something.'

'I should have done that then and there. I just – I panicked. I begged Mum not to tell Dad. But she's done it anyway,' Serena says darkly.

'Have you told Billy you're not coming tonight?'

'No,' says Serena.

'Don't you think you'd better? He's been planning your special night for ages. God, he's going to be gutted. I wonder if I should go anyway. I mean, I'd much rather go with you, obvs, but I don't want to miss it.'

Serena looks at her friend. 'No. I haven't told him I'm not coming, 'cos I am. I'm in so much shit at home that whatever I do will make no difference.'

Georgie looks at her in alarm. 'But they'll worry about you.'

'No they won't. I'll text them later, to let them know I'm safe. That I'm with you. I'll tell them you're having a "family crisis,"' she makes inverted commas in the air with her fingers, 'and that you need me. I mean, I'm nearly sixteen. If I want to stay over at a friend's house, they can't stop me.'

'But you won't be at a friend's house.'

'Duh, but they won't know that. Besides, I will be at a friend's house. A friend of Billy's. Your mum's out tonight, isn't she? So they won't know we're not at your place, safely watching telly in our PJs like good little girls.'

'What if they come over?'

Serena considers. 'Then they come over. They'll find the place empty, and we can say that they turned up just when we went to pick up our pizza.'

'So you've thought of everything.'

'No one will know where we are. Not your mum, not anyone.'

'Don't you think that's kind of … I dunno. Creepy? It's the sort of thing that always goes horribly wrong.'

'Only in the movies. You worry too much. Everything will be fine. There's just one problem.'

'What's that?'

'I brought my outfit for tonight, but I blew a wodge on a matching undie set and I left it at home. I'm such a twat.'

Georgie leans forward. 'What're your undies like? The ones you're wearing now, I mean?'

Serena looks glum. 'Boring old pack-of-five M&S. I was planning to change at yours. You know, keep the new stuff fresh. I didn't want to get them all sweaty playing hockey.'

'Well you can't borrow mine.'

'Well duh, I know that.' Serena is tall and slender, with a C cup. Georgie is petite, and as flat as an ironing board.

'It doesn't matter to blokes. I read this article in GQ and only a couple of the blokes took any notice. Most of them were way more interested in what was under the undies. Besides, he said he loves you, didn't he? He won't care what you're wearing.'

'D'you really think so?'

'Yeah, I do. But seriously. You should go home tonight. I've got a bad feeling about you coming.'

The inkling that her friend wants to go to the party without her only grows stronger and fuels her determination. 'Come on, drink up, we're going. I'd rather my dad gave me a bollocking for bunking out than for receiving porn.'

'Now he's going to bollock you for both.'

'Somehow, that doesn't seem so bad.'

CHRISTINE

Christine is buzzing with sugar and E numbers, only compounding her misery. Now she couldn't force down another crisp or piece of chocolate if her life depended on it. She has stashed the rest of her contraband – a couple of packets of salt and vinegar, a giant Galaxy bar and some marshmallows – at the very back of a kitchen cupboard, the one with all the bottles of cleaning agents. She knows it'll be quite undisturbed there. She has thrown away all the wrappers and covered them with newspaper for good measure. She's put a chicken in the oven to roast for dinner, and the savoury smell of the gravy, normally so wholesome, is starting to fill the kitchen and is making her feel sick. She feels bloated and unclean.

She really wishes she hadn't eaten all that crap. She didn't go for her run that morning either. She's disappointed in herself. She's dreading Giles coming home. She wonders if he has spoken to Neveah today. Maybe he's gone to see her. How would she know what he does while she's stuck here at home? She's also not looking forward to the coming confrontation with Serena. She hopes Giles comes home first, although they may start raging at one another again, and they have to keep their shit together for Serena's sake.

She doesn't know what to do with herself. She's done all the prep work for supper. She's got new potatoes ready to boil when everyone's home and green beans topped and tailed, waiting to be steamed. Normally she and Giles would share a bottle of wine with dinner, but that feels a bit fucking chummy now. Besides, it wouldn't sit well on top of a bellyful of junk. He'll probably be gagging for a drink when he comes home. He can bloody well drink alone.

She glances at the front door. Did she hear footsteps? Only someone walking past the house. There's some mail on the mat that she's ignored all day. Normally, she likes dealing with papers as soon as they arrive, but today … Well. She couldn't be bothered. She picks it up.

There are statements from the bank and BT, a request from their energy company to make an appointment for an engineer to install a smart meter – they've been ignoring this for years – and a letter from the National Parole Board. She gets frequent letters from Victim Support, which is how she joined her weekly group. This is different. She opens it and scans the contents. Then she has to read the letter again, more slowly the second time.

Apparently, it is the duty of the National Parole Board to inform her that Mr. Ian Johan Durandt is eligible for a parole hearing in four weeks' time. She is entitled to attend or send a representative. In any event, they will inform her of the outcome.

She's known this day will come. He's served around half of his sentence. That's what happens, apparently, when prisons are full. They have to let a few of the bad guys out. Then they waltz around masquerading as normal, until they just can't help themselves, and they take a wrecking ball to someone else's life.

She heaves violently into the kitchen sink, then straightens up, supporting herself against the sink edge, taking in great gulps of air. She tears off a square of kitchen towel and wipes her mouth. While she's rinsing away the mess, she hears the sound of a key in the lock. Footsteps.

'Darling, are you all right?' When she turns around, Giles is behind her, full of confusion and concern.

'It's a great way to lose a few pounds before a show,' she says. She points to the letter and begins to cry.

NEVEAH

'He's a fucking wanker,' says Sharna. 'He should man up and talk to you.'

Neveah doesn't bother to defend him. Her desperation to speak to Giles, to explain, has now been overtaken by a weird kind of apathy. She can't bear the idea of never seeing him again, of him thinking badly of her. But there's no fix for this. There's nothing on earth she can do or say to make this better, other than invent a time machine.

'How many times have you tried to call him?'

'Enough to know he ain't picking up.' She wants to add that she doesn't blame him, but she knows how that'll go down.

'You know, we should report him. He's nothing but a fucking paedo.'

Finally, Sharna has said something that rouses her. 'No way, Sharn. Don't you dare say anything. You promised.'

'Okay, okay. I won't,' Sharna says, without conviction.

'I have so pulled a number on him and I've been sussed. I just wanna give myself a massive kicking for –'

'For what?'

'I dunno. For everything.'

Neveah wants to explain, that she really needs Giles. That he's ... essential to her now. But what's the point? Sharna doesn't even want to understand. She's spoiling for a fight, gagging for a bit of drama. She doesn't give a stuff about the cost, especially not to Giles.

'D'you wanna come back to mine? My dad's picking up a curry on the way home. It's movie night.'

Sharna and all the members of her family are incapable of sitting through a film without constantly shouting instructions to the characters or commenting on the action, the plot, the appearance of the actors, their talent or more usually the lack of it, the special effects and whether they're realistic or not, and ceaselessly tell each other off for doing all of the above. Normally, Neveah finds it funny.

'Nah. Thanks, Sharn. I'd rather stay here.'

'Come on. You don't want to rot here all by yourself. Come and crash for the night.'

'I hate curry.'

'It's not about the food, you numpty. You can eat cheese and crackers, I don't care. I don't want you crying into your pillow by yourself all night. Sometimes it's not good to be alone, you know? Your mum'll be out 'til stupid o'clock. It's a Friday, remember?'

Neveah wants to be with Giles so badly that she can't think straight, but if she can't have him, then she'd rather be alone.

'I'll be a right old misery-guts. I can't stand the idea of sitting with your family, having to pretend everything's normal.'

'Well, how about we don't pretend everything's normal? How about we tell 'em what's been going on? That you've been dumped by some rich old white dude –'

'Sharn, I told you, it's not –'

'I'm just saying,' she says, head wobbling from side to side, 'he can't get away with shagging you every which way for months then chucking you like you're a piece of dogshit. I bet if you were white, he'd have called you.'

'It's not like that.' Neveah wants to explain to Sharna that *he* isn't like that, but Sharna's not listening. 'Sharn, if you tell anyone he could get into serious trouble. Lose his family.'

'Why are you so worried about his family? It's not like he is.'

'He could go to jail!'

'And serve the fucker right.'

Neveah groans. 'Stop it. You're doing my head in. Okay, I'll come. If only to keep an eye on that big gob of yours, seeing as you can't watch it yourself.'

Sharna grins. 'You know you love me really.'

GILES

'You've got to calm down, Chrissie. You'll make yourself ill.'

'I can't bear not knowing where she is. Not after what I saw on her phone last night.'

Giles sighs. 'I don't like being in the dark either, but they all make a break for it sooner or later. She's with Georgie, that much is clear. Georgie's a sensible girl. Hell, Serena's sensible too. They'll look out for each other, I'm sure. We just have to hope for the best. All we can do is wait.'

They're back home after driving over to Georgie's place. Georgie's brother had answered the door, munching on a thick piece of buttered toast.

'Everyone's out,' he'd said. 'At least I think they are. Hang on a sec,' and he'd gone to the foot of the stairs and shouted Georgie's name to the rafters. He'd cupped his ear to listen for a response, which didn't come.

'Do you have any idea where they might be?'

'Nope. Sorry. I jumped in with a mate driving down from Durham last minute. I only got in half an hour ago and no one knows I'm here yet.'

They know Serena is with Georgie because her school satchel had been dumped with Georgie's under the hallway table.

Normally only a fifteen-minute drive, it had taken them over half an hour because of an accident on the Cromwell Road. All the way back, Christine had been frantically calling or texting Serena, Georgie and Georgie's mum, without luck.

Giles hands Christine a cup of tea.

'We should have asked him if they'd left a note,' she says.

'They're not likely to have done that, are they?'

Christine knows he's right. 'I can't stand the idea of her being with someone who doesn't love her. Someone who respected her would never send her that filth.' She starts crying again. 'I don't want her going through what I did, or anything close to it.'

Giles is helpless. He wants to comfort her, but he's lost the right to go anywhere near her. He forces the thought aside and gets out of his armchair to sit next to her on the sofa. He takes her hand.

'Chrissie, I hate the idea of it too, but I wonder what we would have been like if we'd grown up with phones and technology the way the kids do these days. Maybe we'd have been sending each other that stuff left right and centre, and thought nothing of it, who knows? The chances of her going through what you did are incredibly slim. You know that, don't you? I wish I could say what happened to you was a one-off. I know it's not. I know that too many women and girls go through similar things on a far too regular basis, but statistically –'

'Fuck your statistics!' she yells and snatches her hand back. 'We don't know anything about this guy. He could be a – oh, I don't know – a fifty-year-old architect.'

He stares stonily at his cup. He says nothing to defend himself.

'I wonder how Neveah's parents feel about her relationship with you? I'm sure they won't be delighted to find out some middle-aged bloke has been pawing their daughter. I assume they don't have a clue about your existence.'

Giles closes his eyes. He knows better than to even attempt to answer this question, studded as it is with potential landmines, especially with the revelation that his own daughter is the object of someone's deviant fantasies. Neveah's parents were of purely academic interest to him in that they had produced the marvel that was Neveah. Beyond that, he certainly had no desire to ever meet them. He couldn't imagine wasting his very limited and precious time with Neveah on making small talk with her parents. The fact that he was married would have made it an awkward non-starter on all sides. Now of course he knows that on top of the slightly delicate issue of his marital status was the massively inconvenient clanging fact that she was underage. His parents are both dead, so he has never had to consider introducing her, even hypothetically. The very idea is unthinkable, laughable even. Would his mother have seen through Neveah's veneer of sophistication? Probably, he admits. Clear-eyed and utterly unsentimental, she would have seen the relationship exactly for what it was. When he'd gone through his diary and reviewed every encounter, every conversation, it's impossible not to be struck by how young Neveah is. Now he knows, he can't see her as anything other than fifteen.

'Well, do they?'

He looks up and says, 'I never gave it much thought, to be honest. I haven't known her that long.'

'When did you meet her?'

'A few months ago.' Thanks to the letter he'd composed on the train, he knows that it's been five months and three weeks. It's hard to believe that their first meeting is so recent, as she has become such a big part of his life. *Had* become, he corrects himself.

'How often did you see each other?'

'A few times a week, we –' Their relationship was all about stolen moments; it was a battle to find enough time to get together. 'I was at work, and she –' he pauses.

'Was at school.' Christine says flatly.

'Yes. Exactly. I believed her without question when she said she was busy with meetings and clients and whatnot during the day.'

What a credulous twat he is. He wants to say as much, but he's afraid it will sound self-pitying. Which it is. 'The few times we saw each other during the day were for business meetings. She must have bunked off school. Or used her free periods. Or whatever. I guess I'll never know.'

'What do you mean you'll never know?'

Giles stares at her. 'I can't speak to her anymore. Not ever.'

'Is that because you don't trust yourself?'

He carefully considers his response. In this respect, he certainly can trust himself. He is recalibrating every memory he has of Neveah, and doesn't even want to think of her in sexual terms anymore, but he wonders whether Chrissie will believe him. Before he has a chance to answer, she asks, 'Do you love her?'

He is silent, knowing that whatever he says will damn him.

'Well do you?'

'God, Chrissie, whatever I felt for her, I can't call it love.' He is reluctant to explain how everything has changed, how every memory he has of Neveah has been coloured by the shattering revelation that she's a child.

'Did you ever imagine any kind of life with her?'

'No, I –' he stops to consider. He wishes he could tell Christine that he had wanted to end things with Neveah. That he had told himself to do it. But Chrissie knows him. She'll know that if he'd wanted to stop seeing Neveah, he would have done it.

SERENA

Serena's smoking in Deacon's kitchen. Actually, it's his dad's kitchen, but Deak's in charge as his dad's away in Somalia. At first, he'd forced all the smokers outside, trying to keep some vague semblance of order, but now it's a free-for-all. He's given up policing everyone and even he's puffing away inside the house now. Billy's told her that Deak's parents had him when they were only teenagers. His dad's in the army, and she's not sure of the details, but his mother's dead. She doesn't know him well enough to ask, but maybe that'll change.

Tonight's been a revelation. She finds she can hold a cigarette between her fingers for ages and take a tiny puff very occasionally and still look like the real deal. No one's checking. No one's keeping count. If she takes a drag and blows it out without inhaling, it comes out in a kind of cloud, like an engine belching which gives her away as an amateur, but if she inhales it, even in minuscule doses, she can blow it out in a continuous stream. She's glad she's been practicing, as her throat is becoming habituated to it, and she can inhale without coughing. She never realised how useful smoking is; that you can take a drag and look knowing, arch, flirty, serious, superior, that you can do it to emphasise a point, to cover up an inanity and to fill a silence.

She's having such a cool time. Everyone knows that she and Billy are together, but they aren't joined at the hip; she's sitting on the kitchen counter looking like she owns the place and no one's minding. She's talking to a bunch of seriously interesting people. They're chatting about live bands and art, vlogging and climate change and porn and veganism, gap years and working vs uni and whether the Mona Lisa's a fake. These are people who are fully launched in the world, they're working, they've left school and they're earning money and doing cool things like making music and films and documentaries on their phones and she finds that even if she has no clue about a particular topic, she can nod at the right time or look sceptical or raise an eyebrow or take a judicious drag of her cigarette or a long cool sip of her cider to imply she does.

There are some things she isn't volunteering: her attendance at a private school, any chat about her parents and exams, and she's blunting the edges of her accent and is becoming ever so slightly Estuary, but she's doing it so subtly that no one except Georgie could call her out on it, and there's no danger of that as Georgie is doing exactly the same. Georgie looks like she's having a good time. She's wearing a close-fitting magenta shirt which suits her boyish slimness, and she's chatting to some earnest-looking rake thin guy in a black polo neck who looks like a young Steve Jobs.

Serena's relieved that Georgie isn't listening into her conversation, as her friend knows her too well, and would see through all her tricks to blend in, and while Georgie would never out her, just the fact she would witness it would hamper her, and stop her from doing it so well. So all is cool. All for the best in the best of all possible worlds.

Serena's feeling good about her outfit; a cute short blue denim dress with a zip from top to bottom. She's making her little crowd laugh, she can be funny when she gets going, and she's got a warm glow inside her after a couple of glasses of vodka and coke. She's drinking a bottle of cider right now, and Billy's in the living room chatting to a group of his mates who went to the pub first and have just arrived. She's really keen to find out who they are, but she's giving no sign; she'll wait and he'll come through soon enough, there's no hurry, and it gives her a buzz of anticipation that he'll bring them to her in his own good time and will introduce her as his girlfriend. God, he's so lovely. His wavy dark hair gives him the air of a pirate. He's tall with good shoulders, with the muscles of a dedicated cyclist. She's so lucky.

The noise from the living room's getting louder. The place is really starting to fill up. She doesn't see how she and Billy are going to get any private time together, but she finds she doesn't mind. They're here, they're together, and all the pressure, the build-up to this evening, the hallowed space of 'Deak's spare room', which is actually his dad's room, all of this stress has fallen away. She doesn't know why she's been worrying about tonight for so long. Billy's cool. His friends are cool. Fuck, *she* is cool. And Deak's room is where everyone has chucked their coats. She's made it here tonight, she hasn't let Billy down and it looks like she's off the hook. She can take the secret of her grotty old M&S knickers to her grave.

She has deliberately not looked at her phone since she texted her parents at around half past six. She and Georgie got themselves ready in a hurry and went to Pizza Express rather than get their usual takeaway. She couldn't risk her parents driving round and finding them still at the house. Every now and then she feels her phone vibrate, but she prefers not to look. It'll only make her anxious. There's no point checking for missed calls and texts if she has no intention of responding. She's told them she's safe. That's good enough. She'll get an uber back with Georgie when they're good and ready. At some point tomorrow, she'll be royally in the shit, but she'll cross that bridge when she comes to it.

CHRISTINE

Christine has just tried Serena's mobile again. Her phone record helpfully tells her that it's the sixteenth attempt. She feels a coruscating anger against her daughter. Serena has always shown a sensitive understanding of her mother's unique fears. She's normally so careful to communicate that she's safe, heralding her comings and goings with brief texts: 'Here xx', 'Leaving now xx' 'Back in 20 xx' ... so it dismays Christine that this constant stream of contact has been abruptly terminated, that Serena is allowing her to deliberately stew in her own peculiarly paranoid juices, and there's not a thing she can do about it. Except wait.

The fact that she's angry contains a germ of reassurance. Anger means her daughter is thoughtless, selfish, callous, wilful, disobedient, headstrong. It tells her that her child is a typical teenager, and will do typically teenage things, and will emerge unscathed, as teenagers typically do. Anger dilutes the fear that her daughter is being abused, violated, humiliated, mentally and psychologically harmed by someone who has no respect for her and no regard for her feelings, who looks on her as a thing. Who will treat her with contempt, possibly even violence. The image she saw on Serena's phone ... the girl, the woman, the owner of the torso being so ruthlessly and efficiently fucked in that video is someone's daughter, someone's sister, maybe even someone's mother.

That kind of lovelessness is violence to Christine.

Ian Durandt's dominance in her mind had waned as her strength had grown, but thanks to the notice of the parole hearing, the fact that he could soon be out … he's elbowing his way back to top billing, jostling for space with her cheating husband, his beautiful teenage mistress, their absconding daughter and the shadowy misogynistic tosspot wanker likely victimising her right about now. That's quite a long shit list. She laughs. It sounds like a bark.

Ian was one of Christine's students when she worked as a lecturer in modern languages. He grew up in Zimbabwe, on a rural farm in the middle of nowhere, the only child of a South African father and a French mother. He was raised speaking French, Afrikaans and English, plus Shona and Ndebele. After a couple of months of sharing a house in London with a student from Milan, Ian accumulated conversational Italian, and was soon reading Dante in the original. 'Just for fun,' he said when asked.

He was tall and good-looking, with a devilish smile and an untameable cowlick in his fair hair. He was highly attractive to women. 'To us blokes, too,' sighed Fred Bunting, Head of the Department and Christine's boss, 'but he's a bit of a ladykiller, from what I hear. That cowlick's his secret weapon, if you ask me. The girls can't leave off trying to straighten it.'

Not only was Ian's facility with languages uncanny, his contributions to class discussions were always original and entertaining, and his written work was notable for its insight and sensitivity.

A few months after Ian's enrolment, it became clear that he had a serious problem with alcohol.

'Yup, his bad fairy left him a little present at his christening,' Fred said, after Ian had gone on the first of his rampages. 'Someone that brilliant's bound to have a screw loose.'

While drunk, he threatened a night bus driver who refused to accept him as a passenger. Ian was arrested, and used his one phone call on Fred, as Ian had no family in the country. Fred was happy to oblige. He loved being in the thick of things. He helped Ian with his statement, and thanks to his intervention, Ian escaped with a caution.

Polite and good-humoured while sober, Ian was a storming maniac when drunk.

'Like Jekyll and Hyde,' Fred said, shaking his head and blowing out his chubby cheeks. 'You know, I'd quite fancy him if he wasn't so volatile,' he said conspiratorially to Christine, 'but I like the quiet life.'

Ian had a habit of developing obsessive crushes on women. Along with his good looks, he was flamboyant, charming and clever, but there was a flipside: he was possessive and overbearing and had little respect for the conventional boundaries that underscored human relationships. One of his early girlfriends on campus was a shy, softly spoken girl from Glasgow.

'Yes, such contradictions really do exist,' Fred laughed.

At first, the girl was flattered by this handsome, exotic and highly attentive specimen who showered her with flowers and presents and took her on extravagant nights out that she could never afford on her own. Warning bells sounded when he started turning up unannounced at the flat she shared with three other students at unsociable hours, and as she told Fred, she became 'spooked' when he demanded a key so he could 'keep an eye on her.' She admitted to Fred that his intensity terrified her.

'If I gave him my soul, it would never be enough.'

On the night she broke up with him, he woke her and her flatmates, as well as half the street, by banging on her door and shouting that if she didn't let him in and take him back, he'd kill himself.

One of the neighbours yelled from an upstairs window: 'Is that a threat or a promise?'

Fred dined out on this story for weeks.

Ian's next relationship was with a glamorous divorcée ten years his senior, who worked front of house for a top end restaurant in Notting Hill. She was the mother of an eight-year-old girl who captivated Ian, and for a while he could not shut up about the girl, banging on about how wonderful she was, how he was so grateful to be given the chance to take a hand in her upbringing, as her own natural father was 'a deadbeat' and 'worse than useless' ... Unfortunately, this relationship took the same predictable turn as the others, and the police were called when Ian went on a rampage in the restaurant where his now ex-girlfriend worked, incurring considerable damages and a lifetime ban.

By now, the university authorities were on high alert. As Fred described it, he 'fell on the boy from a high height' and warned him that the very next infraction would be his last.

'If it were up to me, you'd be booted out, and justifiably so.'

Ian vowed to change and swore off alcohol. Being incapable of half measures, he abruptly turned teetotal, and cut himself off from all social activities, only leaving his digs to attend lectures. He threw himself into his studies and turned his attention to Christine.

'Uh-oh,' said Fred. 'You watch yourself. He likes you, I can tell. You're arousing his passion.'

'Only his passion for learning, Fred,' she laughed. 'He loves Rimbaud almost as much as I do.'

'You know, he scares me. He's the sort of –'

'What?'

'Let me put it this way. If I ever open the papers to find that he's chopped someone to pieces in a murderous rage, I wouldn't be entirely surprised.'

'You can't be serious. Don't you worry, Fred. I'll do nothing to encourage him. Except intellectually, of course.'

'I'm not sure he's able to differentiate. To him, female attention of whatever kind merely serves to fan the flames of his monstrous ego.'

She looked up at him, surprised. She loved Fred because he was always funny, gossipy, arch, ironic. He was hardly ever serious, and seldom unkind.

The two of them had ample reason to regret not trusting his instincts.

Christine never let on to Ian that she was so intimately acquainted with the details of his life, as she didn't want to destroy his faith in Fred.

Ian began to seek Christine out. He loitered after class to chat and would walk with her from one lecture hall to another, as if he had no better place to be but by her side. She knew she shouldn't encourage him, but he was interesting, funny, and she enjoyed their conversations.

Truth be told, she was flattered by the attention. She and Giles had been married for ten years, and they were happy, of course they were, even if they took each other a little for granted. God, what a cliché …

Ian turned up to the French Society she chaired, even though it was an extra-curricular club for students reading other subjects.

'What are you doing here?' she asked him. 'French is your mother tongue. You're not going to get anything out of it at all.'

He raised an eyebrow and gave an arch half smile. 'Isn't that for me to judge?'

She shrugged. 'Suit yourself. Don't blame me if you're bored to tears.'

'Listening to you? That won't be possible.'

'You should file a complaint,' said Fred.

'That he's killing me with kindness? Blitzing me with flattery?'

'It's his pattern of behaviour, that's all I'm saying.'

'Fred, I'm married. I'm fifteen years older than he is. There's no way –'

'Chrissie darling, he's not a rational person. He's an obsessive narcissist. Leaving aside the fact that you're married, he's not remotely concerned about whether the two of you are a suitable match, or if you have a realistic long-term future. He has set his sights on you, and he won't be satisfied until he gets what he wants. He's all softly softly now, but he's going to cross a line one of these days. *'No'* is not a word he's used to hearing.'

As if determined to prove Fred's powers of prediction, Ian hung around after her next lecture, and invited Christine out for dinner. 'I've got a few thoughts about dissertation topics, and I'd love to discuss them with you.'

'Why don't you email me your ideas? I'll consider them and send you feedback.'

'I'd prefer to bounce them back and forth. You know, have a brain-storming session. We could go to L'Etranger. Their steak tartare is to die for.'

'Thanks, Ian, but it would be much better if you scheduled a special tutorial during working hours. You're entitled to two a term.'

He looked hurt. 'You and I are friends now, aren't we?'

'We're friendly, Ian, but it's not appropriate for us to have dinner alone together.'

His face reddened. 'We're above that kind of bullshit. We have a connection, Christine. We –' he broke off, visibly struggling to define their 'connection' in words.

'Ian. It's six o'clock on a week night, and I should be getting home to my husband and daughter.' She kept her tone light. 'Let me rephrase that. I *want* to get home to my husband and daughter. They hardly see me during the week as it is. You've got bags of time to think up dissertation topics. You've got a wealth to choose from, and talent enough to do them all justice.' She paused, wanting to make her point, but delicately. 'You're in a special stage of life. You have no particular responsibilities, other than to yourself, and you should make the most of it. Gather ye rosebuds while ye may, and all that.'

He recoiled as if she'd spat at him. 'That's such patronising bullshit. You have no idea what I feel for you.'

She sighed heavily. 'You should focus your emotional energy on someone who's able to reciprocate. Someone age appropriate, for a start.'

'Do you think for one second that I care about age?'

'It's not everything, but it's something. In this case, it's irrelevant. I'm a staffer and you're a student. Not only that, I'm a married woman. A mother.' She wanted to say that even if she wasn't any of these things, she wouldn't be interested, but she didn't want to be unkind. 'You're clever, Ian, and a great conversationalist, and you come up with some wonderfully interesting and original ideas, and I love chatting to you, but the only interest I have in you is intellectual. Sorry.'

The look that crossed his face was one of fury. He made a huge effort to rein himself in. 'You can't mean that. I know I'm special to you, as you are to me. I –'

'Stop it, Ian. You've told me how you feel and I've responded. Please don't make my position any more difficult than it already is. If you continue pressing your case, I'll have to report you for harassment, and I really, really don't want to do that.' She was going to add that he was in enough trouble as it was, but again, she stopped herself.

He looked at her as if she'd electrocuted him. 'Fine,' he said. 'Thank you for making the situation crystal clear.' He turned on his heel. As he got to the door, he looked over his shoulder and hissed: 'Bitch,' injecting the word with almost comically camp venom.

'I was flabbergasted,' she later told Fred. She acted out Ian's mini tantrum.

'Cheeky little bugger. You should report him,' Fred said, after he stopped laughing.

'Honestly, I can't be arsed. These things make life more interesting. He'll settle down, really he will.'

For a few weeks, every time Fred left her office, he'd dramatically turn on his heel and hiss, 'Bitch!'

And the two of them laughed like drains.

Ian continued to attend Christine's lectures, but avoided any kind of personal contact with her. He shot her moody, smouldering glances full of hurt and resentment. Christine did not engage or give him any sign that she noticed his non-verbal screeching, but she discussed all the minutiae of his behaviour with Fred. Sometimes it was funny. Other times, disturbing.

Then Ian's focus abruptly switched. He started going out with Trudi Morensi, an Italian American girl from Brooklyn, who was in London for a year doing a Masters in Modern History. Trudi was a couple of years older than Ian, a striking girl with dark hair and a ready smile, fond of red lipstick and dramatic clothes. Big-hearted and brashly confident, she seemed to sprinkle some of her popularity and social ease on Ian, and the pair became a glamorous fixture on campus. It appeared that Ian was growing into his full potential, keeping his demons in check, and he even remarked to Fred that Trudi had 'tamed' him.

After dating Trudi for a couple of months, Ian sent an email to Christine:

Dear Christine
Heartfelt thanks for being so gracious when I laid my
cards on your table. I thought I was offering you the very best,

a royal flush, not appreciating that you were committed to a
full house already.
   Ian xx

'I'm not sure the poker metaphor is entirely appropriate,' said Fred. 'What's he trying to say? That you can't accept the best because you've already settled for less?'

'I think he's trying to be poetic, Fred,' said Christine.

Ian followed up his note with a visit. 'You were right about everything, Christine. I'm embarrassed by my behaviour, and I'm sorry.'

'Don't give it a second thought,' she'd reassured him.

'Friendly relations are restored,' she remarked to Fred. 'Friendly, but not over familiar.'

Which was just as well, as Christine was directing *Tartuffe*, the language department's end of year play, and Ian was playing the title role. The cast had a heated discussion about which translation to use, and Ian persuaded them that Donald Frame's rendition most closely maintained the beauty and elegance of Molière's original verse, without sacrificing the humour and the wit.

'It's got to be funny,' he argued. 'If we find it funny, so will the audience.'

At the same meeting, the cast decided on Amnesty International as their chosen charity, again persuaded by Ian, who spoke eloquently about what they were doing to counter atrocities committed daily in his homeland of Zimbabwe. He was especially outraged about sexual crimes committed against women.

Christine sighs ruefully. Even now she can appreciate the irony and still be objectively horrified by the waste of such stunning potential. She checks her phone in case a message has come in from Serena. Still nothing.

During rehearsals, Ian delivered his lines with a distinctly French inflection and flavour, rounding the flattened vowels of his own strong Zimbabwean accent. He effortlessly shifted into the skin of his character, oozing piety and hypocrisy through gesture and expression, and displayed a gift for comic timing. Christine worked closely with him during the readings and rehearsals. He never gave her a single uneasy moment. She often accompanied the cast to the pub after rehearsals. Ian always ordered a 'full fat coke.' He maintained his teetotal status, even when Trudi was by his side, merrily guzzling red wine.

'That stuff does terrible things to me,' he said and laughed along with everyone else when Trudi drawled, 'Don't you worry, honey, I can drink for the both of us.'

Thanks to Trudi's unique marketing skills, every ticket for the play was sold.

On the night of the performance, before curtain-up, Christine and Trudi had to calm Ian's nerves. They were in the large communal dressing room backstage with all the other cast members putting finishing touches to costumes and messing around with hair, wigs and applying make-up, whiteface and beauty spots.

The space had always been communal, operating on the unspoken understanding that no one was to stare or flaunt; the girls in particular were good at getting changed under layers, occasionally flashing a glimpse of underwear or skin. Haste neutralised the sexuality of stripping. There was a buzz about the room, which flared with high spirits and adrenaline, chattering and giggling, at odds with Ian's white-faced catatonia. One of the girls had brought in a few bottles of cheap supermarket plonk and a stack of paper cups. 'For a bit of Dutch courage,' she said, as she shared it out liberally.

Ian was in a corner, nauseous with fear. He leaned forward in an old armchair, rocking back and forth. Trudi was perched on the arm, rubbing his back. Christine pulled up a stool and took his clammy hand in her own.

'You're so talented. You're going to be amazing. You *are* Tartuffe.' What had she seen when she looked into those eyes? She had asked herself that question so many times, but the truth was she hadn't seen anything. She'd been looking into the eyes of a scared kid. To say that she had stared into the evil, unreflecting blackness of some Charles Manson-ish monster would have added relish to an anecdote, but it wasn't the truth.

'I need some of that wine,' he said. 'Just to take the edge off.'

'Seriously?' Trudi responded. 'But what about all the stuff we talked about?'

'Will you get me some?'

'Ian, you're just having some kind of panic attack.'

'Please, Trudi.'

'You can get through this without a drink. You sure can. You told me not to buckle, remember? No matter how much you begged me.'

'Don't be such a controlling cunt!' he screamed. 'Get me a fucking drink!'

Christine withered in shock. The room fell silent. Dropping the C bomb was all too commonplace on campus, but the vitriol that accompanied it was not. Trudi got to her feet and stalked out without a word.

Ian was visibly shaking. Christine watched Trudi withdraw, admiring her dignity, then stood up herself.

'You can't speak to people like that. Stage fright is no excuse.' She injected steel into her tone, conscious that others were listening. 'I'll leave you to it.'

His hand shot out and snatched her own. Then he said in a low voice, 'Please. Don't go.'

She disengaged her hand. 'If Trudi comes back, and I wouldn't blame her if she ran a mile, you ought to apologise.'

'Oh, she'll be back, all right,' said Ian, with a toss of his head.

'I wouldn't be so sure,' said one of the girls, glaring at him. Two high red points appeared on her cheeks. 'That was disgusting.' There were loud murmurs of assent.

Ian got out of the chair and made a beeline for the wine, filling a paper cup to the brim. The girl who had supplied it watched him resentfully. He downed it, then lifted the bottle to pour more, but stopped himself. He put it down then wiped his mouth with the back of his hand. He looked around, taking in the sea of glowering faces. His nerves seemed to have vanished.

'Guys,' he said, meaning the girls as well. 'I want to apologise.'

'Tell that to Trudi,' someone said.

He closed his eyes and nodded, then held his hands up in a mea culpa. 'That's so true. She was only trying to help me. She loves me, and I'm a dick. I'm sorry for wrecking the vibe in here. It was great until I blew my stack.'

He sounded pompous, but sincere, and he turned to leave the room.

'Where are you going?' Christine asked. 'The show starts in ten minutes.'

'That's all I need,' he said, and winked at her. His pre-performance catatonia seemed to be another demonstration of his exceptional acting ability. He liked attention and wasn't too fussed about how he got it. His little act had commanded the single-minded devotion of his girlfriend and his lecturer for half an hour. Yes, he's brilliant, she thought to herself. But he's fundamentally immature. And he really is a bit of a dick.

Curtain call approached, and there was no sign of Ian or Trudi.

'Shall I go and have a quick look?' asked Sarah, the girl who was playing Dorine.

'Yes. Please do. Actually, on second thoughts … I need all those in the first scene to stay here. Ralph, can you go?' Ralph was playing Orgon and wasn't due to appear onstage until the third scene.

'Sure thing. What if he's done a runner?'

It was a good question. Talent and reliability are not always comfortable bedfellows.

'We'll cross that bridge when we come to it.'

The next ten minutes went by in a panicked flurry, with cast members dashing in and out, various people sending hasty texts and making urgent calls to anyone able to help search for 'the Lesser-Spotted Dick' as Ralph had dubbed him.

Eventually Fred came in to investigate the delay. She explained the problem. 'We could start the play. He's not due to appear until the third scene, but if he hasn't turned up by then, we're stuffed.'

'Or you could do it,' said Sarah.

'What?'

'You can be Tartuffe. You know every word. Spoken by every character.'

'Well, yes. But –'

'Genius,' said Ralph. 'Problem solved. All you need is a black frock coat. There are at least three in the dressing room that will fit. The boots you're wearing can work. And look. He's left his wig on the armchair. Let's hope he doesn't have nits.'

Christine hesitated. 'But it's a student production, I'm –'

'Look, it's either that or we have to call it off, which will be a great shame when we have a packed hall full of ticket-paying people,' said Fred. 'Let's not dither anymore. We have to clear the chairs at the end of the evening before the cleaners come in, and I don't want them having to hang around. In any event, he may well turn up for his cue. Either way, we have a play, and that's what we've all come for.'

There was no point in protesting further. Filling in for Ian was the pragmatic thing to do. She'd been in the Dramatic Society when she was at university, and it was true that she knew the play backwards. What choice did she have?

'Okay, fine,' she said.

'Perfect. That's settled then.'

Ian did not reappear by the time Tartuffe was required on stage. Christine waited in the wings for her cue, heart hammering, determined to ape Ian's every gesture. She oozed onstage, as Ian had done, and before she even raised the first laugh from the audience, she found that she was enjoying herself. She loved Molière. She loved the play. She loved the language, the poetry, the cleverness, the wit... she loved her character, for all his slippery deceit, and for all these reasons, she played an excellent Tartuffe.

During the interval, Christine and the rest of the cast were in high spirits, toasting each other with paper cups of wine. Over the chat and the laughter, she heard shouting coming from the stairwell outside.

'Get off me, you fat old queen!' Then the door to the dressing room burst open.

It was Ian.

'You fucking bitch!' he screamed at Christine and advanced towards her. Fred was right behind him and grabbed his arm, just as Ralph stepped in front of her.

Even at that stage, she didn't believe he would actually physically harm her. Fred and Ralph knew better. She marvels now, at how secure she had always felt, how she'd taken her physical safety absolutely for granted. Tears spring to her eyes. What an idiot she was.

'Calm down, Ian,' she said. 'You can do the second half.'

'He'll do no such thing,' said Fred, chiming with a 'No way,' from someone and a 'You've got to be kidding me,' from someone else. Fred continued, 'Ian, I suggest you take yourself off to your digs and have a good hard think about your behaviour and the way you address people. I'm going to recommend a disciplinary, and let's face it, it'll probably be your last. Putting aside the offensive homophobic remark addressed to my good self, I heard you swore aggressively at Trudi, and I've just witnessed your hostile verbal abuse towards Christine, not to mention your threatening physical stance. She only took over your character because you decided to go AWOL before your cue.'

'I was only ten minutes late. You should've waited for me.'

'Do you think the world revolves around you? There are two hundred people in that hall. And twenty odd of us in this room. What about the cleaners who have to wait until we're finished arsing about? Should the poor sods all stay late, miss their night buses home, just because you believe you're exempt from the conventions that regulate everybody else?'

It was clear that was exactly what Ian thought. He was puce with rage, unable to formulate a response.

Ralph said, 'And her Tartuffe's better than yours, mate.'

Ian exploded with a deep throated scream, elongating every word: 'Fuck you all, you fucking bastards!' and he stormed towards the door. Unfortunately for him, he pushed at it, even though it was clearly labelled 'Pull' and someone giggled.

He quickly rectified his mistake, but no matter how swiftly he had run up the stairs, he would have heard that single giggle multiply into a roomful of raucous laughter. Even Christine couldn't help laughing. She felt sorry for him, of course she did, but the absurdity of his error, on top of his ridiculous outburst, the impotence of his rage ... well, it was so ludicrous. The way he'd spoken to Trudi, to Fred and to her ... he really needed to learn an important lesson ... that jaw-dropping arrogance which Fred had so rightly called him out on ... the best revenge was to forget about him for the rest of the evening, to do whatever she could to make sure everyone enjoyed being part of the performance, and not allow him to spoil their night. So they finished the play to triumphant applause, went *en masse* to the pub afterwards, and no one saw Ian for the rest of the evening.

Except Christine.

He attacked her as she walked from the pub to her car. She decided to get the tube home rather than drive, as she judged she was probably over the limit, but she had left her book in the car, and wanted it for the journey home. She had been reading *The Lovely Bones* and was engrossed by the depiction of Susie Salmon's short life and the disintegration of her family after her brutal rape and murder.

If she believed in a God, it could only be one with a sick sense of humour. As with every other detail of that evening which she has since replayed in her mind so many times, if she'd been reading something less enthralling, would she have gone straight to the tube, saving herself the four-minute detour to her car? Would it have made a difference? She was full of triumph after a deliciously successful evening and was in no hurry to call time on it.

Now, she's aware that the author of that book mistakenly accused an innocent man of rape, condemning him to sixteen years in prison. Sixteen years! And Ian Durandt may soon be out after seven.

Her filmic recollection of the events of that night falters during the attack itself. Her shrink has told her that this is normal. The brain repels traumatic memories to protect the integrity of the organism,

125

but of course she knows exactly what happened and in what order, as it was repeated endlessly in court.

He hit her savagely across the jaw, then forced her on to her knees and shoved his penis into her bleeding mouth. He held her head firmly with both hands and thrust back and forth into her face so mercilessly she vomited. This only enraged him further, so he ripped her shirt open, then bent her face down over one of the vehicles in the car park and raped her from behind, screaming obscenities, and when he was done, he turned her over again so she lay face up on the bonnet of the car.

'Look at me,' he said, smiling, and he playfully slapped her left cheek with his open hand. She flinched, so he backhanded her viciously on the right. She turned her face away. 'I said look at me!' he screamed. 'What are you?' he demanded.

She didn't understand.

'You're nothing!' he told her. 'What are you?'

'I'm nothing,' she said, tasting blood.

'That's right,' he nodded with exaggerated approval. 'You're nothing. You're a piece of shit. Tell me what you are.'

'I'm nothing. I'm a piece of shit,' and she swallowed blood and a loose tooth.

It didn't matter what she said. He continued hitting her. She could not protect herself, as he held her arms down.

Finally, he got tired. Or bored. He threw her down on to the concrete and kicked her side. She made herself as small as possible, but he kicked her in the back, knocking the wind out of her so badly she fought to breathe.

'Stay here. Don't move,' he'd growled, 'or I'll fucking kill you.'

She lay where she was, half naked and shuddering in the cold for what seemed like an eternity, too terrified to get up in case he came back. Eventually, before she lost consciousness, her lizard brain forced her to get to her knees and to crawl from the car park to the main road, where someone found her and called an ambulance.

Christine's lifeline is starkly divided between Before and After.

Her physical recovery was rapid, but mentally she disintegrated.

She sees that now. She hadn't fought him off. She made no effort to stop him. She could have bitten his dick off when he forced it into her mouth, as the defending barrister had so helpfully pointed out. But she didn't. She did whatever he told her to, said everything he wanted. She had wilfully walked to a deserted car park late at night without a second thought. She may have repressed some of the details, but she remembers the feel of the freezing hard gravel against her cheek and her arm and naked hip bone, the smell of dirt and leaves and wet asphalt, the icy fingers of a December night clawing into her bones.

She doesn't even remember the pain particularly, but sometimes she wakes in the night with his voice in her head. *Fucking bitch. Stinking whore. Dirty cunt.*

What she remembers is the fear, the sheer terror that he was going to kill her, and the knowledge that she would have done just about anything to keep herself alive. She despises herself for it, for her failure to understand that he *was* killing her. Her body survived, but he'd destroyed her sense of self, her persona, her trust in the world and her standing in it. He had told her that she was nothing, a piece of shit, and she had believed it was true.

SERENA

Serena and Billy are playing a drinking game with a bunch of his mates in the living room. They're sitting around a glass of beer bouncing a coin off the wooden floor in the hope that it lands into the glass. If they succeed, they win the right to nominate someone to down the beer. If they fail, which is far more likely, they have to down it themselves. The more they drink, the more their skill deteriorates and the louder they become. They incur a drinking penalty if they refer to each other by their usual names. Instead, they have each been assigned aliases, various terms for the female sexual organ. 'Beef Curtains.' 'Labial Loveliness.' Serena is 'Your Vag.'

There's a lot of squabbling about the most successful technique. Given the variables – the coin, the power and accuracy of the throw, the thrower's level of sobriety – it's utterly random. There's a lot of cheering and jeering going on.

'Go on, babe,' Billy says, sweeping his piratical mane away from his face. 'It's your go.'

'Drink!' yells Deak. 'She's 'Your Vag,' you numpty.'

Serena picks up the coin and tosses it. It's going wide, but it hits a wine bottle and ricochets straight into the glass of beer.

'Beginner's luck, you jammy cow!' says Stickman.

'Drink, Stickman! That ain't her name!'

'You drink, Beef Curtains! You just called him Stickman!'

Nominating someone is fraught with risk. If you choose someone with a talent for bouncing the coin, then they have ample opportunity to extract their revenge. Billy's mate, Stickman, is rubbish at the game, but nominating him seems ultra-mean, as he's so pissed he can hardly stand.

He's the runt of the pack, the one everyone picks on, the object of collective scorn. They haven't even given him a clever name. He's simply 'Fat Cunt'. He doesn't seem to mind. He's taking it all in good spirits, but that kind of sustained abuse has got to take its toll, surely? She can only assume his nickname is ironic, as he's extremely round-faced and plump.

'Billy –' says Serena, desperate to get away.

'You gotta drink, Your Vag,' says Deak. 'It's 'Beef Curtains' to you.'

She takes the glass and begins to drink it. It does not sit well on top of vodka and cider. She stops and coughs.

'You gotta drink it all, Your Vag! Or you get a refill!'

She raises the glass to her lips, but her body refuses to accept it. She has a belly full of acid already.

'I gotta go to the loo,' she mumbles, and escapes.

'Beef Curtains, you gotta drink for your bird,' Deak laughs.

Serena takes herself to the kitchen, clutching her cider bottle. It's made of clear glass, otherwise she'd pour it down the sink and top it up with water instead. She's lost her spot on the counter. She casts her eyes around for a friendly group to attach herself to. The smoke is making her feel queasy.

Georgie is having an animated chat with a couple of girls, one with gorgeous long fair hair who is with a good-looking black guy with long dreads. They're having a laugh. Serena feels that the natural order is a touch subverted. She's usually the lively one, good at making conversation with anyone about anything. She wants to join them, but she feels oddly inhibited. She's not on top form.

'Hi guys,' she says, aiming for breeziness, but her pitch is too loud.

Georgie introduces her. The girl with the long blonde hair is Fern. Her friend is Harriet. The guy with them is Fern's boyfriend, Josh.

'Are you okay?' asks Fern.

'Yeah, I'm fine,' Serena says, although she's swaying and she's having difficulty focusing. There's a chair in the corner of the kitchen which has a box of beer on it. Josh sets the box on the counter and brings the chair over. Fern takes her cider bottle away and fills a glass of water for her. Serena wants to kiss them both.

'God, Serena, you're so out of it,' says Georgie. 'Do you want to lie down somewhere?'

'Nah, I'm okay. I'll drink this, then I'll be back in the game. What're you guys talking about?' She's trying to enunciate, but her words are eliding.

'Music,' says Fern. 'Josh runs a vinyl stall with his dad at Camden Market.'

'You into vinyl then?' says Serena.

'I wasn't 'til I met him,' she laughs. 'Now I'm as much of a geek as he is.'

Serena's sipping the water slowly, and her body's gratefully absorbing it. Josh opens a window, and a cold but merciful breeze cuts through some of the smoke. She starts to relax. Georgie is talking about her older brother, who's reading Astrophysics at Durham.

'... so this guy on his course seemed perfectly normal, but he had a total nervous breakdown when he realised how insignificant he was in relation to the universe.'

'That's so funny, 'cos it's so obvious, isn't it?' says Josh.

'What?'

'How insignificant we all are. It's like that machine in *The Hitchhiker's Guide to the Galaxy*.'

'Is that a film or something?'

'It's a series. My dad made me watch it. The effects are seriously lame, but it was funny. Anyway, this machine– I can't remember what it's called –'

Serena says, 'It's the Total Perspective Vortex.' She wonders if she should mention that the series came from the books, that she's read and loved all of them.

'It speaks!' says Georgie, and everybody laughs. Serena smiles.

'That's it, yeah,' says Josh. 'The Total Perspective Vortex. Anyway, it's used as an instrument of torture, and anyone who's put into it goes mad when they realise how tiny they are compared to the universe.'

'Whoa,' says Georgie. 'It must be a thing then, if the idea has made it into a TV series.'

Serena's about to say that the one thing living organisms can't afford to have is a sense of proportion when Billy lurches into the kitchen.

'Babe,' he says, and tries to kiss her. He misses and hits her ear. He smells of beer. He has sunk a boatload, and he's spilled some down his shirt. 'Come wi'me, babe.' He takes her hand. He jerks on her arm as if it's a tug 'o' war rope. She offers only fractional resistance, but he drops her hand, careering back into the counter, knocking over a couple of empties.

'Fuck,' he says, and rubs his back. He blinks furiously in annoyance, as if she deliberately pushed him. His mouth is open, slack, as if it belongs to a fish.

'Sorry, babe,' she says, then blushes, as she's never called him that before. It strikes a false note, which she attempts to giggle off. She wants to stay where she is. She has warmed to Fern and Josh, and Harriet seems nice even if she doesn't say much, and Georgie's with her, and they're having a nice talk and not calling each other 'vag' or 'cunt', and she wants him to go back to his mates, as she's sober enough to see that he is mortifyingly smashed.

He staggers to her chair and takes her hand. She has an instinct that if she resists, he could make a scene, and she doesn't think she'd be able to bear it.

'Later,' she says to no one in particular, and she follows him.

'You okay?' says Josh. 'You don't have to go with him.'

'Yeah, I'm fine thanks,' she says over her shoulder.

'That's her boyfriend,' she hears Georgie say. She hopes like hell that Georgie doesn't tell them anything about her and Billy's plans. Not that they'll come to anything. They're both too pissed and the set-up's all wrong.

He drags her upstairs into one of the bedrooms and shuts the door. The lights are dim, and he pulls her towards the bed. The duvet cover is black with a huge white skull and cross bones on it. On the wall is a massive poster of a mountain range.

'Is this Deak's room?' she asks.

''S'is dad's.'

'Billy, I don't think we should be in here.'

''S' fine. C'mere, you're beau'iful,' he says, and pulls her onto his lap. 'Kiss me.'

She kisses him. She sees in the dimness that there's a light by the bedside. She leans over to turn it on.

'Yeah, tha's cool,' he says. 'I can see you better now. Kiss me again.'

She breaks away just in time, as a huge burble of beery air comes up his gullet. She winces. 'Billy, I'm sure Deak's dad wouldn't be too impressed that we're in here. I don't feel good about it.' She makes a move to get up, but he pulls her back.

''S'okay,' he says, soothingly. 'No one's gonna come in. We ain't gonna do nothing neither … let's just lie here an' have a cuddle.'

She relents. 'Promise?'

'Yeah, babe. Promise. C'mere.'

They stretch out on the bed and he takes her in his arms. She nestles against him. That's better, she thinks. This is nice. Really nice, and she relaxes. She's still feeling fuzzy after all the booze.

'We'd better not fall asleep,' she whispers.

131

'We ain't gonna do that,' he says.

It's fine, she thinks. He said we wouldn't do anything. He's my boyfriend. We've got all our clothes on, it's all good. It's nice lying on a real bed kissing, knowing you're safe. She wasn't sure what to expect from 'their first time' at Deak's place, but being in a room next to a bathroom with no lock, and with at least fifty drunk or stoned people in the house wasn't exactly it. But it's okay. She's fully clothed. Even if someone walked in, all they'd see is her and Billy snogging.

He starts kneading her breast over her dress. She hopes he won't get carried away. She doesn't want to have to say no, but she really, really doesn't want to have sex. They're both wasted. And she doesn't want to have sex here, but a feel is fine. She tries to relax into it. She imagines herself as if she were a character in a movie. She shifts closer to him and hooks her leg over his, nudging his calf towards her with her heel, encouraging him to shift his leg between hers. It's as if they've choreographed the move, and she feels a tiny thrill, as the film in her head is sexy. It's romantic. They're looking good …

'So sexy,' he breathes, and she feels that thrill again, as it's so clear they're in tune, in sync, they're good together, it's all cool, they're feeling good, looking good, they're smoking hot. She wants him to know that she wants him, so she arches her back, and gently strokes his hand, the one that's kneading her breast. He'll know what she means. She's telling him she loves what he's doing and in normal circumstances would want to go all the way, but not now. Obviously.

He deviates from her beautifully choreographed mental movie by lifting the hem of her mini dress and putting his hand over her crotch. Her hand flies to his to push it away. His arm locks. It's like tensile steel.

'Not here, Billy. Not now,' she whispers.

He relents and runs his hand over her leg instead. That's better. That's okay. She slips back into her movie. They kiss again, and she pulls ever so slightly away from him. She needs to gently disengage. They'll go back downstairs in a minute. She and Georgie should go home. She needs to sober up. She's exhausted. She has pushed her parents to the very back of her mind, but she knows she's got a confrontation ahead of her and she badly wants to sleep. She hopes Georgie's okay about leaving now. She props herself up on her elbow.

'Billy, I've got to go home,' she murmurs. He doesn't reply. Instead, he pulls her towards him and rolls on top of her. She struggles beneath him, but he's so heavy she can hardly move, and she can't protest as he has clamped his mouth over hers and is pushing his tongue down her throat. She doesn't panic, even though he stinks of beer, and he's entirely ruined her movie. He's pissed, that's all. She's teased him too much, but he'll calm down, she knows he will.

She makes a supreme effort to move her head to one side. She could bite down on his tongue, but that would be ridiculously over-the-top hysterical. She's his girlfriend. She loves him.

He lifts her dress again and pulls her tights down. They're not coming off without a fight, so he gives a concerted yank, taking her knickers down most of the way with them. He breaks off from tonguing her to look down at what he's doing. She tries to lift her legs up to stop him, but she's trapped beneath him.

'Billy, stop,' she says. It's hard to be heard over the sound of the music but with or without the noise, he's not listening.

She lifts herself up, but he pushes her down and pins her arms above her head with one hand, and with the other he undoes his jeans, letting his dick spring free. He can't part her legs far enough, as her tights are at half mast, so he lets go of her arms to rip them off completely but doesn't quite succeed. She seizes her chance to spring from the bed, it's only three or four paces to the door, but her stupid tights stop her from moving her legs properly and he catches her before she tumbles to the floor.

He pulls her back to the bed and finishes the job, ripping her tights and knickers off while she's on his lap.

'Billy! No! Stop!' she cries, and it works. Her panic registers, and he stops abruptly, as if electrified. He puts his hands in the air as if he's in a Western and she's holding a gun to him. She doesn't dare move. Slowly, he puts his arms around her.

'Shhh, babe. You're okay. We don't have to do anything you don't want to. Sorry, baby. I didn't mean to scare you. I love you, babe. You know that.'

On red alert, she is conscious of his hard dick against her naked thigh. She listens to him whispering to her, and she realises that she has completely overreacted. For a moment, she actually thought ... God, she's a twat.

He nuzzles her neck. He runs his hand over her back and her legs and starts to kiss her. It's not a beery tongue twister like it was before. It's gentle, it's nice. It's everything kissing should be. She's wary at first, but at last she responds. This is Billy. Her boyfriend. She's on his lap, in his arms and he's promised her that they won't do anything she doesn't want to do.

So it's a shock when within a blink he has flipped her on to the bed, pulled her dress up, pushed her legs apart and shoved himself into her, rutting like an animal, stifling her cries with his mouth.

CHRISTINE

Christine has fallen into an uneasy doze on the sofa. She wakes up to the sound of the front door opening quietly. The hallway light comes on.

'Serena. Is that you?'

The girl gives a start at the sound of her mother's voice. Her eyes are unnaturally bright. 'Mum!'

Christine has so many things she'd like to say that the words crowd each other out.

Without a word, she gathers her daughter up in a hug. Serena is now taller than her. She smells of beer and cigarettes. Christine doesn't care. Thank God she's safely home.

'Are you okay?'

Serena nods.

'Let's go to bed,' says Christine. 'We'll talk in the morning.'

'Okay,' says Serena, but she clings on to her mother, as if not wanting to let go.

SATURDAY

MARIE

Marie's coming round to consciousness. She's in bed, which is a bonus. When she's on her own, she often falls asleep on the sofa with the telly on. She's still in her bra, knickers and tights, so she feels constricted and sticky, and, as is usual after a night shift, slightly hungover. The curtains are closed and it's lovely and warm, and she could easily slip everything off and roll over and go back to sleep, but she wants to catch Neveah before she goes out. Besides, she's busting for a pee.

She slips on her dressing gown and goes to the bathroom. As she pees, the air fills with ammonia. Christ on a bike, she needs to drink something. She forces a sip of water down, straight from the tap. She has a vile taste in her mouth, so she brushes her teeth, giving them a good going over, especially as she can't remember cleaning them the night before. She splashes water on her cheeks, and it's so cold it makes her gasp. She looks in the mirror and chides herself for going to bed yet again without taking her face off. Her dermatologist keeps telling her off about that. She has dark smudges under her eyes, and it's hard to know if they're due to make-up or exhaustion. She looks knackered. Shit, she *is* knackered. She can't remember the last time she had more than a single night off in a row. She tells herself, as she does practically every morning, that she should go easier on the booze. Have a glass of water between the cocktails. She doesn't exactly get wasted when she's at the club – her boss Mike wouldn't stand for it – but she never goes a night without drinking something, and she can put an awful lot away before she starts to get silly.

Neveah's door is closed. It's not like her to still be in bed. Maybe she's working. She's always studying. It's a wonder to Marie that she ever gave birth to a creature so unlike her. If she hadn't actually been present at the birth – which would have been hard to avoid – she would have sworn that Neveah was a changeling.

She turns the door knob slowly and pushes the door open. The room's empty. It's in darkness, as the curtains are drawn, so she turns on the light. The bed looks as if it hasn't been slept in, but it's impossible to tell. Neveah's such a neat freak. She may have made it before she went out. Unless she stayed out last night. Marie's narked off. She had put Blue off coming back in case Neveah was home. Neveah should fucking well tell her if she stops out. She's probably at Sharna's. Or maybe she's with the bloke Sandra told her about.

She is so not looking forward to telling Neveah that Blue's back in her life.

She takes a step further into Neveah's room. She has an irresistible urge to snoop. There's a single wardrobe at the foot of the bed, which is tricky to get into, as there isn't enough space for the door to open fully. Just clothes in there, as far as Marie can tell. God, it's a pain in the arse to get into. It would be better if the door were taken off. Maybe she'll suggest it. Or she could look at Freecycle for a wardrobe with a sliding door. That would be much better. Then there's a chest of drawers groaning under a pile of books and files. Marie pulls the top drawer open. Knickers, bras and socks, that's all. Neveah's socks are obediently paired. How the hell does she manage it? The other drawers contain nothing but clothes. The desk has more files stacked on top of it, neatly arranged in magazine racks. Neveah doesn't have room for a chair, so she has to perch on the bed and pull the desk towards her whenever she wants to use it. She has to take all the files off first. Apart from the files, the desk is clear, as Neveah usually works with her laptop in front of her. The laptop's not here and Marie hasn't the foggiest what the password is in any case.

Marie has to acknowledge that anyone living in such a tiny space really has no choice but to be super-organised. Neveah has a small cactus on her window ledge that Archie had given her for her twelfth birthday. It's still alive. Amazing. Marie has often bought plants at the local market to liven up the flat with a touch of greenery. The place is too bloody dingy though, and she forgets to water them, so all too soon they turn brown and lose their leaves. Neveah's room is the only one that gets any sun.

There's a blown up black and white photo of Jackie framed and hanging on the wall above the bed and a notice board above the desk with various bits of paper and a few photos pinned to it. Neveah's school timetable, a revision schedule, a strip of photos of her and Sharna mucking about in a phone booth, a postcard Jackie once wrote to her from Edinburgh – the only one he's ever sent her so far as Marie can remember – a selfie of her with Marie … at least there's a photo of her in there, even if she's never made wall status, she thinks sourly. There's a professional looking picture of Neveah with Cha-Cha and Cha-Cha's younger sister. Whatsername. Angelet, something like that. Cute little thing. There's a colour chart of the periodic table, conjugations of the French verbs avoir, être and the modal verbs, whatever the fuck they are. Marie would love to be able to speak French. She'll take a class someday.

Marie opens the top desk drawer. It contains nothing but stationery. Pens and pencils, a few sharpeners, rubbers, a ruler, a protractor and a calculator. She's about to open the others, when one of the files on the chest of drawers catches her eye. Nestled in between Geography and History is a folder with no label. Marie eases it out but upsets the pile, and the stack of files and a few of the books cascade to the floor. She curses as she picks them up. She opens the folder and sits on the bed to look inside. It's full of statements. In date order – typical – and she sees that Neveah has recently received two payments from a company called Hawthorne's. The most recent is for £3,000. The other is for £2,000. Marie is shocked, but she's also thrilled, exhilarated. She sees that there are a couple of smaller amounts that have been paid in from a company called Sweet Street. The amounts vary. She flicks back through the pages, going back months, and she sees that Sweet Street make regular payments into Neveah's account. Some in the double digits, but most are between two and three hundred. One's for £534 and another's for a whopping £830. The debits are to Boots, Tesco Metro, Liberty, WH Smiths… She's spent £412.98 at Selfridges. Marie had asked her about those Patrick Cox shoes and she'd said they were from a charity shop. Marie had believed her, the conniving little bitch. Neveah's current balance is £7,533.53. The devious little sh –

'Mum! What are you doing in my room?'

Marie's chest seizes up in fright, but she needs only a second to recover herself. 'What are you doing with all this money? What the fuck is going on, Neveah?'

'I've earned it.'

'What d'you mean, you've earned it? You've got a fortune stashed away here.'

'Yeah, I've worked for it. Social media, SEO and website design.'

'What, and this is how much you get paid?'

'Yup. And I'm saving it up for university.'

'That's all very well, but you're living under my roof, young lady. You know that money's tight, and you've been sitting on all this cash without once thinking of helping out?'

'Mum, in case you haven't noticed, whenever there's food in the kitchen, it's 'cos I've bought it. I buy all the bog roll, the shampoo, the conditioner, the shower gel, the toothpaste …'

'With that much stashed in the bank I should bloody well hope you could buy a few bits and pieces.'

'I pay for my phone and the Wi-Fi –'

'You expect me to pay for your phone?'

'No, Mum, I don't. Like I said. I pay for it myself. Have I ever asked you to pay for it?'

'And it was you that wanted the Wi-Fi put in.'

'Yes, so I can work. And you and your mates use it all the time, but do you hear me complaining? I've paid for the last two EDF bills as the statements were red, I covered your last mobile phone bill as you were gonna get cut off and I am always lending you money. Whenever you ask for it. A tenner here, a twenty there, and you never pay me back. And I don't ever nag you for it. So you can't sit there on my bed rummaging through my stuff and tell me that I don't do my bit.'

Marie feels a surge of fury, stoked tenfold by the certain knowledge that she's in the wrong. 'Are you saying I'm a scrounger? I pay the rent round here, in case you've forgotten.'

'Which is heavily subsidised by the council. Plus you're getting child benefit and a universal tax credit. Which would be cut in a heartbeat if they found out what you're really earning.'

'Are you threatening me?'

'No, I'm not bloody threatening you. Don't be so stupid.'

'Don't call me stupid!' Marie screams.

'Well, don't accuse me of dumb stuff then. Someone could dob you in for not declaring your earnings. You could get a massive fine. Go to prison, even. Mike's taking advantage by paying you in cash.'

'Well aren't you the little financial whizz kid. The cash suits him, and it suits me.'

'You just don't want to stand up to him. He saves a bomb by not paying you right. You think he's gonna come back to you, but –'

'It's got fuck all to do with you. And besides, we're getting off point here. You can't expect to hoard all this cash and not pay more of your way round here.'

'I've already told you how much I put in,' Neveah hisses. 'This is my uni fund, and you're not touching it. I am not gonna piss my life away.'

'Like I'm doing, you mean?'

Marie is incensed, filled with a horrifically impotent kind of rage. Not only because of the money. It's the colossal unfairness of it all. She's feeling like a horrible old skank, and Neveah is standing in front of her in a righteous fury, looking all dewy and fresh, stuffed to the brim with collagen, luminous with youth and health. She's living from hand to mouth, and Neveah has seven grand stashed away to launch herself into her glorious future. She works like a dog serving drinks and snacks, hour after hour at the club every night, and Neveah taps a few buttons on her laptop every now and then and tsunamis of cash roll into her account. She, Marie, has taken Blue back, after two years of being signed up to no fewer than five dating sites, lurching from one lousy date to the next, yet the blokes crawl over broken glass to beat a path to Neveah's door. And they should save themselves the bother as Miss Priss is never interested. Saving herself for her Sugar Daddy, no doubt.

'I didn't say that. Look, Mum,' says Neveah in a more reasonable tone. 'You know it's not cool going through my stuff, but I'll park it –'

'Oh, that's very big of you,' says Marie bitterly.

'I'll put the kettle on. There's no point us talking until we've calmed down. If you're worried about money, let's go through it. There are so many ways you could save a bit. You spend a fortune boozing it up with your mates, and what do you get out of it? You end up paying for the booze and the pizzas and the fags and the gear … every time Faisal comes round it's you reaching for your bag, not anyone else … Archie pays his way, but all the others are freeloading. When's the last time they bought you a drink? Took the party to their place?'

'We don't pay for the drinks at the club. You know that.'

'Yeah, but nine times out of ten you all go out afterwards. You haven't come straight home in living memory. You need to rob a bank to pay for a round in Soho, 'specially after midnight.'

'It's only 'cos I need some winding-down time, I …' Marie tails off. Suddenly she feels exhausted. How can she explain that if she doesn't pay for the first round, then her mates would likely go straight home? Sometimes she can't bear the idea of coming home to the silence of an empty flat. To Neveah's closed bedroom door. Besides, she's known for being generous, and it makes her feel good. She follows Neveah into the kitchen and leans against the counter. It's a tiny galley space with no room for a table or chairs. Neveah fills the kettle and flicks the switch. She's brought home a flimsy blue plastic bag dangerously stuffed to bursting with sliced bread, butter, strawberry jam, a packet of extra mild cheddar – Neveah *knows* she prefers Extra Mature – a couple of Pot Noodles along with a pint of milk, a small bag of sugar and a jar of instant coffee. All bought and paid for by her oh-so-solvent daughter. Neveah busies herself putting it all away and she opens the packet of bread and flips past the crust and puts a couple of slices in the toaster. Marie chews her thumb while she watches her. She's tempted to give full rein to her peevishness and make a point of refusing any coffee or toast, but she's hungry. She needs to hang on to some of her dignity.

'So where've you been, then?' Marie asks.

'At Sharna's.'

'You didn't have breakfast there?'

'Yeah, I did, but I went to the pool with her this morning. Mum, you do know it's lunchtime, right?'

Marie is sick of being wrong-footed. 'So you weren't with your fancy man, then?' Neveah stops what she's doing, as if she's been turned to stone. Marie is astonished to see her daughter's eyes suddenly brim with tears. In spite of herself, she feels a pang of pity, but she quells it. 'I know all about it, you know.'

'There's nothing *to* know,' says Neveah, who seems to have mastered herself.

'Oh,' says Marie, injecting a highfalutin tone into her voice. 'That's not what I heard.'

Neveah's lip trembles. Her whole body is in a state of visible tension. Again, Marie represses an urge to give her a hug. The toast pops up, but Neveah doesn't move. Marie gets two plates out and opens the packet of butter and reaches for a knife.

'Giles, isn't that his name?' Suddenly she makes a mental leap, links what Sandra had told her with the bank statement. 'Giles Hawthorne.'

Neveah masters herself. 'He's a client of mine, that's all.'

'A client. Really. What kind of client? What do you do for him to earn money like that? Sounds a bit fucking fishy to me.'

'I told you. Digital marketing.'

'And how did you meet this *client*?' She roughly butters both pieces of toast.

'Sweetman passed him on to me. He had too much work on.'

Sweet Street. Of course. 'And if it's all so kosher, why didn't you tell me about it?' Neveah says nothing, but Marie knows exactly why. She was worried that Marie would try and commandeer the cash. Marie feels another stab of fury, only amplified by the fact that this worry is entirely justified. The girl's not sixteen yet. Surely she, Marie, has rights over that money? How can a child sit on a small fortune, while the parent is living from one pay packet to the next? 'Seriously. Why didn't you say anything?'

'Because now you know about the cash, you won't rest until I've handed it over. You don't give a stuff if I go to uni or not.'

'That's so not true. Of course I care!'

'You wouldn't do anything to stop me, but you wouldn't bust a gut for it, either.'

'If it's so important to you, darling, then let's factor it into our plans, but seriously, think about it. Uni's years away, sweetheart. There's a lot we can do with seven grand right now. I could pay off some of my Barclaycard. We could maybe take a holiday ... you've been nagging me to do that for ages.' Marie takes a bite of her toast and thinks about the money she's forced to chuck at accumulated interest every month. It's criminal what they're allowed to charge, it really is. She thinks about her last appointment with her dermatologist, who had mentioned restatylane fillers. God, if she'd had the money she would have forked it over on the spot. Her wardrobe needs a spruce-up too ...

'Mum, I'm really sorry, but I've got plans for that money. Even if I paid your credit card off –' she shuts up.

'What?'

'Nothing.'

'Go on. Say it.'

Neveah sighs. 'If I gave you every penny I had, it still wouldn't cover what you owe. You can get cards that are interest free for a whole year. If you transferred your balance –'

'When do I have time to sort stuff like that out?' she says resentfully, taking another bite of toast.

'If you didn't have to pay interest, and paid down a bit every month, you'd soon dig yourself out of the hole. It's hard to see why I should pay your card off if you can't be arsed to help yourself.'

'You patronising little shit. You try working nights. I'm on my feet for hours. Sometimes I come home so shattered I can barely remember my own name.'

Neveah raises an eyebrow. 'You sure it's the work doing that to you?'

'When you start working full time, maybe you'll understand.'

'Yeah, you're right,' Neveah says. 'I don't know anything about work.' She picks up her tea and toast and heads for her room.

'Hang on a minute! I haven't finished yet!'

'I have.'

'We haven't discussed your Mr. Hawthorne yet.'

'There's nothing to discuss.'

'There bloody is. Has he been shagging you?' Neveah stops in her tracks and turns around.

'What makes you even think that?' Her voice wobbles.

Marie puts another slice of Mother's Pride in the toaster. Now she's started, she's got a taste for cheap buttery carbs.

'Intuition,' she says smugly. Marie doesn't know anything about Giles Hawthorne, except for the fact that he's middle-aged with a posh name and he's got enough wonga to shell out thousands on digital marketing. 'Do I need to remind you that you're underage? And if there's something dodgy going on between you, then he's gonna be in a serious amount of trouble.'

Which he may be willing to pay a serious amount of money to stay out of.

SERENA

Serena is lying in bed. She'd got up in the morning to scrub herself in the shower, but instead of getting dressed afterwards, she dragged on a clean onesie and crawled back under her duvet. She can't face going downstairs. Seeing her parents. Behaving normally. Apart from the shower, she's been in bed all day. She's slept a little, but mainly she's been thinking. Her mum's worried about her, but she's accepted that she's 'a bit under the weather.' Her mum thinks she's hungover. She probably is, but that's not what's eating her.

She hears the landline ringing. Shortly afterwards, her mum knocks on the door.

'That was Georgie, just ringing to check you're okay. She says you're not answering your phone.' Serena doesn't reply. 'Are you sure you're all right?' her mum asks.

'Yeah, I'm sure,' she croaks.

'Hundred per cent?'

'Just tired, that's all. I may be coming down with something.'

'What happened to you last night?'

'Georgie and I went to a party. I'm sorry, Mum.'

Her mum sighs. 'What happened at this party? You seem …'

'What?'

'Out of it. Spaced.'

'Nothing. Honestly. We had a bit to drink, that's all.'

Christine sits down on the bed and smooths Serena's hair from her brow. 'Why didn't you answer your phone last night? Your dad and I … we were out of our minds with worry.' Her gentle concern makes Serena feel so guilty. Yelling and screaming would be preferable. It's what she deserves. Serena takes her mum's hand and squeezes it.

'I'm so sorry, Mum. I should have sent you a text.'

'Yes, you should have. You should have come home,' Christine had said.

'I know.'

'Why have you turned your phone off now? That's really worrying,' Christine smiles, trying to sound light-hearted.

'It's on silent. The noise is giving me a headache.' In truth, she doesn't know how to respond to Billy's texts. She needs more time to think.

'Maybe you should get some more sleep.'

'Yeah. Maybe. Thanks, Mum.'

And Christine leaves Serena in her darkened room alone with her thoughts.

Serena is facing a forked road, and she can't decide which way to turn. She's going over what happened in Deak's dad's bedroom last night in her head again and again. She can't stop thinking about what Billy did. He's her boyfriend, so surely it must be okay. But the fact that she's framing it as something that Billy did kind of makes it not okay. She didn't do anything, and wasn't it supposed to be a mutual, reciprocal thing? Actually, she corrects herself. She *did* do something. She led him on. She acted like a sex kitten, so she shouldn't be surprised that he lost control of himself. *Lost control of himself.* He shouldn't have done that. Isn't she victim-blaming herself? She specifically told him that she didn't want to have sex. She was clear. At least she thought she was clear. She didn't want to have sex in that room, in those circumstances, at that time. He should have respected that. She can't stop thinking about the film that was playing in her head. She'd cast herself as a vamp, a sultry seductress, in charge, completely in control … until suddenly she wasn't. Until she'd been flipped over and shagged like a rubber doll.

Why did he do that?

She'd said no. He'd promised her that nothing would happen without her say-so. Even in her head, she's playing word games with herself. She's sugar-coating what he did. *Without her say-so* … in other words, without her consent. He'd lied to her that he wouldn't do anything she didn't want to do, and he'd had sex with her after she had specifically told him no.

Okay. That's fucking awful, she thinks. But what is she going to do about it? She has to face facts. How can she explain what happened to anyone else? Will anyone believe her? And should Billy be accused of one of the worst crimes a person can commit against another without killing them, just because he made a bad judgment call at that particular moment with his own girlfriend when he was drunk? This is potentially life-changing stuff for both of them. He could justifiably say to anyone who asked him that they had planned to have sex at Deak's party for weeks. Even her best friend would back him up.

Every time she thinks she has everything straight in her head, the picture changes.

Even if she had been writhing on the bed naked and begging for it, teasing him to within an inch of his life, if she'd changed her mind at the last possible second, he should have accepted it. She remembers a photo she'd seen once, of a striking dark-haired young woman who had walked the streets of Cologne naked wearing nothing but a sign: *Wir sind kein freiwild* … 'We are not fair game, even when naked'.

She cringes to think about the excruciating moment when it was all over. He had flopped on top of her and had nuzzled her neck. 'You're beautiful, babe,' he'd said.

She squirms in her bed now at the memory. That was her cue to tell him that he was a rapist scumbag. That he'd forced himself on her like a lust-crazed animal. That he had basically wanked inside her, that he should rot in hell for what he'd done.

But she hadn't said any of those things. She had lay there beneath him, pinioned beneath his weight, buzzing with shock and electricity, feeling his dick shrivel and wither, wet against her thighs like a luke-warm slug. Why hadn't she responded in a righteous fury?

She'd been too embarrassed.

What the fuck was wrong with her?

She hadn't wanted to seem weird.

Even then, in her shock and confusion, the fork in the road was shimmering clearly in front of her. She could have gone one way, or she could have chosen the other. It had to be a quick decision, and she'd made the wrong one. She'd turned her head towards him and kissed his temple, then had stroked his back.

After all, he was her boyfriend and he loved her.

How pathetic.

The right path would have been painful and humiliating. She should have extricated herself, grabbed her clothes and … what? Raised the alarm at the party? Screamed rape? Whatever pain and humiliation she might have gone through would be better than feeling like this. Confused. Muddy. Degraded. Worthless.

She should have gone straight to the police and made them swab her for evidence. He hadn't used any protection. There would have been plenty of evidence that sex had taken place. But there was not a bruise on her. Would they have believed her? And now she's had a shower …

She could be pregnant. She should get hold of a morning after pill. A pregnancy would be an unmitigated disaster, of course it would, but she can't summon the energy to get worked up about it. She can't bring herself to get out of bed. She has some time before she has to take a pill. A couple of days, something like that. She'll worry about it tomorrow. There are pharmacies open on a Sunday all over London. She'll have to figure out a way of getting her hands on the pill without telling her mum. She hopes it's available to the under sixteens without parental consent. She's sure it is.

Billy has been sending her frequent texts.

U my sexy babe

You taken over my head!! When I gon cu?

U ok? Sup babes?

His texts are all accompanied by emojis, pornographic pictures and gifs. A girl stroking her own breasts. A close-up of an ejaculating penis. A guy taking a girl roughly from behind. The girl's loving it, of course. In Billy's world, the girls love whatever is done to them. She deletes them all immediately. Billy's behaving as if nothing has changed between them. Is it just her, then? Is she massively over-reacting? Maybe he was too drunk to know what he was doing?

She burrows further into her duvet. Was she actually raped? If she herself doesn't know the answer to this question, then how can anyone else be the judge? When she replays the events of the previous evening, even taking the disastrous sex out of the equation, she can't help concluding that Billy's … a bit of a dickhead. The game he was playing with his friends, the name calling, the way he got so stupidly drunk. She remembers how embarrassed she'd been when he had pulled her away from Georgie and the others. 'You don't have to go with him,' Josh had said. He'd seen right through Billy. She's so stupid. A fresh wave of shame engulfs her.

She should snap herself out of this state. She's only a victim if she plays that card. She can choose to keep it to herself. She can still feel a dull burn between her legs, but really, how has he harmed her? It's not the pain that bothered her. The wax strips brandished by the kind Vietnamese lady in the waxing salon had been far more painful. Everyone loses their virginity at some point. Some people have terrible experiences. The girls in Rotherham, groomed and abused and passed around like sex toys ... the poor Yazidi girls, routinely raped and beaten and treated as subhuman, the monstrous things happening to women in parts of Africa, the Uighur Muslim women in China ... in the grand scheme of things, what does she have to complain about? She could just shut the fuck up and get on with her life. She doesn't have to see Billy again. She can tell him where to go.

In her mind's eye, she replays the picture of herself kissing his temple and stroking his back. She never wants anyone to know how badly she's let herself down. Overriding everything is how her mum would react. She'd be devastated. Just at the point where she'd started to recover. To go out by herself. Nope. No way. The idea of her mum knowing is unthinkable. Christine's voice echoes in her head. 'If he had any respect for you, he'd never send you stuff like that.' She sees now that her mum was right.

Her phone's still on silent, but she sees it light up. Another text has arrived from Billy. She picks it up.

Pressie for u babes xx

He's sent her a video. The opening still is of a bed. No prizes for guessing what's coming, she thinks. She's about to delete it, when she sees that the bed has a giant skull and cross bones on it, and there's picture of a mountain range on the wall. Her scalp prickles as she presses play.

NEVEAH

Neveah can't stop herself from obsessively checking her phone, in case some phantom text or voicemail could slip past all the notifications, which she has repeatedly checked are all on, and at maximum volume. She doesn't know what to do with herself. There's no point working on Giles's stuff, as she doesn't know if she still has a job. Oh come on, Shitferbrains, she tells herself. Course you got no job. She doesn't have the head space to focus on her schoolwork. She's tried reading, but she's not absorbing anything, and the words periodically morph into dancing tadpoles, as she keeps welling up. What's the good in crying? Pointless. But she can't stop herself. She can't even leave her room to watch telly, as she can hear her mum's watching one of her old movies. She hears Addison deWitt's cutting tones: *'You're maudlin and full of self pity. You're magnificent.'*

She can't stand the sight of her mum right now. She's from a different planet to everyone else. Seriously, where does she get off snooping in her room, throwing her weight around, taking ownership of the money that she, Neveah, has worked her arse off to earn? Everything Neveah has ever achieved, it's been in spite of Marie, she thinks furiously. It's Sandra who has always been there for her, her two Grannies and people like Mrs. Markham and Mrs Beck. Sweetman and Laura. And Giles. The only good thing her mother has ever done for her is to leave her alone. That she has done in spades, ever since Neveah was tiny. The conversation they had that afternoon is the longest they've had for ages. 'Can't it wait?' 'Not now, darling.' 'Later, sweetie.' That's what she's used to hearing from her mum. But over time, she has learned to make the best of it, and, lately, to work it to her advantage. She has always been free to do her own thing in peace. But now that Marie's suddenly sniffed a bit of cash, and now she knows about Giles ... her mum is gonna gnaw at her like a dog with a bone.

149

The need to see Giles, to speak to him, to touch him, torments her like a physical ache. She's never told him she loves him. It's such an overused phrase, worn to death. Melodramatic. Needy. Who says 'I love you' to anyone without expecting it to be parroted back? Now her chance has been snatched away. What difference does it make? Even if she said it now, there's no way in a million years he'd ever believe her. She badly wants him to know. A distant voice in her head asks her how the fuck does she know what love feels like? It feels like this, she tells herself. It feels like you can't breathe when the one you love is out of reach. She can't bear for him to think badly of her. She desperately wants to explain. He must think she's been using him all this time. And that same distant voice tells her that maybe she had been. At least to start with. She wants him to know she's sorry she lied. He must understand why she could never have told him the truth. First off, he would never have hired her. And he'd never have touched her if he'd known she was only fifteen. Would he?

The two halves of her carefully separated life have smashed into each other. Her financial plans are shot to ribbons, although she's finding it hard to really care about that just now. She would happily make a bonfire of all of it if it meant making things right with Giles. But there's one thing she promises herself. No way in fuck is her mother getting her hands on any of it. Her phone rings. It's him. Feverishly, she reaches to answer.

'G,' she says.

He sighs audibly. 'Hello, Neveah.'

The two of them are both silent. Then they both speak at once. She says, 'G, I'm so sorry –' and he says, 'I was ringing to –' then they both stop and then she says, 'You first,' at the exact same moment that he says 'Go on,' and she's overcome by misery and finds she can't speak, and tears start rolling down her cheeks. They are both silent again, before she lets out a sob, then she shuts herself up, as it's manipulative to cry, to play the 'Poor Me' card. She's not the victim here. She has lied about everything from the first moment they met. There's no way to make this right.

There's a knock on her door. 'Vay, sweetheart. You okay?' Oh God. It's Marie, using her *concerned* voice. The door opens. Marie has her *concerned* face on too.

'Hang on,' she says into the phone, then covers the mouthpiece to furiously whisper, 'Mum, leave me alone. I'm fine.'

Her mother appraises her, takes in her tear-streaked face, her wobbly lip and raises her eyebrows in an 'oh really' look.

She pulls the door towards her until it clicks shut. 'G?' she says, in a whisper, as she can't be sure her mum isn't listening in outside.

'I know you've been trying to call me,' he says. 'I've been so blind. So stupid and blind. We can't see each other anymore, but I –' he falters. She waits, swallows her despair. 'I wanted to say goodbye to you. And to tell you what you've meant to me. How you've made me feel. How much I love –' he stops. 'How much I loved our time together.'

'G, don't say we can't see each other anymore,' she whispers urgently, horribly mindful of her mother hovering outside her door. 'I can't bear it. We don't have to – you know. We don't have to do anything. I just need to see you. I need you, G. Don't cut me off. Please.'

'The world doesn't work that way. This has to be goodbye.' There's a drawn-out pause. 'Neveah…' he takes in a deep breath. 'If I can ever help you. If you ever find you need me, you know how to find me.'

'G! Wait!' but he's gone. A sob catches in her throat. It's as if she's being suffocated alive and can't take in enough air.

Marie swoops in and perches on the side of the bed, and puts her arms around her, and rocks her from side to side. Neveah is rigid. She is going to explode. Trapped in that tiny space with her mother… there's not enough oxygen for them both.

She drops her phone on the bed and staggers past Marie to get to the bathroom. She grabs a tissue and blows her nose, then splashes cold water on her face. She leans against the sink. Marie follows her and rubs her back while she towels herself dry. Once she would have lapped up this kind of attention from her mother.

'D'you want a coffee, darling?'

She nods. Not because she wants one, but because Marie can't smother her while she's mucking about with jars and milk and sugar. Neveah hears the sound of water drumming into the bottom of the kettle.

She wants to be alone, but she knows she'll get no peace until Marie's found out what's eating her. She joins her mother in the kitchen and leans against the counter while Marie busies herself with mugs and spoons as the water boils. She has to keep dabbing at her eyes as the tears won't stop.

'So he's dumped you then,' says Marie with a matter-of-fact shrug of her shoulders.

Neveah is suffused with fresh fury. 'He hasn't dumped me,' she says indignantly, although that's exactly what he's done.

'There's no shame in it, sweetheart. We all get dumped from time to time. He's a total shit.'

'He's not! He's –' Far from it. He hadn't said a single word in anger. Instead he'd told her – God, she wishes he'd said it. She wants to hear it from him so badly that … fresh tears spring to her eyes as it begins to dawn on her what she's lost. She'll be sixteen in three months. Old enough to see him properly. Old enough to get the hell away from Marie.

'You may not think so, but he is, you know. When I was your age, I was preyed on by an older man.'

'He never preyed on me!'

'That's the thing, sweetheart. They're so clever … they've been around the block a few times, so they're good at making you feel so special that you don't realise what they're doing. Using you, that's what.'

'He has not been using me! I …' She wants to say she loves him, but she can't bear to be mocked for it.

'So you have been shagging him, then?' Neveah doesn't say anything, which Marie takes as her answer. 'Thought so,' she says as she pours boiling water on granules of instant coffee.

'What difference does it make?' says Neveah fiercely.

'Nothing, just that… I've been so worried about you, sweetheart.' Neveah raises her eyebrows. 'You haven't been yourself lately.'

Like you'd know, Neveah thinks sourly, but says nothing.

Marie pours milk into both cups and stirs sugar into them, her face a cartoon of maternal anxiety. 'I thought it was maybe your exams coming up. I know you take that stuff to heart. I've spent so much time worrying about you working too hard and not taking care of yourself –'

'I can't say I've noticed.'

'– and all along you've been groomed and taken advantage of by some horrible old creep.'

'He's not an old creep.'

'You may not think so, darling, but in the eyes of the law –'

'Since when has the law bothered you?' says Neveah.

'It's there to protect girls like you. You being underage and all. We should report him.'

'No way! Mum, don't you dare say a word to anyone.'

'Why the hell not? It's disgusting what he's been doing.'

'I lied to him about how old I am. I said I was twenty-two.'

Marie laughs. 'And he believed you?'

'Why wouldn't he? I was all poshed up carrying a briefcase.'

Marie raises her eyebrows, then shakes her head. 'Ignorance is no excuse in the eyes of the law.'

Neveah's heart gives a lurch. She's heard this phrase before but has never paid proper attention to it. Now the starkness of its meaning is being ground into her face. If anything happened to Giles because of her, because of the lies she's told … What can she do about it, except deny, deny, deny? In effect, tell more lies. In a daze, she realises that Marie is still talking and tunes in. '… because young girls don't have any experience, it makes them suckers when older men focus on them, flatter them, make them feel like a million dollars. The law's there to protect you from disgusting old paedos like him.'

'What about Blue?'

Marie stiffens. 'That was different.'

'How? I mean, I know it was different. But I'd love to hear why you think so.'

Blue is a taboo subject. Other than the screaming match which took place immediately afterwards, they have never talked about what happened.

'Don't make me say it, Neveah.'

'Say what?'

Marie pauses before she speaks. 'You know.'

'What do I know? You think I led him on?'

'You know you did. I was happy with Blue.'

'You make it sound like I had a choice. I was twelve! I told you again and again I didn't want to be left alone with him. But you wouldn't listen. Night after night, off you'd go to the club, leaving him in charge when I told you I hated being left with him. I mean, who does that? Who leaves their creepy alcoholic boyfriend to babysit their twelve-year-old daughter?'

'We were going to get married, for fuck's sake. Why wouldn't I?'

Neveah laughs. 'I asked you not to leave me alone with him. To any normal person, that would have sparked off a warning bell. Not you, Mum. You were too busy playing happy families.'

'If you'd told me –'

'I did, remember? But you didn't believe me. You said I was being silly. I was 'exaggerating'. He was a 'really tactile guy' who was 'just being affectionate'. Every night, he'd get drunk and he'd start on me. He'd always get wasted first. Maybe 'cos even he had to get properly tanked before he could do something so wrong. Then he started bringing Connor with him. Mum, that was so fucked up.'

Connor never did anything to her, hardly spoke to her, and would sit on the sofa and watch telly or play his stupid video games while Blue molested her, sometimes in Marie's bedroom, sometimes in hers. Neveah doesn't know how to explain to Marie how much Connor's presence disturbed her and amplified her shame. 'And now I have to sit in a class with him at school knowing what he knows. How do you think that makes me feel? Blue abused me, Mum. Night after night for weeks.'

'That's a word that's chucked about a bit too much for my liking.'

'What else would you call it?'

'I know what I saw.'

'You think I chose that?' She wants to scream that only the most deeply warped and fucked up individual would ever blame a twelve-year-old for being abused. It's clear to Neveah why even the low-grade wankers her mother tends to date decide to steer well clear of her sooner or later. No matter how attractive she is, how much fun she can be on a night out, how much cash she splashes on drinks ... ultimately, her narcissism, her neediness, her distorted values, her fundamental expectation that others should take care of her, her absolute denial of any kind of responsibility for anything ... these are all factors which are bound to poison the most promising of relationships. 'You –' Neveah shuts up. She knows a nuclear button when she sees one.

'No, go on. Tell me,' says Marie, crossing her arms. 'I'm all ears. Let me hear what my guru of a daughter has to say about my many flaws.'

'It's hard to believe that you somehow think it's okay for Blue to molest a twelve-year-old.'

'I didn't say that. I chucked him out, remember?' Even for Marie, sticking with Blue after he'd had sex with her daughter was a bar too low. 'I was happy, Neveah. Did that not ever occur to you?'

She's about to say that it's a worthless kind of happiness that's built on a lie, but Neveah takes in Marie's defensiveness, her anger, her resentment, her inability to see any other perspective but her own, and realises that there's no point in holding up a mirror to her, as she will only ever see what she wants to. 'You know what, Mum? I begged Blue to leave me alone. But even if I hadn't, even if I'd come on to him, he shouldn't have done what he did because I was only twelve.'

Marie turns to her in triumph. 'By the same token, even if you lied to this Giles guy about how old you are, legally you're still a child. And it doesn't matter how much you think you love him, he has broken the law. End of.'

'There's a world of difference between Giles and Blue and you know it. If you report Giles then all that other stuff about Blue's gonna come out.' She doesn't need to add that Marie is hardly going to emerge smelling of roses.

Marie says nothing, which tells Neveah that she's thinking exactly the same thing. She's all hot air, Neveah decides. What good would it do her to report anyone, other than bring a heap of shit on both their heads? Neveah stands up straight and puts her cup on the counter.

'Where are you going?' Marie asks. 'You haven't finished your coffee.'

'I need some fresh air,' she says. 'I'm going out. I'll see you later.'

'No you won't. Mike's asked me to come in early today.'

'Tomorrow, then. I'll stay at Sharna's again.'

'You may as well move in with her,' says Marie bitterly.

Gimme half a chance, Neveah wants to say, but she buttons it as per usual.

BILLY

Billy holds the shop door open with his foot while he reaches outside for the metal pavement banner advertising 20% off all cycle wear and yanks it inside. He's never been more relieved to finish work. Saturdays are always flat out, this one more manic than usual, and he had to get in early this morning accompanied by the king of all hangovers. Andy and the others have been calling him The Stud and Lover Boy all day, and while Billy's not always the sharpest tool in the box, he senses it's not entirely good-natured. They've not stopped looking his way and laughing. There's an edge to it. Something doesn't sit right.

He quickly checks his phone before he locks up the cash register. It's on silent while he works. He has seventeen missed calls. That's a lot … none of them from Serena. Fuck. He has a creeping feeling of anxiety. Normally, she replies within an hour or two, sooner on a weekend when she doesn't have to bother with school. It's been so busy he's only had a chance to send a few texts. He was very, very drunk last night. He doesn't remember exactly how things went down in Deak's dad's room, but after watching the video from start to finish a couple of times, he kind of knows he didn't put his best foot forward. He shouldn't have got so wasted. He wonders if she came? Somehow he doesn't think so. He should have taken more trouble to make sure she enjoyed herself.

He regrets sending her the video. He should have binned it and set the whole shebang up again for next time. Put in a little more time and effort. But there will never be a next time. You can only lose your virginity once.

He wishes he could explain to her how much she'd turned him on, how he just had to dive in ... it's like a caveman thing. She should feel good about it. How can he get that across when she won't respond? He loves watching the bit where she pulls his leg in between hers. And his favourite bit is where they're lying together after it's all over, and she kisses him, with her arm around his back. That's so cool ... that's where he'd cut the video he sent her. Other bits in between he wishes he could rescript, redirect, shoot again, especially the part where she bolts for the door and he pulls her back. That's so ... not cool, and he holds his breath through it, taking in air only when they start kissing again. And after he'd cut it, when they're putting their clothes back on is all a bit of a confused blur, and he wishes she looked more relaxed, more free and easy, more like a woman whose had a *proper seeing to*. He can't help clocking that the expression on her face, even though it can only be seen for a second or two, is grim and stunned. She didn't come, he concludes.

'You coming to the Eagle, Lover Boy?' asks Andy.

It's their ritual after work on a Saturday.

'Yeah, in a minute,' says Billy. He's going to sneak off to the loo and watch the video again, from start to finish. 'I can lock up. See you there, yeah?'

He grabs his phone and pulls the bolt across the door of the highly utilitarian staff bog which smells exactly as expected, being used exclusively by seven male members of staff under the age of twenty-three. He makes himself comfortable. No reason not to multi-task.

Before he pulls up the video, he checks who the missed calls are from. Seventeen is a lot of missed calls … three from his mum. She never calls him at work. Several from his mates. A couple from Auntie Jen. Still none from Serena. Then he sees he has 327 notifications. Fuck. That's a lot. The signal's not the best, and by the time he's managed to open the app, it's gone up to 352. There, on his feed, is the video; the opening still is of a bed in a dim bedroom with a big skull and cross bones and a picture on the wall of a mountain range, with a big white forward arrow, a massive call to action, practically screaming to be pressed. Billy's lucky he's sitting where he is, because his stomach liquefies.

Oh my fuck. Did he post it? How could he have been so stupid? It was only ever meant to be him and Serena that ever saw it. Maybe when he was pissed? How long's it been up? He checks out the comments. They are littered with laughing, screaming and vomiting emojis.

Billy mate, WTF?

Has anyone reported this?

Is this for real?

And the award for the worst porn movie ever goes to……. Drumroll LOL

OMG this is so wrong DELETE! DELETE! DELETE!

To the little hottie in this video.. call me, darling. I can show you a better time.

Billy, your a numpty

This is disgusting and should be taken down.

Smokin' hot bird... what's she doing with Neanderthal man??

Are we witnessing what happens when cousins fuck?

So glad there are no records of my early forays into sex... I'd die of shame.

At least he got it in, cos that's all he done right!

This fuckwit probs thinks he's some kind of stud

Poor chicklet! She deserves better. Does she even know???

His heart lurches to see a comment from his Auntie Jen:

OMG Billy what is this????!!!!! Your mums gonna kill you and when she's finished, I am

He can't stop scrolling. He's getting horrifyingly raw feedback. The mocking of his performance is hard to take, but even harder are the comments slut shaming Serena.

Classy bird. Slutty McSlutface

Oo let the dogs out? Ooo oo oo

Class act – they deserve each other. This is disgusting.

He's locked in a waking nightmare.

His phone's still on silent, but it buzzes. It's his mum again. Auntie

Jen's right. She's going to kill him. Shit. He can't take the call. Not now. He clicks on 'Settings' to delete the video, but the signal fails at the same moment his battery dies.

Hastily, he cleans himself up, even washes his hands, picks up his stuff and sprints to the pub. Andy's at the bar, getting the second round in.

'Mate, I'm in deep shit,' he says.

'What is it, Lover Boy?'

Billy tells him.

Andy smirks. 'Relax. It's a fine piece of cinema.'

'You've seen it?'

'Sure. We all have. You only just cottoned on?'

Billy's guts twist. 'Did you post this?'

Andy grins. 'Shouldn't leave your phone lying around.'

'Seriously, did you? Without telling me?'

'What? And have you take it down?'

'Too fucking right I'm taking it down. Give me your phone. Mine's dead.'

'Come on … not yet. There may be a couple of anti-social hermits in the Outer Hebrides that haven't seen it yet.'

'Stop pissing about, Andy. Fucking take it down. If not for me, for Serena.'

'What about her?'

'She doesn't deserve this. She didn't even know about the camera.'

'Sorry, mate, but any little slag that gets her kit off at a Friday night party is kind of asking for it, don't you reckon?'

CHA-CHA

Cha-Cha is sitting with Angelique on her toddler bed.

'What's that, Angel?'

'It's a dragon.'

'What's he doing?'

'He's talking to the dinosaur.'

'What's he saying?'

'I don't know, silly. I can't read.'

'Sure you can. See that letter? It's a 'D'. 'D' for dinosaur. And that one? It's the same. 'D' for dragon. See? That's how it works. Each letter stands for a sound.'

'What's that letter?'

'It's an 'R'. D-R-A-G-O-N. Get it? Dragon.'

The little girl repeats each sound, then squeals. 'I can read, Cha!'

'Yup. You can. Well done. You can read the rest yourself. I'm gonna go watch –'

'No, you're not,' calls Sandra from the bathroom, and Cha-Cha rolls her eyes and settles back on to the bed. She really wants to watch 'Strictly', but Sandra's making her put Angelique to bed while she's mopping up the spillage from her bath. Cha-Cha was supposed to supervise but was busy playing Snake on the crummy old mobile she's being forced to use for a month. Her mum has confiscated her iPhone and has put her SIM card into a cheap pay-as-you-go which can only make and receive calls and texts. The phone's so old that it needs a specially shaped piece of plastic to make her SIM card fit. She's got no internet. No Instagram. No Snapchat. No Candy Crush. But even this useless little piece of shit phone has a game on it. Only one, but it's quite cool.

She's grounded for a month too. Normally she goes out to a café a couple of times a week with her mates, but now she has to come straight home from school, and she's not allowed out on weekends except to go to her football practice and her Saturday gymnastics, and has to get straight on the bus home when the classes are over. 'Do not pass go, and do not collect two hundred,' her mum had said, wagging her finger at her. She didn't have a clue what she was on about.

'Guess what, Angel?' Cha-Cha whispers.

'What?' she stage-whispers back.

'Mummy's a D-R-A-G-O-N.'

'I can hear you, you know,' says Sandra, and the two girls giggle.

'She's not,' says Angelique.

'You've never seen her when she's mad. Like, properly mad. I have.' Which is perfectly true. Sandra had given her a rocket when she turned up at Granny South's on Thursday night. Cha-Cha has not dared to own up about the dress. Thank God she'd already changed out of it and was in her pyjamas by the time Sandra arrived. She'd managed to stuff it behind the bed in Granny's spare room before her mother had turned up to frogmarch her home. And now the dress is festering in its hiding place, just waiting for its moment to explode. If the destruction of her mother's dress is added to the tally of her crimes, she'll be grounded for the rest of her life.

She obediently reads the rest of the picture book to Angel.

'I'll take over now,' says Sandra.

Cha-Cha cuddles her sister and scarpers downstairs in time to watch a rumba. She settles against a cushion on the sofa, pulling a blanket over her knees.

Twenty minutes or so later, Sandra comes down to join her.

'She asleep?'

Sandra nods. 'She doesn't fight sleep the way you used to. You were a –'

'Yeah I know. A nightmare.'

Sandra smiles, and pulls Cha-Cha towards her. 'Yes, you're a nightmare, Charlotte Sansom.'

Cha-Cha snuggles into her mother.

'Mum?'

'Yes, sweetheart?'

'I know I'm grounded, and I know it's totally fair enough,' she says quickly, 'but I was just wondering ...'

'Yes?'

'When can I see Dads again?'

Sandra sighs, and takes a while to answer. 'You know, your dad is not a bad man. He loves you and Neveah. I used to love seeing him with her, because I thought I was getting a sneak preview of what he'd be like when we had kids. We used to see her every weekend.

Marie never minded. I thought I was so lucky meeting a man who was a good father to a cute and lovely toddler with an ex who wasn't difficult. I used to change her nappies, bathe her, feed her, the lot. He did everything he could to avoid being alone with her. I assumed that it was a man thing, but now I know that's not true. Look at Leon with Angel –'

'Leon, Dad of the Year,' Cha-Cha pouts.

'Knock it if you want, but I'll take Dad of the Year over Stud of the Year anytime.'

'Mum!'

'You know it's true. Your dad doesn't stick to relationships for long. You should see the current one. She's like a twiglet with boobs. On the night you went AWOL, she had a right go at me. She was like a crazy little bantam hen.'

Cha-Cha laughs. 'Wish I'd seen that.'

'Anyway, to answer your question, I don't want to stop you seeing your dad, but it is absolutely not on for you to be in night clubs getting drunk with revolting old blokes slobbering all over you. Seriously, I could have killed your dad. I don't care if he was on stage. If he was performing for thousands at Wembley Stadium or the flaming Albert Hall, he should have stopped his set to look out for you. Frankly, I'd rather put Herod in charge of childcare than him.'

'Who?'

'Never mind. Thank God Neveah called me.'

'Neveah's such a bitch. If it wasn't for her, you'd never even know I was out.'

'Don't call your sister such awful names. She was in pieces that night. And she did the right thing. Which is more than can be said for your dad. You know, your dad grew up without a father, and Granny South spoilt him rotten. She did him no favours. Even now, she'd wipe his bottom if he asked her.'

'Mum!' giggles Cha-Cha.

'When we got together, he didn't even know how to make a cup of tea.'

'Are you being serious?'

'Yes, I bloody well am. I'd get up at the crack of dawn and go out and do a full day's work, and when I came home, you should have seen the state of the place. It always looked like a frat party had been going on. I tried really hard to be supportive where his music's concerned. I know it's a hard business, and he's talented, but –'

'What?'

'Like I said, it's a hard business. Then there were the clothes. Your dad's a preener. He'd spend a fortune that we didn't have on new threads. He'd trawl round the markets and the vintage shops, always after a particular look, which he could never describe. He'd say, 'I'll know it when I see it, sweetness.' He'd try on different outfits in different ways and would stand posing for ages in front of the mirror. I never got a look-in. It wasn't just for his adoring audience at his gigs. He was the same stepping out for a pint of milk.'

Cha-Cha giggles again.

'He'd never hang anything back up, he'd drop them on the floor, where they'd stay until I picked them up. We had some fun together, don't get me wrong. No one is better to be around than Jackie when things are going well. It's just that …' she tails off.

'What, Mum?'

'Well, things don't always go well, do they? We were both chuffed as anything when we found out you were on the way, but then I lost my job and it's not easy finding another one when you look like a beach ball with arms and legs. Your dad wasn't bringing in any money and he's not exactly cut out to be a stay-at-home dad. I wouldn't let him look after a gerbil unsupervised. I was desperate.

'Couldn't Granny South look after me?'

'She was working herself then. She only retired ten years ago, and as soon as she did she decided to take to her bed and wait for Death. Lucky for her, Death's got other ideas.'

'So what happened with Dads?'

'He spent my redundancy money on a new guitar.' Cha-Cha gasps. She wants to ask what redundancy money is, but she doesn't want to ruin Sandra's flow. Her mum's not normally this forthcoming. Sandra laughs. 'I did not find it funny at the time, let me tell you. We had no income and a baby on the way, but what did that matter? Jackie needed a new guitar, so a new guitar he must have.'

'Wow,' says Cha-Cha. She's well impressed by this dedication to his music.

'And he did it without even asking me. That's what comes from having a mother who never says no to you. You get this weird sense of entitlement. Kids who have parents who say no are the luckiest ones in the world.'

'Well, I've really hit the jackpot then,' says Cha-Cha. 'I never realised how much you hated Granny South.'

'I don't hate her!' says Sandra, sounding shocked. 'She's a lovely old girl. She's had a hard life. Your grandfather died in a factory accident when Jackie was tiny. And I don't know if I ever told you, but Jackie was an identical twin. His brother died at birth.'

'Really?'

Sandra nods. 'I don't know how one person can cope with so much suffering, but you hear of far worse. I've wondered sometimes, if that's the reason he can't settle on one woman. He's looking for something that he'll never find.'

'That is so sad, Mum.'

'Yup. It is. And I'm sorry to say that you and Neveah have paid a really big price for it.'

GILES

'Would you like some supper? I could whip up some spag bol?' Giles asks Christine. She's huddled in the far corner of the sofa, hugging a cushion to her chest and staring into space.

'No thanks. I'm not hungry.'

'Do you think Serena wants anything?'

'She went out.'

'I thought she was in bed. Has she made a miraculous recovery?'

'Something like that. She said she needed to see Georgie. She seemed agitated, but she left in such a hurry I couldn't find out what was bothering her. She'll be back later.'

They're both conscious that they have avoided a conversation with Serena about her going AWOL, but she's been so contrite and they've both been too distracted. No one has the stomach for a fight.

'Okay. Are you sure you don't want anything?'

'Sure. Giles?'

'Yes?'

'Have you spoken to her today?'

'Not much. She's behaving very strangely, isn't she? It's not like her to –'

'Not Serena. Have you spoken to … to Neveah?'

Giles sits down. He wants to lie. 'Yes. I called her. Just to say goodbye. It's all over now.' Baby Blue, he thinks inappropriately.

'How did she take it?'

He doesn't know how to answer without either glorifying or diminishing the relationship. He doesn't know which is worse. 'I don't know. It was a really short conversation.' *I need you, G. Don't shut me out.* A lump rises in his throat.

'Do you think there's any danger of her being vindictive?'

'I don't think so, no.' *We don't have to – you know. We don't have to do anything.* 'I'm sure she won't be.'

'She can do a lot of damage if she wants to.'

'She's not like that.'

Christine gives him a withering look, then she crumples into tears. 'Why did you do it, Giles? Just when –'

'When what?'

'Just as I was climbing out of the hole I've been rotting in for so long.'

'I didn't go looking, I promise you. I don't know what to say. I'm sorry, Chrissie. I really am.'

'And why her, of all people?'

Again, he's conflicted. The usual lies employed in this situation won't do him any good. He can't say that she meant nothing to him. Christine would see through that in an instant. He sighs. 'She's bright and clever. We crossed paths when I was –' Shut up! He thinks to himself. He's in a minefield. He decides against telling Christine that Neveah made the first move. Instead, he says, 'I was flattered that she was remotely interested.'

'And of course it helps that she's young and gorgeous.'

Giles keeps quiet.

'Does she know about me?'

'You mean that I'm married? Yes.'

'Did you tell her about … us? About our situation?'

He sighs. Of course he'd told her.

'Well, did you? *My wife was viciously raped and is too traumatised to have sex*, is a little more original than *my wife doesn't understand me*,' says Christine bitterly.

Giles takes her hand while he considers very carefully how to answer.

'Are there any others?'

'No.' He's too demoralised to even inject a hint of outrage into his reply.

'You sure? You may as well make a clean sweep of it now.'

Giles is tempted to laugh and ask if she thinks he's had a full frontal lobotomy, as only then would he be dumb enough to confess all. He knows that however royally he has fucked things up, it's always possible to make a bad situation worse.

NEVEAH

Neveah rings Sharna's doorbell. Her brother Earl answers.

''S'Vay,' he shouts to no one in particular, and rushes back to the telly.

Sharna and her mum are in the kitchen.

'Hello, darlin',' says Sharna's mum, Dee, rising to hug her. 'Long time no see.' It's what she always says, her little joke, but Neveah knows there's something wrong.

'Yo, Vay,' says Sharna. Neveah notices she can't quite meet her eye. She looks at her friend sharply.

'Sit down, sweetheart,' says Dee, as she fills the kettle and flicks the switch on. 'We need to talk.'

Neveah looks daggers at Sharna, who gives her a guilty shrug.

MARIE

The club is busy, but Marie's escaped for a smoke on the roof terrace. She'd lied to Neveah about being wanted early at work. In fact, her hours have been cut. She doesn't know what she'd do without this job. She's sure that it's Mike's girlfriend, Selma, who's behind it. She's started throwing her weight around. Marie has an on/off thing going with Mike but he hasn't come near her for a while. Probably terrified Selma will find out. Just as well. Now she's back with Blue, it would only complicate things.

Neveah has brought up stuff that Marie would rather not have to think about. Where does she get off saying that she tried to tell her what Blue was doing? But there's a doubt gnawing at her. She has a feeling there's a sliver of truth to it, and it's eating away at her. She remembers that Neveah had told her she didn't like being left alone with him. Did she tell her she was being abused? If she'd only told her straight, then she, Marie, would have kicked him out way sooner. Of that she's certain. Did she tell her? She shudders at the memory of Neveah and Blue together. She'd pay good money to get that image erased from her brain. She has a chance now with Blue. In the cold light of day, she kind of knows that getting back with Blue is – well, she'd best keep her eyes wide open. That's one problem. The other is... she doesn't know how to square it with Neveah. She doesn't need her fucking permission, she thinks furiously. Still ... there are things she can't possibly explain to the girl. That Blue is like a sodding lifeline to her. She's been single for two years, and it's bleak out there. She's not getting any younger, and –

'You look proper deep in thought,' says Peaches. 'You got a light?'

Marie passes her lighter over. 'Yeah. I had a barney with my daughter before I came in tonight. She's at that age, you know.'

'How d'you manage having a job like this with a kid? It's mad.'

Marie shrugs. 'You just get on with it, you know.'

Peaches laughs and shakes her head. 'Hats off to you.'

Marie wonders whether to tell Peaches, then thinks why the hell not. She takes a deep drag.

'She's been seeing someone. Some bloke who's much older than she is.'

'Like how old?'

'I haven't met him, so I dunno exactly, but her step-mum says he's middle-aged.'

'No way! That's disgusting.'

'That's what I thought. Anyway, the guy's dumped her, and she's heartbroken. At least she thinks she is.'

'Ouch. Poor girl. That's the pits. I wouldn't be her age again, not if you paid me.'

'I wouldn't mind,' says Marie. She'd play things very differently if she were given a second chance. 'Also, I found out today she's got money. Like, a lot of money. He's been paying her.'

Peaches's eyes widen. 'Get outta here! You mean-'

'No, no, nothing like that. She's shit hot at website stuff, you know, the whole digital malarkey. He hired her to do all that.'

'Phew! I thought you meant she was on the game or something. Good on her. I wish I knew something about that digital stuff.'

'Yeah, me too.'

'She get paid a lot for it?'

'Too right. She's got over seven grand stashed away.'

'No way! That is awesome. You can retire, baby!' says Peaches, and bumps her hip against Marie's. The two of them laugh. 'Why's he dumped her?'

''Cos he found out she's underage. He thought she was some hotshot businesswoman.'

Peaches cackles in delight. 'Fuckin' A! Holy shit, that is just beautiful. You should be proud.'

'Yeah, I am, but she's sitting on it all. She wants to use it for college.'

'Fair enough, I suppose.'

'D'you think? I've got bills pouring in, and I'm in debt up to my eyeballs, and she's hogging a small fortune all to herself. I mean, she lives with me and I pay for, like, literally everything,' Marie's colour rises, not that Peaches can see, 'and she went mad when I suggested she should chip in once in a while.'

Peaches shrugs. 'It does seem a bit wrong though. She's still at school.'

'What difference does that make?'

'I dunno, really. It just does. She's got a dream and she's going for it. I mean, it's not like you're on skid row, is it? It'd be like, I dunno, like nicking her paper round money.'

Marie feels a stab of annoyance. 'If she was getting up at stupid o'clock and jumping on a bike to deliver newspapers, that would be one thing, but she's sitting pretty in a nice warm bedroom, that I'm paying for, fannying about with a laptop and gets paid megabucks for it.'

'All right, all right … when you put it like that … What a shame he's dumped her, eh? Sounds like she was on to a good wicket.'

'Yeah, I know,' says Marie, who couldn't have put it better herself.

'Poor kid. I hope she's okay. Being dumped sucks. Maybe she should sue him. For wrongful dismissal or something.'

Marie is silent.

'Or maybe he'd be willing to stump up a bit of cash. You know. To stay out of trouble,' says Peaches. She pulls a lipstick out of her bra and smears it on.

'Hm,' says Marie vaguely.

'We better go back in, or Mike'll be on the warpath. Even worse, Selma.'

But Marie's deep in thought and isn't listening.

SERENA

Serena screams, then collapses on Georgie's bed in floods of tears.

'Ohmigod, ohmigod, ohmigod.' She's hyperventilating.

Moments later, Georgie's mum, Leila, pokes her head around the door. 'What's going on?'

Georgie looks helplessly at her mum as Serena wails like a wounded animal.

'Get her some water,' Leila says to Georgie, who scuttles downstairs to the kitchen.

Leila sits next to Serena on the bed and puts her arm around the shuddering girl.

'What's the matter, darling?'

Serena can't stop sobbing, and she shakes her head desperately.

'It's okay,' says Leila soothingly. 'Nothing can be that bad. What's up?'

Georgie comes back with the water and plonks it so hard onto the chest of drawers next to her bed that some of it spills. Leila rubs Serena's back while she bawls uncontrollably.

'Do you know what's going on?' she asks Georgie.

Georgie hesitates, then blurts: 'Last night she and her boyfriend had sex, and he filmed it and he and his mates have posted it all over the place.'

'Shit,' says Leila. 'Did you know he was filming it?'

Serena shakes her head violently, still unable to speak.

''Course she didn't, Mum. How could you even think that?'

Leila raises her eyebrows in a *You Kids* expression. 'There are laws against posting things like that without your consent. You know, the revenge porn thing. Sexploitation. Do your parents know? We'd better call them. The police too.'

Serena grabs her arm, her face a mask of horror. She staccatos: 'No. No. No,' then collapses into a long fit of sobbing. 'I can't tell my mum. She'll – it'll kill her!'

Leila's expression shows that she is grimly aware of how Christine will react. 'We don't really have a choice. How do you think she'll feel if she finds out some other way? If you want to get the stuff taken down, and stop these boys from spreading it, then we've got to call the cops and we can't do that without telling your folks. Best ring them now and get it over with. She's stronger than you think, you know.'

'No! Please!' says Serena, even though she recognises with a crippling bleakness that Leila is right.

'Georgie, will you get my phone? It's in the kitchen,' says Leila firmly.

Serena feels the walls closing in on her. She just wants to die.

BILLY

'What were you thinking?'

'I dunno, Mum. Honest, I never posted it. I swear. I just wanted it –'

'For what? What in God's name would you want it for?'

'I thought– I thought she'd like it.' Billy's crying now.

'You really don't know anything about girls, do you? Your Auntie Jen is proper fuming. Kyle saw it on her mobile.'

'What the fuck –'

His mum, Elaine, smacks him lightly round the head. 'Don't you use that filthy language. You know he's always on her phone. She's told Nanna, you know.'

Billy's almost sick with shame. He hunches over his knees and sobs.

'Billy, you are a prize pillock, and that's the truth. I'm ashamed of you, son. I never brought you up to treat women like that. However bad you're feeling, she'll be feeling it a hundred times worse. A girl's reputation is worth more than diamonds, my boy, and thanks to you, hers is trash.'

Billy cries pathetically. 'What should I do, Mum?'

She sighs sadly. 'I dunno, love. You could start by apologizing.'

'She won't take my calls.'

'Can you ruddy well blame her? Why don't you write her a letter?' Billy's never written a letter in his life. 'I mean,' Elaine continues, 'it's a bit like sticking a plaster on a broken leg, I'll grant you, but it's a start.'

SUNDAY

NEVEAH

Neveah gets another text from Sharna, which she ignores. She's doesn't see how their friendship can survive. Neveah loves Giles, however pointless that is, and Sharna has stuck two fingers up to what's closest to her. What she's done could ruin his life. The sense of betrayal is immense, and only amplifies Neveah's isolation.

One by one, she's losing everyone she cares about.

She could go to Laura and Sweetman's, but they'll give her a lecture about Giles. Laura's been sending her *concerned* texts. She'll steer clear of Sandra and Leon too. San's also been firing off worried texts and left a couple of voicemails for her, that she'd 'like to talk'. She can't explain to Sandra what Giles means to her. Everyone will look at her and Giles through their own skewed little lens. There's not a soul she can talk to who would even try to understand.

Her mum hasn't surfaced yet. It was past 3am when she finally crawled in. She doesn't want to be around when Marie finally drags her carcass out of bed. It shouldn't be a surprise to Neveah that her mother has shown herself to be a money-grubbing monster. Whatever happens to her, she darkly vows, she will dedicate her whole life to being everything Marie isn't.

She can't stand being in the flat. She's having a hard time being inside her own skin. Cha-Cha had told her that Granny South wasn't well. *Maybe she's depressed*, Giles had said. She's been so wrapped up in her own troubles that she'd forgotten about that conversation.

She decides to go and visit her. She'll take a packet of Jaffa Cakes. If Granny won't eat a Jaffa Cake, then maybe she really is ready to kick the bucket.

BILLY

Billy's still in a state. He calls Stickman.

'What a shower, Billy, mate,' says Stick. 'I saw the whole thing.'

'I know. It's mental. I'm in so much deep shit.'

'Why the fuck did you post it?'

'I didn't. I swear on my mother's life. Andy did.'

'That figures. You know he was watching it in real time at Deak's? He was showing everyone.'

'Oh my fuck. Snakey little shit,' he says, with venom. 'Listen up, Stick, I need a favour. I need you to help me write a letter.'

Stickman is the only one of his friends who can string a sentence together. He's even won a competition for an internship at an online magazine.

'What kind of letter?'

'I want to write to Serena. To tell her –' Billy pauses as his voice is wobbling so much, '– that I'm sorry.'

'Okay. Why don't you write it, and I can edit it?'

'You can write something she'll know is, like, real. With poetry and everything. You were always good at English and stuff. I've been a fucking twat, and I don't blame her for ignoring me. But it's killing me, Stick. I feel so bad.'

'Billy, mate. Tell her exactly what you just told me. That you've been a twat. That you don't blame her for being a bit fucking miffed. It needs to be short and sweet but mostly, it's got to be from you. Look, I can help you, but she needs to believe you wrote it, and she won't be expecting sodding Shakespeare.'

MONDAY

NEVEAH

Neveah has pressed the snooze button on her phone alarm three times. She's normally showered and dressed and getting her breakfast and packed lunch ready by now, about to head out for the bus, but she's lost all sense of purpose. She's exhausted. She hasn't slept properly since Thursday.

She is so miserable.

She turns the alarm off and goes back to sleep but is plunged into a dream of being buried underground. She wakes up in a panic and forces herself out of bed. She'll swallow down some instant coffee with extra milk and sugar and get her sorry arse to school.

She's stunned to see Marie in the kitchen, perched on the counter in her dressing gown, the smell of coffee thick in the air. Marie has never, in living memory, been up before her, unless she hasn't yet gone to bed.

'Mum!' Neveah feels that her mother is intruding in her space/time continuum.

'I was wondering whether to come in and get you up. I heard your alarm going, but I thought I'd best leave you to it.'

'Why did you think that would be best?'

'Oh, you know.'

Neveah doesn't but can't be arsed to push.

'You all right, sweetheart? Have you been crying?' Neveah guesses she must look dreadful. She doesn't bother replying. She hasn't seen Marie since Saturday and still feels pretty frosty towards her. 'You can talk to me, you know,' says Marie. There it is again. Her *concerned* voice.

Neveah doesn't engage. Instead, she asks, 'What are you doing up?'

'I've got a lot of stuff to do,' Marie says, deliberately enigmatic. 'You know. Organise a few things.'

Knowing it will needle Marie, she asks no further questions. She makes up her coffee with extra sugar, and goes to the fridge to get the milk, but there isn't any.

'Sorry, darling,' says Marie. 'I finished it. I'm on my third coffee. I'm wired. You know, big day and all that.'

Neveah is seriously annoyed. She swallows it. 'Why is it a big day?'

'I don't want to say too much now. You know. In case I jinx things.'

'Do you have an interview or something? Are you thinking of leaving the club?' She knows Marie's in a bind. She isn't qualified for anything else, and while Mike pushes his advantage, he pays Marie more than she can get elsewhere.

'Nah, I don't think I'll be doing that anytime soon, but I need to do some stuff. It's time I started considering my future.'

My future. Not *our* future or even *the* future. Not that Neveah's remotely surprised. Her mind whirs. Marie's up to something. 'Cool,' she says noncommittally and takes a sip of coffee. 'Fuck!' Without milk it's scalding and burns her mouth.

'Language, sweetheart,' says Marie mildly as she scrolls through her phone.

A dark rage flares up inside Neveah. Imagine what life would be like with a mother who actually gave a flying fuck about her. A mother that would save her a drop of milk for breakfast would be a good start.

MARIE

As soon as Neveah leaves for school, Marie picks up her phone and googles: 'Are parents entitled to their underage children's earnings?'

It's a mixed bag.

'If parents are in severe financial hardship or at risk of losing their homes, then it is reasonable to take charge of income or assets belonging to all family members, including those of underage children.' Hmmm. She's broke, but like Peaches said, she's hardly on Skid Row.

'If a child lives with his/her parent(s), benefiting from housing, heating, electricity, clothing, food etc, and the child earns an income, then it is reasonable for the parent to claim a part of that income for household upkeep.'

She can't deny that Neveah contributes to general household upkeep. In fact, the little cow has pretty much ground it into her face that she puts in far more than her fair share.

She reads some of the threads attached to the posts. The threads all have one thing in common: the rapid descent into insults and name calling. It's a minefield.

'You can take your kid's phone away as a punishment or confiscate a laptop to limit screen time, but this doesn't mean you own these things if your kid has bought them with their own money.'

Marie thinks about this. It has never occurred to her to curb Neveah's screen time, or to control her behaviour in any way whatsoever, except when she was much younger, obviously. By never exerting any kind of parental power over Neveah, she has lost the authority to ever do so now.

'Parents may take nominal ownership of a child's assets, but those assets will revert to the child at the age of eighteen.' Bingo, she thinks. Neveah's only fifteen. Three more years of earnings potential. She'll have to play it very carefully. Neveah could flat out refuse to work, and there's not a damn thing Marie could do about it. More likely, she'd work in secret. When it comes to technology, Neveah runs rings around her. She'd be untouchable.

She reads a couple of case studies; parents and children fighting over laptops, phones, stereos ... a son suing his mother for spending the cash in his childhood savings account. A daughter forced to work by her parents, who took all her earnings and refused to feed or clothe her ... all resulting in bitter lifelong recriminations on both sides.

Marie has a feeling that spending hundreds on a dermatologist, on cosmetics, fashion items – no matter how much of a requirement they are for her work – not to mention booze, the weed and the odd bit of Bolivian marching powder, will not make a strong case for financial hardship in court, especially as she's taking cash in hand from Mike while claiming benefits. Plus, getting the law involved only risks the whole Blue horror coming out. She does not fancy the world and his wife finding out about that. Especially as Blue's back in her life.

She looks out of the window down to the concrete playground that Neveah has long grown out of. She feels a little strange. She's been too wired to sleep and has been staring at a tiny screen for too long. Definitely OD'd on the coffee. She puts her cup down. Her sense of righteous indignation about Neveah's cash suddenly shrinks in importance. Who's she kidding? She can't take charge of Neveah's money. She'll be kicking a hornet's nest if she even tries. She knows she doesn't show it enough, but she loves her daughter, and it suddenly hits her how little time they have left together. She'll be off to great things soon, leaving her, Marie, far behind. She googles the minimum age for a child to leave home. Sixteen. Holy fuck. In three months' time, Neveah can officially leave home. If she wants any kind of relationship with her in the future, she can't nick her money. She should support her in her uni dream, no matter how much it sticks in her craw.

It's clear the girl is miserable and unhappy because of this Giles bloke. Despite all their harsh words over the weekend, she does feel sorry for her, and she really had tried to reach out that morning, but Neveah's still mad at her, and if she's honest, the feeling's mutual. The best way forward is not to throw her relationship with her daughter under a bus for the sake of a few grand. Not when there's a much bigger pot to play for instead.

She remembers what Peaches had said. *Maybe he'd be willing to stump up a bit of cash. To stay out of trouble.*

Her phone doesn't have much battery left, so she plugs it in before she searches for Hawthorne Associates, as she'd seen on the bank statement. The website declares itself to be under construction, but the contact details are easy to find. There's a mobile and a landline. Heart thumping with caffeine and adrenaline, she dials the mobile number. It rings twice before she panics and kills the call. She needs to calm down first. Plan what she's going to say. She takes a deep breath. *I'm* not the one in the wrong here, she thinks. She exhales, then jumps in shock when her phone trills into action. It's him. Calling from the mobile she's just dialled. Fuck! She should have withheld her number. She quickly jabs the red X and turns the phone off, as if it has personally offended her.

She's flooded with the spirit of combat, but it's tinged with fear. Almost in a daze, she wanders to the bathroom and turns the shower on. She likes to be drenched in water so scalding that her skin turns a livid pink. She leans against the shower wall with her hands, her arms extended, and lets the water roll over her, wallowing in the sensation of liquid heat running down her body. Her mind buzzes as she considers her options. She washes her hair roughly, taking out her agitation on her scalp, then works her way downwards, soaping vigorously as she always does.

He must be minted, she thinks, as she washes between her toes. He has his own business and can fling cash with abandon at Neveah. The money he's given her has effectively put her own daughter out of her reach. She feels a patch of rough skin on the underside of her right foot. She reaches for the pumice and rubs it as if it's the face of her worst enemy. Giles Fucking Hawthorne. With a name like that he can't be anything other than a public school posh boy who has swum since birth in a pool of privilege. She's come across plenty like him at the club. Men who take whatever they want and never pay the price. He's a marauding paedophile who has preyed on her baby. He can't get away with it. She decides against shaving her legs. She'll do herself a mischief the way her hands are shaking. She wants to be cool and noir, but she knows that what she's planning to do has a name and that it's against the law. She's seen it done a dozen times in her beloved black and white movies, always with style and a slick smile. *'Why make me your victim?'* Ziggy asks Carla, the impossibly elegant casino singer in *Blackmail*. *'Because you have the kind of bank account I've learned to love, Mr Cranston,'* says Carla, as she takes a languorous drag of her cigarette. Marie has to summon up some of that flair if she wants to pull this off.

Her heart is pumping as she rubs herself down with a patchy old blue towel. Everything in this place has seen better days, she thinks with bitterness. Including you, says a cruel voice in her head which is sounding off more and more these days. She's afraid. But chances like this don't come along every day, and she's more afraid of missing it. It's Giles Hawthorne who should be scared, she thinks viciously. He should be fucking petrified.

GILES

Richard Fox, Giles's lawyer and long-time friend, pours coffee from a silver pot into two cups and hands one to Giles. He slides the milk jug across.

'Now I understand why you wanted to see me so urgently. It's a bit worrying, I can't pretend otherwise. You've laid yourself open to a charge of statutory rape. Made yourself a target for the girl –'

'She's not remotely like that. She –'

Richard holds his hand up to interrupt. 'She may well be a good-natured girl who's happy to watch you waltz into the sunset with a wave, but my role is to imagine the worst-case scenario. If you're reported, the police will get involved. You've also got to think about your reputation. However you spin it, it doesn't look good. Does Chrissie know?'

'Yes. She does.'

'The full story?'

Giles nods.

'Well that's something. How did she take it?'

'As you'd expect,' Giles says grimly. 'It'd be bad enough if she only had this to deal with, but she's beside herself with worry about Serena –'

'Serena knows?'

'God, no, and I don't suppose Chrissie will tell her unless ... unless she decides to leave me.'

'Is that likely?'

'How the hell do I know?' Giles runs his fingers through his hair. 'Serena's in a mess of her own. Her boyfriend made a secret recording of them having sex and the little shit has posted it on the internet.'

'Oh my God. The poor girl.'

'Yes. She's in pieces about it.'

'Has he been on the scene long?'

'A few months. We didn't know he existed until Saturday. He's a little below stairs, apparently. A bit older. Works in a bike shop. She thought we wouldn't approve, I guess, but so long as someone's fundamentally decent –'

'Which he obviously isn't. How old is he?'

'Twenty-one.'

'Not too bright either. Teenagers getting it on is one thing, but six years is a big enough gap for him to be done for statutory rape. And he's broadcast his crime. Even if she wasn't underage, posting without her consent is a crime in itself. When did it happen?'

'Friday night, but it only came to light on Saturday. That's when I called you.'

'Sorry I didn't get the message sooner. The signal at the cottage is terrible, and to be honest, Rose and I were on our own for once and had gone to ground. Next time email me.'

'Well, there's hardly going to be a next time, is there? Both scenarios are so fucking off the scale extraordinary that –'

'Well, yes. Sorry.'

Giles takes in a deep breath and exhales noisily. 'No, I'm sorry. I know perfectly well what you mean. It's just that finally, finally, Christine seemed to be recovering from the attack, and everything looked like it could get on an even keel, but because I'm a fuckwit, and because Serena's a horny brainless teenager who picked a fucking wrong'un –' he pauses, unable to end his sentence in a way that adequately conveys his contempt.

'Did you call the police?'

Giles reddens. 'Under normal circumstances, of course I would have called them. But Serena begged me not to. All she wanted is for the video to be taken down.'

'Has it?'

'Yes, but we have no idea how many people have seen it. God, Richard, she's in a state. You should see her. She's not in school today. She's a total mess.'

'I can imagine. What a shocking violation.'

'Exactly,' says Giles bleakly.

'She does know, doesn't she, that just because he's taken the video down, doesn't mean it's been deleted? It could have been forwarded multiple times. The porn sites are shit hot on the issue of consent, but it could be forwarded on WhatsApp or appear on the dark web.'

'What can we do?' says Giles dismally. 'It's like throwing confetti into a gale then trying to collect all the pieces.'

'I know someone. A digital specialist. She can track its progress. She may not be able to mop up everything, but she can do a lot of damage limitation. She can get in touch with website owners and order deletion, that sort of thing. I'll give her a ring.'

'That would be brilliant.'

'And you should go to the police.'

'God, Richard. How can I do that when I'm potentially guilty of the same thing?'

'You shouldn't conflate your position with his. There's a world of difference. He knowingly had sex with a minor and publicised it. In your case, you had a relationship with someone you believed to be of age.'

'*Ignorantia juris non excusat*, as you well know.'

'Normally, yes, but there are mitigating factors in your case. In the first instance, you met her in a business context, correct?'

'Yes. She came to my office during working hours to pitch herself as a digital marketing guru.'

'How did she find out about you?'

'A friend recommended the company she works for.'

'Even better. So she turned up representing a company. Which one?'

'Sweet Street Media.'

Richard jots the name down. 'I'll check it out. Did she provide you with a business card?'

'Yes.'

'And she came frequently during working hours?'

'Yes. Of course, because I'm a credulous, cretinous and gullible twat, it didn't occur to me that she was bunking off school.'

'Did you keep a record of your appointments?'

'I have every meeting on my phone diary. As soon as I found out how old she was, I made a full contemporaneous note, which I have here.' He digs into his briefcase and hands an envelope over.

'Okay, good. I presume she at least *looks* of age?'

'God, yes!'

'Did she give you any documentary evidence that she was over sixteen before you had sex?'

'I didn't ask for ID if that's what you mean. She told me she was twenty-two. She said she'd gone to uni to do computer science –'

'Did you check that out?'

'No, I didn't. I have a hundred better things to do than check out the provenance of every service provider I hire. She was extremely good at what she was doing, so I didn't care. In any case, she'd already told me she hadn't graduated. She said she'd dropped out of uni as she didn't want to bankrupt herself paying for a course which wasn't teaching her anything she didn't already know. That sounded entirely plausible. Knowing what I do about your average uni course … she told me she'd been freelancing for Sweet Street for years, had started when she was still at school. The guy who runs it is a friend of her father's.'

'The whole thing's extraordinary. Didn't she ever let her guard slip?'

'When I think about it, she could be a little, well, gauche, I suppose. She's completely ignorant about food and wine. She's never travelled.

I doubt she could name a single opera apart from Jerry Springer, but seriously, Richard, the same is true of half the adult population in this country. Saying all that, she knows things I wouldn't expect a fifteen-year-old to know.'

'Do you mean sexually?'

'God, no. I hope I'm never drawn on that.'

'You may be, if it ever comes to court.'

'Christ,' says Giles. 'I fucking hope not.' He'd rather go to jail than betray her like that. 'I mean she has a surprising amount of general knowledge. She's actually a reader. How many kids know Emily Bronte, for instance?'

'Is it on her GCSE syllabus?' Richard asks drily.

'Well, fuck, isn't hindsight a marvellous thing? Poetry. Sylvia Plath, for instance. Emily Dickinson. Dylan Thomas.'

'Probably on the syllabus too.'

'Well, yes,' he says despondently. 'She has an encyclopaedic knowledge of Film Noir. She can quote whole chunks of dialogue from the Hitchcock movies verbatim. Modern history. We had a long discussion about Antony Beevor once. I mean … does that sound like a fifteen-year-old to you?'

'Well …'

'I mean, she's clever. She thinks about things, but she has never pretended to be anything other than a girl from *Sarf Lundon*. There are other things… her knowledge of music, for instance. She's like a walking jukebox. Jazz. Reggae and ska. All the Motown classics. Sam Cooke, Ella Fitzgerald, Billie Holiday, Nina Simone… no matter how obscure, there's not a B side she doesn't know. Her dad fronts a band and –'

'She's not –'

'Not what?'

'You know.'

'You know what?'

'Black?'

'What's that got to do with anything?'

'Well, is she?'

'Her dad's Jamaican and her mother's Irish but they both grew up in London. So what?'

Richard pauses before he answers. 'It just makes the position ... more ambiguous. I don't want to put the frighteners on you, but the cops are keen to show they take sexual crimes of all stripes seriously. After Rochdale and Oxford, bagging a few white scalps will make them look more even-handed.

Giles's blood pressure spikes. 'Fuck!'

'Black people have been targeted and singled out by the cops unfairly for years. It shouldn't be a surprise that it can work the other way, too.'

Giles digests this. He'd always thought police treatment of minorities was monstrously unfair. But he doesn't much like being the statistic that helps to balance the score.

Richard continues: 'This is why we should just hope like hell this whole sorry saga never sees the light of day. If it does, don't answer a single question from the police without calling me first.' He sighs. 'What was the other thing?'

'What other thing?'

'You said you needed to see me about three things.'

'Oh, God yes. If we didn't have enough shit to deal with, we've received notice that Ian Durandt is coming up for parole. He's served half his sentence.'

Richard inhales deeply and raises his eyebrows. 'Troubles come not as single spies, but in battalions.'

Giles doesn't bother correcting the quote. 'Yes, exactly.'

STICKMAN

Stickman is working at *The Biscuit*, an online freezine monetised by advertising revenue. He's one of five interns. He's been there for fifteen minutes and is already on the back foot. He'd been told to arrive by 8am in the morning. 'You're the last to get here,' said the girl who let him in, even though he'd been bang on time. The other four had arrived way earlier and had been assigned to various tasks. Making hot drinks. Photocopying. Filing. Cutting out pictures. Yes, really. He'd been told dismissively by some beanpole in black to 'Go and organise the stationery cupboard, Fatboy,' only to find there wasn't one.

Now he's in a meeting with the other interns and the news team.

'When your fortnight's up, we'll keep one of you. Maybe,' says the scarily immaculate Fiona *Call-me-Fi* Marron, the founder. They're pitching story ideas to Fi and the beanpole, who's a staff writer. They're in a hangar-like garage in Wapping, but Stickman's sweating, and his stomach is churning, even though he's 'never knowingly underfed' as his mates like to say, and he had a big bacon and egg butty for breakfast. Mitzi, a bright little posh girl, wants to investigate the companies that are 'charging like wounded rhinos' for removing the lethal cladding from high rise buildings.

'Obviously it's of public interest when they're the same companies that installed the stuff in the first place. I've got a couple of interesting leads who can give a new perspective…' and she rattles them off as she flicks her hair back and pushes her glasses further up her nose. She's talking to that roomful of people, including Fi, as if she's known them her whole life. Fuck! All the tea he's drunk is pressing on his bladder. He wishes he'd had a piss before he sat down.

'Yup, if you make it short. Anything else?'

'A story on dyslexia.'

'What's the angle?'

'There's a pilot study taking place in three schools in Oxfordshire, where teachers are identifying learning difficulties as soon as kids start in reception, so they can take action before they fall behind and become labelled, bored, or disruptive.'

Fi makes a face. 'Well whoop-de-doo.'

'The Dyslexia Society aren't supporting it.'

'Why?'

'They say it's an invasion of family privacy, but I think it's because they regard it as an existential threat. If the pilot works and takes off, dyslexia won't be such a life-changing problem anymore. They're more interested in receiving cash than spending it properly.'

'What a bunch of arseholes. Like all charities.'

'Yup,' says Mitzi, as if she and Fi were best buds. Bet she went to private school, thinks Stickman. 'It could be an opening to investigate other charities which purport to solve problems that they actually perpetuate.'

'Okay. Look into that. How about you, Steve?'

Stickman isn't used to being called Steve. There's nothing wrong with his vocab, but he can't imagine peppering his sentences with words like *existential* and *purport*. 'Um,' he looks at his notes. 'London grime nights and the rise of the spoken word. I've got some pictures.'

'Okay. Anything else?'

'A story about a guy who dug up a huge second world war bomb in his veg patch.'

'I'm sure I've read about that somewhere,' says Mitzi.

'Better make the pictures funny,' says Fi, unimpressed. Stickman's losing her... she's turning towards Asif, the guy next to him. He feels a sinking in his gut. Then he has a flash of inspiration. 'Sextortion,' he says. 'Sexploitation.'

'I'm sorry?' says Fi.

'A private sex video that's gone viral,' says Stickman.

'You mean like that film with Cameron Diaz?'

'Yeah, except the girl didn't know she was being filmed.'

'Oh God. Poor thing. Who filmed her?'

'The boyfriend. Then the video got pasted all over the place.'

'What a dickhead,' says Mitzi. 'Without her consent, that's against the law. Has it been taken down?'

'Yeah, but it's been copied and uploaded on multiple sites.' Stickman doesn't actually know if this is true. 'He's lost control of it now.'

'Yup. We can run with that. Good. Very topical. If you can get some interviews, that would be dynamite. Pictures, too. We can pixelate the girl's face, obvs. Get moving on it. I want that in today.'

Stickman almost faints with relief.

It's Asif's turn. 'A tribute to Stormzy called Klowdzy, who's coming up with his own original music…'

Stickman's brain is buzzing. He can't see how he'll get Billy's girl to agree to an interview, but he'll come up with something.

MARIE

Marie has decided to go to Giles's office. Why give the bastard advance warning?

She needs to look good. She rifles through her wardrobe. The burnt orange Karen Millen number is too dressy. The black Roland Mouret is a mite tight at the best of times and is off the table when she's having anything remotely approaching a fat day. She'll have to get Neveah to stop buying Mother's Pride. Black's a cliché, in any event. A midnight blue lace dress from Fenwick's … she decides on an old favourite, a dark grey Nicole Farhi which whispers rather than shouts sex. She got in the sales. She bets Giles Hawthorne's wife doesn't have to wait for the sodding sales.

She rehearses what she's going to say as she blow-dries her hair. God, her roots really need touching up. Her hands are steady as she puts her face on, but her nerves are jangling. What if she fucks it up? What if he calls her bluff? Would she really be willing to report him, and have her life dragged through social services, the police, the courts? All their dirty linen … The lawyers and the judges are all public schoolboys like him. It's a closed shop. People like her don't stand a chance. What if he reports her for blackmail? It's infuriating. For the first time in her life, she has some leverage on someone and she's too chickenshit to use it.

She's slowly simmering with the injustice of it all. She's flooded with a tide of resentment which is only partly directed at Neveah, who just has to click her chewed up little fingers to land a man like Giles Hawthorne. An architect. Loaded, by the looks of things. It's not as if Marie doesn't fish in the right pools. She meets plenty of rich men at the club, but they're usually married or arrogant wankers or both. They talk a good game, but when push comes to shove, all they want from her is a legover, and when she gives in, as she sometimes does, she ends up feeling properly shit about herself. She's sick of being used. That includes Mike. As well as not paying her properly, he'd taken advantage of her loneliness. Completely led her down the garden path. She could have done amazing things at the club with Mike if she were his partner. They could have been great together, but guess what? He'd rather be with a fishwife like Selma.

Then there's Blue. All she's ever wanted is someone to walk through life with. Someone *solvent* to walk through life with. Is that so much to ask? Blue's got wads of cash. He's a bog-standard plumber who started calling himself a heating engineer and bought a fleet of white vans, slapped logos on them and filled them with Szymons and Bogdans who work the length and breadth of London for pennies while he rakes it in big style. It's not what you'd call glamorous, but she can live with that. What she couldn't live with is a man who would shag her daughter.

But that was then.

She's staring forty in the face. The dating apps she's signed up to haven't helped her. It's a desolate scene out there. She's in debt, has no savings, no assets, no pension and a penchant for the finer things in life, some legal, some not.

It's not exactly accurate to say that she and Blue had been engaged to be married. But they'd talked about shacking up ... he'd always put her off, saying that Connor needed to get used to the idea of not having his dad to himself. As if Connor gave a toss about anything except for guns and ammo and Assassin and Fortnite ...

Blue had often complained about her working nights, that if it were up to him she'd keep her evenings free, had hinted that if they took things further ... he'd never outright offered to keep her, but what else could he have meant? It was all academic, really. Neveah fucked everything up good and proper. Deep inside, Marie knows Blue is squarely to blame, but in the freedom of her own head, she's judge and jury.

She has always wanted to be married. She wants to tie the knot with Blue. She's not stupid. She can't see him getting down on one knee in a hurry. Unbidden, her mother's words echo in her head: 'Why buy the cow when you get the milk for free?' And she knows that he's a hard dog to keep on a leash. But she'd make him happy if he'd let her. She'd look after him. Keep an eye on him. And she'd have some status. She'd have *rights*. If she's willing to forgive him for his little flingette with Neveah … she shudders again at the memory of the two of them together. Fuck. She'll have to get over it somehow.

Coming back to her current problem. How is she going to confront Giles? What if he denies it? What if he… then it comes to her. She doesn't have to threaten him. Not at all. She's a distraught mother with an emotionally damaged daughter. An emotionally damaged *underage* daughter. He can fill in the blanks for himself.

She can't afford a black cab so she orders an uber. She could jump on the tube, but that is so unstylish. Plus, she's in a pair of killer heels and must keep walking to an absolute minimum. A sexy prowl round his office is absolutely all she'll be able to manage. A message pings on her phone telling her that her driver, Kamal, is four minutes away. She throws on her long red coat which she'd pinched from the cloakroom at work – it had been left for weeks without being claimed – and belts it around her waist. She glances in the floor length mirror propped against the wall by the front door. She is so Hollywood, she reassures herself. She holds her breath down the four flights to the outside as the smell of piss in the stairwell's so bad and the sodding lift's out of order, as per usual.

GILES

Giles is at work when his phone rings. It's Christine.

'Giles? You've got to come home. The police are coming round.'

His chest freezes. 'You've got to be kidding me.'

'It's about the video. They've come to talk to Serena.'

'I'm on my way.'

He grabs his jacket and shouts to Julie, his assistant, that he's going home. He sees when he gets outside that traffic is at a standstill, so he strides towards the tube. He gives himself a savage mental kicking for not reporting Billy and Videogate to the police himself. His failure to report it does not put him or Christine in a particularly good light. He has a presentiment that the one horror show will spill over into the other.

MARIE

Marie gets into Kamal's car in a high dudgeon.

'Where in the bloody hell have you been? The app said four minutes, then every time I looked at it the time kept going up and up.' She's bloody freezing. Her striking red coat offers little in the way of warmth, and her feet are now like ice blocks.

'Sorry, Missus,' says Kamal, which makes Marie even madder. She's not even considered a 'Miss' anymore. 'Traffic's mental. 'S'roadworks, innit. The whole city's being dug up.'

SERENA

'The video was taken down by the moderators,' says the WPC. Serena can't remember her name. 'They got loads of complaints and got their act together PDQ. They're not always that quick, believe me. Because of Serena's age, we have to consider this child pornography, so the person who filmed it and distributed it is in a world of trouble. Even though it was taken down, it was still viewed multiple times.'

Serena squirms. Like she needs reminding. She's sitting on the sofa at home with a parent to either side of her. They want her to tell them 'in her own words' what happened on Friday night. With her parents listening. She didn't think her humiliation could get any worse. She's torn between blabbing about rape, or keeping her gob shut as she'd promised herself. Apparently, Billy's guilty of statutory rape anyway. What difference does it make if she tells them she clearly said no but he stuck it in regardless? Won't she look like she's crying rape to moderate her own shame? It's real classy, shagging a boy at a party on a Friday night in a jampacked flat.

Her cheeks burn. He hasn't just raped her. Thanks to him, she's being dragged through the dirt too. If Billy had listened to her, she wouldn't be in this position. If he hadn't filmed her, she wouldn't be sat here having to blurt out deeply personal stuff to two strangers in uniform. In front of her parents. She has done nothing wrong, but she's being punished over and over.

MARIE

It's amazing how much you can loathe a perfect stranger without exchanging a single word. At first, she was glad of the warmth, but now Marie's been sitting in Kamal's overheated metal box for forty minutes, for a trip that should take no more than twenty, listening to his shite hip hop, breathing in his synthetic forest pine air freshener, mingled with the smell of stale fags and his horrible aftershave, cursing him under her breath every time the lights turn red, and especially when he lets someone cut in front of him which is practically all the time. She's fuming. Her grandmother used to drive like an arthritic snail but had more balls behind a wheel than this muppet.

Fuck it. She gets her cigarettes out. She's about to light up when Kamal catches her eye in the mirror.

'No smoking, missus,' he says.

'It's like sitting in an old ashtray in here.'

'I do what I like in me own motor.'

'Oh come on! Don't be an arse. Just let me –'

He has a clear bit of road ahead of him and is about to shift into a so-far unprecedented third gear, when he mutinously pulls over. 'Ride's over, missus. App'll charge your card to here.'

'Fine!' Marie shrieks. 'I'll put them away. For fuck's sake, put your foot down.'

But it's too late. Half of London is bearing down on the back of his car. He waits patiently for the multitudes to pass, obediently indicating, before he sedately pulls out into the road, taking his place right at the back of the long snaking queue of traffic, which comes to a dead halt long before the lights change again to red. Marie boils with impotent rage. She is so not going to give this little prick a tip.

SERENA

'How long have you been seeing Billy?'

'Around six months. I met him at the cycle shop. I took my bike in for a new wheel, and he asked me out for a drink.'

'Weren't you worried about the age difference?'

'I liked it. Boys my age are so lame, you know? Besides. Billy's not really like your average grown-up.'

'Have you had sex with him before?'

'No!' Serena squirms. 'We – we'd talked about it. He said he was happy to wait.'

'Until you were old enough, you mean?'

'Well, not really. We did talk about – ohmigod, this is so awkward. Mum, Dad, can you go and make a cup of tea or something?'

'Can you question her without us present?' Giles asks. 'As she's a minor?'

'Yes, absolutely. As long as you're happy with that, Serena.'

'God, yes.' She sees her dad is as relieved about absenting himself as she is. She picks up her mum's hand and gives it a squeeze. Tears, never far away, spring up to her eyes. 'Sorry, Mum.'

Christine reluctantly gets up and follows Giles out.

As soon as her parents are out of the room, Serena turns to the officers and says, 'Okay, so I know you've seen the video, and you're going to find this really hard to believe, but– before I tell you, I have to say that I never thought Billy was a bad person. I mean, I thought I loved him. I can see now that he's a bit childish, and I thought he behaved like a twat at the party even before he got me up the stairs, but if you play that video and you turn the sound up, maybe you'll hear that I told him clearly to stop. I know the music was loud, but I didn't want him to do it.' She starts to cry again. 'To be fair to him, we talked about having sex at the party. It was a big build-up for both of us for ages. It was like, some kind of romantic pipe dream, but when we got there, the vibe was all wrong. He was seriously wasted, and he didn't seem to care, but I did. I mean, I'd had a lot to drink, and at first it was cool, I was buzzing, but then I felt really ropey and just wanted to go home. Besides, the house was rammed. There was no lock on the door. I didn't want anyone walking in on something so– you know.'

'Intimate,' supplies one of the coppers.

'Yeah. That's how it's supposed to be, isn't it? Intimate. Something cosy shared between two people? Well, that's not what this was like. It's like I wasn't a part of it. As if he suddenly turned into a different person. I was shocked. You know the bit where I … you know, the bit where I – you know,' she's so ashamed she can barely speak, and the tears threaten to spill again.

The two coppers look at each other.

She controls herself. 'When it's all over, I kiss him. I cuddle him, too. That's because I was shell-shocked, and I didn't quite understand what had just happened. I wanted things– I wanted us– you know, I wanted to feel normal. That's why I did it. I mean obviously I wish he hadn't had sex with me that way, and I definitely wish he hadn't filmed it and shared it with half the fucking universe, but more than anything, I wish I hadn't kissed and cuddled him afterwards. I'm such a twat. I shouldn't have put myself in that position in the first place. My mum – my mum was raped and it ruined her life, and all she's ever wanted is for me to be safe, and I let myself down, but more than anything, I let her down.'

The WPC gets out of her chair and sits next to Serena and puts her arm around her shoulders while handing her a tissue.

'He didn't have sex with you, Serena. He raped you. It's true the sound isn't good on the video, but– look, whatever it shows, it's irrelevant, as you're underage and that makes him guilty of statutory rape. No ifs, no buts. It doesn't matter what you did or didn't do afterwards. Maybe you did kiss him afterwards, but that doesn't appear on the video.'

'What?'

'The video that's been posted publicly has been edited and has been cut pretty much at the moment of – of ejaculation.'

'Are you being serious?' Serena feels a tiny spark of relief.

'You should explain exactly what happened to your mum. Your dad too. They obviously care about you. And you shouldn't blame yourself. Most victims of rape waste a lot of psychic energy blaming themselves, instead of channelling it all into recovering. There's one person to blame here, and that's Billy.'

'What's going to happen to him?'

'We'll take a statement from you now. And then we'll pay him a visit. Your statement and the video more than justify an arrest.'

Momentarily, Serena feels bad for Billy. Then she tells herself fiercely that he deserves every ounce of shit that comes his way.

MARIE

Kamal finally deposits Marie in front of Giles's office. She gets out without saying a word, slams the door and totters on her vertiginous heels towards the revolving glass doors.

Kamal winds down his window. 'Have a nice day, Missus.'

Marie glowers at him. 'Are you actually taking the piss?' She'd dearly love to tell him to fuck off, but that would so not be classy.

'Nah. I'm, like, you know – ah,' he shakes his head. 'See ya, lady.'

He drives off.

Cheeky bugger. Who does he think he is? She decides to have a cigarette before The Big Confrontation. She needs to chill the fuck out. She is so highly strung she's ready to snap.

She lights up and takes a drag deep down into her lungs. She fishes in her bag for her phone so she can glance at the time. She looks up at the back of Kamal's receding car. She's only left the bloody thing on the back seat. Marie is so enraged that she wants to cry.

GILES

Giles and Christine sit at the kitchen table together, waiting to be summoned back to the living room. They're like two countries at war forced to unite in the face of a sudden common enemy.

'We should have –' says Christine, but her sentence peters out.

'Other than lock her up in a tower, we couldn't have done anything differently.'

'We could have taught her how to defend herself, to look out for danger.'

'She can't tiptoe through life. Right or wrong, she's picked up from us that the world is full of dangerous people who will do her harm.'

'That's because it is!'

Giles shakes his head. 'We've all got to take our chances, including her. She'll get over this. We'll hunt the video all over the net – Foxy's on it – and we'll get her some counselling.'

Christine arches her back and brushes her hands together as if ridding them of crumbs. 'Yes! Job done. Bit of counselling… she'll be right as rain.'

'What else do you suggest? Should we cave in to despair?'

'It took me years to recover from rape.'

'There is absolutely no comparison between your experience and Serena's. None whatsoever.'

'She's been violated and betrayed.'

'Yes, she has. But we need to put things into perspective. He didn't viciously beat her and leave her for dead. He didn't –' he becomes conscious that he's raising his voice. 'She had sex with her boyfriend and the little shit filmed it.'

'She's only fifteen!

'Yes, and because of that he's going to feel the full force of the law.'

'Does that give you any satisfaction?'

'How can you possibly expect me, in my position, to answer that question? Intent is everything. I never set out to –' he suddenly remembers the police are in the house.

'Has it occurred to you that you may have done Neveah harm?'

Giles stands up and grips the back of his chair.

'If you're worried that I've taken my hair shirt off, please put your mind at rest.'

'That's not what I meant and you know it. It just seems to me that any reassurance from you that Serena will be just peachy is ever so slightly self-serving, if you ask me.'

'What else would you like me to say? Will it make you feel better if I say she'll never recover and be psychologically scarred for life? Should we slap her into a convent and be done with it? How about a loony bin? Or is it just possible that she's had a vile experience which she'll quickly recover from if she gets the right kind of support from us?'

Christine doesn't say anything.

Giles inhales sharply. 'Chrissie, I'm sorry. I feel terrible about betraying you. As to whether I've damaged Neveah, that's not for me to say.'

'This could completely destroy us. You've made all of us hostages to fortune.'

Like he bloody needs reminding, he wants to snap, but he knows his anger is misplaced. There's one person to blame here, and it's not Christine.

MARIE

Marie's hopelessly out of breath after a doomed attempt to run after Kamal's car. Her ridiculous heels were her first obstacle, her appalling fitness the second. He'd been stuck at a traffic light ahead of her. She'd frantically waved her arms, hoping he'd look in the mirror, but nope ... the lights changed and off the little prick zooted. Stop-start traffic all afternoon, and now just her flaming luck, he has a clear run. She's too vain for glasses and too broke for contacts, so she can't clock the numberplate. His details will be stored on her uber app, she reassures herself.

What good is that when it's on her stupid phone?

She can't think straight. Her need for a nicotine hit is overwhelming. She'd dropped her lit cigarette on the pavement before her pitiful sprint. She scans the ground for it, and sees it smouldering next to a fire hydrant. It's only burnt down a tiny bit. There are people coming out of the revolving doors to Giles's office. Once they've gone… but then more people spill out, and suddenly it's a busy stretch of pavement. Fuck it, no one's paying attention. She quickly looks around, but ultimately she's too embarrassed to pick it up. What a shameful waste. What it costs to buy a packet … it's extortion, it really is.

She lights up a fresh one. She feels utterly naked without her phone. She has no way of even telling the time. She has to get it back. It's not only all the numbers and photos she'd lose, she can't afford a new one. She'd cancelled the insurance on it as she didn't want to fork out an extra six quid a month. She suddenly remembers the Apple pay facility on her phone … that wanker Kamal or whatever his name is could have a field day with that. She can't cancel it without … yup, she thinks. She needs her phone to cancel the payment facility on her phone. It would be hilarious if it were happening to anyone else. She and Neveah don't even have a landline at home. It's a long time since she's had such a lousy day. Things can only pick up from here, really.

KAMAL

Kamal's glad to be rid of Marie. Like sharing a car with a simmering volcano. And her refusal to part on good terms … that's bad karma, that is. As he's waiting at the lights, he sees a flash of red in his rear view mirror. It's her, and no mistake. Waving like a good'un. As the lights change, his eyes sweep over the back seat. Yup. She's left her phone behind. He could pull over, let her catch up. He could even zip around, save her from running. Nah, he thinks. Serve the miserable moo right. He drives on.

MARIE

Marie takes in another deep drag. She'll have to use the bathroom before she marches in to see Giles. She's busting for the loo ... all that coffee this morning's catching up with her, her hair's a mess and she probably looks as demented as she feels. She uses the cigarette as a meditation device. Inhale. Calm. Space. Breathe. Exhale. Her nerves are as frayed as old shoelaces.

She quails at the task she's set herself and contemplates calling it off. No. She's here now. She may as well get it over with. She grinds her cigarette out under her heel and pushes through the revolving doors into a cavernous reception area, with a large, spacious desk manned by several people, and a waiting area, where a few people are sitting on big, squashy sofas. She marches up to the desk, which would not look out of place on the Starship Enterprise, and is about to ask one of the nice smiling young people manning it if she can use the loo, when a tall, well-built young black man approaches her. He's in a white shirt and black trousers and has a walkie talkie strapped to his waist. It's hardly noticeable, but Marie lengthens her spine, pulls in her tummy and elevates her chest. It's hard-wired into her, a conditioned response at the sight of a good-looking man.

'Excuse me, Madam,' he says quietly. 'Didn't you notice the very big chrome ashtray fixed to the wall?'

'Well, obviously I didn't see it. If I had, I would have used it.'

'There's also a big sign by the door requesting that smokers dispose of their litter responsibly.'

'I didn't see that either.' Her voice is wobbling dangerously. She's mortified. Why's he picking on her?

'Please go back outside, pick up that cigarette butt and put it where it belongs.'

He hasn't raised his voice, yet to her, it carries to every corner of this cavernous space, and the young shiny people behind the desk are all looking at her, and all those seated in the waiting area have craned their necks in her direction. She can't even begin to explain to this bossy little Hitler how much he's kicking her when she's already down.

'It's only a fag butt!' she hisses.

'If everyone thought that, we'd be up to our necks in filth. That's why there are laws against littering.'

There's a small part of Marie's brain that recognises that she's in the wrong. It urges her to apologise, to do as he says, to muster as much dignity as she's capable of, get her arse outside, bend down, pick up the butt and put it in the aforementioned receptacle, but an overwhelming surge of cortisol drowns out the molecules of reason.

'For fuck's sake, where do you get off telling me what to do?' shrieks Marie. 'I pay my taxes just like everyone else, and that covers street cleaning.'

'Madam, if you carry on swearing like that, I'm going to have to ask you to leave the building.'

'This is fucking unbelievable! What if I refuse to go?'

To her horror, he moves towards a telephone behind the desk.

'What are you doing?'

'I'm calling the building manager.'

'You what? For a fag butt! You've got to be kidding me.'

Resolute, he punches four digits into the desk telephone.

Part in fury, part in panic, Marie reaches over the desk, slaps at his arm and makes a grab for the phone, which crashes to the floor, landing on his feet.

'Whoa, lady,' he says, gripping his arm before bending to pick the phone up. 'That's assault. Plus damage to private property. On top of swearing, hate speech, littering … I mean, never mind the building manager, we're talking a call to the cops here.'

Desperate, Marie turns to one of the girls behind the desk, who's watching the drama, spellbound. 'You saw the whole thing. Did I assault him? Well, did I?'

The girl's expression hardens. 'Yeah, you like, totally attacked him. Just 'cos he called you out on your litterbugging, you got the hump and flew off the handle. It's, like, totally out of order.' She picks up her phone. 'Don't worry, Terence. I'll call Colin.'

'I'm right here,' says a mild-looking middle-aged man with a bald patch, who appears from a side door. 'What's going on?'

'This lady dropped her fag butt on the floor outside, totally ignoring the sign, and Terence asked her very politely to go and pick it up, and she swore at him and attacked him and went, like, totally postal.'

'That is such a lie!' screams Marie. The mild-looking Colin's lips thin when he looks at her.

'I can't tolerate attacks on my staff. Terence, are you all right?'

Terence is holding his arm as if it's broken. 'Yeah, she –'

'I hardly touched him! He's acting up to make me look bad! I mean, look at the size of him! He could knock Mike Tyson out with his little finger!'

'Please keep your voice down,' says the building manager. 'There's no need to be so –'

'Don't tell me how to behave!' shrieks Marie, who by now has a red klaxon blaring in her head. 'You're a bunch of fucking wankers! You're all ganging up against me just 'cos your pet gorilla here can't mind his own fucking business!'

Beneath all the fury, the small speck of reason in Marie's brain makes a feeble attempt to warn her that she's gone too far, that now would be a really good time to grovel and apologise, but the speck is like an ant shouting to be heard in St. Paul's Cathedral.

Colin calls the cops.

STICKMAN

Stickman's been on Serena's page for no more than ninety seconds when he spots the major issue. He gets a horrible sick feeling in his gut. He's always thought Billy was a bit of a spud, but yesterday it had impressed him that Billy was far more upset on Serena's behalf than his own. He'd been touched that Billy was full of remorse because of the hurt he'd caused, rather than the flack he was getting from all sides. But this is serious shit.

He goes straight to Fi's desk. She doesn't have an office, it's all one big open plan hangar.

'So, there's a problem with the sexploitation story.'

'What's that?'

'I didn't realise before, but… the girl's underage.'

'So he's a kiddy fiddler as well as an untrustworthy pervert. No problem, we run the story but we don't name her. And we should ring the police for good measure.'

'But my m – her boyfriend could get into serious trouble.'

'Serve the sick bastard right. Look, it's the only decent headline we've got for today. Write it up.'

'But –'

'If you don't, then Seb will.'

BILLY

Billy's cashing up some Porelle Dry socks and a helmet for a middle-aged desk warrior when two coppers come in. They wait politely while the transaction is concluded before one of them asks: 'Am I right in thinking that Billy Watson works here?'

'Err … that's me,' he says.

The older copper pulls out his ID. 'I'm DI Thomas. And this is DI Byers. We're arresting you on suspicion of statutory rape.' He recites Billy's rights. 'We'd like you to come to the station and answer a few questions.'

Billy can't breathe. He's afraid to say anything in case he cries.

'Can I get my stuff together?' he croaks, and gestures at the back room.

'Sure. I'll come with you,' says DI Thomas cheerfully.

Thomas shadows him to the back room, where he keeps his street clothes. They all wear cycling wear in the shop. His hands shake as he pulls his trainers off and yanks his jeans on.

He swallows repeatedly to stop himself from crying. Rape! Oh my fuck. He'd never rape anyone. What is his mum going to say?

He picks up his rucksack and follows the two men out. Mercifully, they haven't cuffed him or anything. Andy and the others are all staring at him as he meekly files out. Andy has a weird expression on his face. He's looking at Billy in disbelief.

They don't talk to him in the car. They chat to each other about electric cars, the game coming up on Saturday, how hard it is to get their kids to do their homework, weird babysitters, dysfunctional in-laws, the new recruits and how useless they are … they're happily chinwagging while his world is imploding. Billy wants to scream that he's never raped anyone in his whole life, not ever, that they should be out there looking for real criminals.

They drive to Shepherd's Bush Police Station. When they arrive, he's led into an interview room. He doesn't know if this is good or bad. He was expecting to be put in a cell. There's a jug of water and some glasses on the table. They don't ask if he wants any, just pour him some and push it towards him.

They tell him they're recording the interview. They inform him of his rights, that he has a right not to answer questions without a solicitor present. That it may harm his defence if he doesn't mention anything during questioning which he later relies on in court. He has the right to call a solicitor, or have a duty solicitor appointed, free of charge.

'I strongly advise you to get yourself a solicitor.'

'But I haven't done anything wrong.'

'Billy, I urge you to at least get a duty solicitor.'

He doesn't want a solicitor. Only guilty people need them. He's done nothing wrong. He's feeling sick. His tear ducts throb and threaten to explode. His whole body is in shutdown. They ask him some routine questions, like his name, his date of birth and address. He squeaks out answers. He comes out in a cold sweat.

'Easy, son. Take a sip of that water,' says Thomas.

Billy obeys. They ask him if he's all right, and he nods.

'On Friday 17th February, did you have sex with a girl named Serena Hawthorne?'

'She's my girlfriend.'

'Did you have sex with her on 17th February?'

'Yeah, I did.' Billy doesn't know what else he can say. There's an iPad on the table. On the screen, Billy sees the opening still of the video. His video, with the arrow, the bed with the skull and cross bones, the mountain poster on the wall … it'd be pointless to deny it.

Oh my fuck, please don't tell me they're going to play it here, he prays. It's bad enough that his piss poor performance has been raked over the coals so publicly. If he has to watch it with these two coppers present, the humiliation will kill him. At least they'll see that he didn't rape her. They'll see that she's kissing and cuddling him afterwards. Who kisses and cuddles a rapist?

'She's your girlfriend, you say.'

'Yeah.'

'How long have you been going out with her?'

'A few months.'

'Do you know when her birthday is?'

'Er, yeah. It's in October.'

'October the what?'

Billy's mind goes blank. He should know. Fuck, he can't remember. They can't bang him up for forgetting a date. 'I – I can't remember. I do know it. I – I'm just – you know. Stressed.'

'It's October 7th. Just FYI. Do you know how old she'll be this coming October?'

Billy's stomach turns over, part with horror, and part with relief. He now sees where they're coming from. Of course he knows exactly how old Serena is, but no one's ever bothered about that, are they? Fucksake, she's his girlfriend. Okay, so she's fifteen, but he's not some old nonce. She'll back him up, won't she? They can't break his balls for having sex with his girlfriend. He sees a neat way out for himself. 'Yeah. Seventeen.'

'Do you follow Serena on her social media accounts? Friends, and whatnot?'

'Yeah, of course,' Fuck! He's a twat. 'Not that I'm online all the time, but –'

DI Thomas gives him a sharp look. 'That's not what I heard.' DI Thomas picks up the iPad and presses a few buttons. He comes up with Serena's page. He scrolls back a few months to her birthday. There are dozens of birthday wishes, several referring to her age.

'Like I said, I don't use it much. I send her private messages.'

'Do you do that a lot?'

Billy goes red. 'What d'you mean?'

'When you send her private messages, do you sometimes send her videos, gifs, stuff like that?'

He shifts in his seat. 'Yeah, sometimes.'

'You're rather fond of videos, aren't you Billy?'

Thomas picks up the iPad again, and calls up the video. 'Does this one mean anything to you?'

'Yeah, it does,' he says. 'I recorded it. It's not against the law, is it?'

'No. There are plenty of people who get their rocks off by making DIY movies. You should see some of the rank filth that people happily post of themselves. That's not against the law. But taking pornographic images of a minor is a very serious offence. We're not only talking unlawful sex with a minor, we're talking child porn here, Billy. Do you know what the penalty is for taking illegal sexual images of children? And then you've compounded it by disseminating that video, which is a separate crime. We're talking three crimes here, Billy. A full trifecta.'

'But she's my girlfriend! I love her! It was our first time, and I just wanted the video for us. You know, for it to be something private between her and me, nobody else.'

'Billy, do you know what'll happen if that video is ever viewed by anyone in the States? They'll fight to extradite you. You could end up serving time in the US of A. Far away from your family and friends. That's how serious kiddie porn is.'

Billy breaks down into pitiful sobbing. 'I never posted that video. I swear to you, I'd never do that. It was one of my mates. He set the camera up. He's a techno geek. I didn't know it, but he was watching us live at the party … I didn't even know 'til Saturday afternoon that he'd done it.'

'But it was posted from your phone.'

'He did it. On my phone. Oh my fuck, if you knew how much grief I'd got from my mum, my Auntie, my Nan… you'd know I'd never in a million years post anything like that.'

DI Thomas leans forward. 'Look here, Billy. I'm going to put you in the cell while I take charge of your phone for a spell, okay?' It's not a request. 'The duty sergeant'll pat you down and keep your stuff safe while you're inside. Give you a cup of tea. Then we'll take a statement from you. Do you want to call anyone? Your mum, for instance?'

Billy's mum is gonna kill him, and no mistake. He doesn't have a choice but to call her. But it's Serena he wants so badly to talk to. If he just had a chance to explain… he needs her to know he'd never post anything that would make her look bad. She's always looked up to him. Made him feel so good about himself. He now sees that the camera's the bottom of the league worst idea he's ever had in his whole life. They've got the video. All they need is Serena's birth certificate. He's well and truly fucked. He'd cheerfully strangle Andy then stomp all over his dead body. Even while the surge of anger takes hold of him, he knows he has no one to blame but himself.

NEVEAH

Normally on Mondays Neveah goes to the pool with Sharna then goes home with her for supper, but not tonight. Probably not ever again. Sharna had tried several times to approach her at school today, but nobody does cold shoulder better than Neveah.

She's filled with a strange emptiness.

She's not surprised to come home to an empty flat. She's picked up some more milk, so she goes into the kitchen to put it away. She puts some bread in the toaster. As she's waiting for it to pop up, she checks out the news on her phone. *The Biscuit* have posted a story about some poor teenage girl who's been filmed having sex. 'The girl, who cannot be named for legal reasons …' That's something, Neveah supposes, that they can't print her name. Neveah feels sorry for her, but seriously, what kind of idiot lets themselves – the intercom buzzes.

'Hello?'

'Name's Kamal. Uber? I picked up a lady from outside here today. Marie Ryan. Number 221. This the right flat?'

'Yeah.'

'She left her phone in my motor.'

'Oh right. I'll be right down.'

She trots down the four flights of stairs, holding her breath as usual. Kamal's easy to spot as it's dark and he has his hazards on.

'You her flatmate?'

'Nah, her daughter. Where did you take her?'

'Dropped her in Marylebone. Dorset Street.'

'Thanks a lot, yeah? She'll appreciate it.'

'Dunno 'bout that. You got some manners, darling. Your mum ain't got none, and that's the truth.'

'Sorry about that.'

'Nah, you're all right. You get all sorts doing this job.'

When she's back in the kitchen, she takes a look at Marie's call history and her texts. No texts to Giles, but there's a call to his mobile, and another call back from it.

So that's what she meant by *thinking of her future*. She'd gone to shake Giles down, the devious, money-grabbing cow.

She calls the club. Mike answers.

'How you doing, darlin'? What's going on with your mum? She sick or something?'

'She not there?'

'She's half an hour late. She hasn't called in, neither. Hope she gets her arse in gear. The place'll be jumping soon.'

Neveah explains about the phone. 'She's probably running round in a panic looking for it. When she gets in, can you get her to call me?'

'No problemo, babes.'

Neveah is seized by a powerful desire to text Giles. She wants to warn him. She casts her mind over her conversation with Marie. Did she actually admit that they'd had sex? She'd been so upset she can't fully remember. There would have to be evidence, surely? She doesn't have any Monica Lewinsky-type items hanging around the back of her closet. Her fingers itch to text him. It's not only because she wants to warn him, it's because she wants to be connected to him. Longs for it. But she stops herself. She wipes away an angry tear. They can't be together anymore. Ever. And she'd better get used to it.

She butters her toast and spreads some marmite on it. She takes a big bite.

Marie's phone buzzes. Neveah doesn't recognise the number. She answers, in case it's her mum, trying to locate her phone.

'Hello?' she says, her mouth full.

'Well fuck me, she finally picks up. I'm just seeing to a dodgy old drain round Coldharbour and thought it's probably not the only bit of pipework needs ramming.'

Neveah chokes on her toast. It's Blue.

MARIE

Marie's been held in Marylebone Police Station. She's distraught. 'You gotta believe me. I don't have a racist bone in my body. My daughter's mixed-race. I was with her father for, like, two years. His mum's like family to me. Some of my best friends are black. Indian too. I don't give a stuff if someone's green or purple so long as they're a decent person.'

'So what possessed you to racially abuse some guy who was just doing his job?'

Marie sniffs. 'I didn't mean it like that, I swear.'

'Seems you're rather fond of swearing. I realise the eff word's two a penny now, but some people find it seriously offensive.'

'I was under a lot of stress. My uber driver had just been, like, seriously abusive to me, then he drove off with my phone, which

I so can't afford to replace, then I came into the building, minding my own business and this guy Terence made such a fuss about me dropping a fag butt, and he just wouldn't leave it alone, even after I apologised and offered to pick it up and everything. He's a big guy and he seriously, like, you know –'

'He what?'

'He intimidated me!' cries Marie. 'He can't go round threatening people like he did ...' her voice peters out.

'In what way did he threaten you?'

'Didn't you see him? He's like, huge. He was like a dog with a bone, and everyone was looking at me, and I was just so embarrassed. I guess I – just lost it. I didn't mean it racially, it's just that Colin guy came in and started throwing his weight around, and everyone was like bowing and scraping before him and... that's why I said what I said. I mean, obviously it was insulting, and I'm, like, sorry for that, I really am, but I didn't mean it to be racist. I swear I didn't. I don't know what else I can say.'

'What were you doing there in the first place? I wouldn't have thought it was your usual hangout.'

'What d'you mean by that?'

'I'm only asking what you were doing there. I mean, you're a club hostess who lives in Brixton, so what were you doing in a corporate office block in Marylebone?'

Marie leans forward, an earnest look on her face. 'Another reason for, like, huge stress. Some middle-aged bloke's been sniffing round my daughter. She's only fifteen.'

'What do you mean by 'sniffing around'?'

'I mean having a full-on affair with her. He works there. I was going to, you know, confront him. You know. To see if it was true.'

'So you don't have any evidence?'

'I have loads of evidence! A mother's intuition, for starters.'

'What's this guy's name?'

Marie has sod all to lose now. 'Giles Hawthorne.' Throwing that wanker under the bus may just soften her own landing.

TUESDAY

ELAINE

It's not yet seven in the morning, but Billy's mum, Elaine, is putting together their packed lunches while she's finishing a bowl of Weetabix. Her cleaning shift at the Chelsea & Westminster Hospital starts at eight, and she has to be out of the house in the next ten minutes. She's exhausted. She'd had to wait for hours at the police station before they released Billy, and the two of them hadn't made it to bed until long after midnight.

Rape. It's her worst nightmare.

The story's already out. A couple of the nurses had been talking about it before she'd left work the day before. She'd wanted to curl up and die. They haven't cottoned on it's her son, but it won't be long before everyone knows. It was bad enough that Billy filmed himself with the girl. Fifteen years old … she'd been with Billy's father at fifteen. Times change, though … what mother of a son hasn't felt a finger of fear in this brave new world? That condemns what only comes naturally? Oh God, her boy needs protecting. From himself, most of all.

Billy's still asleep. She doesn't know if he'll go in to work today, but either way, he'll need his lunch. She'll knock on his door before she goes to tell him.

She hears the letterbox snap open and closed, followed by hurried footsteps. It's too early for the post. Before she even turns into her narrow hallway, the acrid smell of dogshit hits her like a smack in the face.

SERENA

Serena has steeled herself to go to school. She's pulsating like a giant nerve. She'll go in, keep her head down, and hope like hell no one says anything. She has to get it over with sooner or later. She saw the write-up in *The Biscuit*. She hasn't been named, but there were enough people at the party who know exactly who she is. Her social media is on fire. It's all spiralling out of control.

As she's getting dressed, Christine knocks on the door.

'Just warning you, sweetheart. It's hit the papers. Maybe you should stay off school today.'

Serena is faced with another fork in the road. She could stay in. And stay in some more. And staying in makes staying in more attractive. Then she'll never want to go out again. She's in the unique position of seeing first-hand what staying in does to someone.

'No, Mum. I'm going to school.' Her voice catches.

Christine hugs her. 'I'm proud of you, sweetheart.'

NEVEAH

Neveah is getting herself ready for school. She's dog-tired and still steeped in a furious anger. She'd fallen asleep in front of the telly waiting for her mum to come home. She'd woken up freezing with a cricked neck in the middle of the night. Her mum's room had still been empty. The treacherous skank was probably with Blue.

As she's about to gather her things together, she hears the door opening, the clanking of Marie's keys as she drops them on the side table by the door, the swish of fabric as she takes her coat off. The change in the flat's atmosphere is instant.

'Vay! You still here?' she calls. Neveah comes out of her room and gives her mother a baleful stare. Marie's eyes are unnaturally bright. 'Ah, thank God. I was hoping to catch you before you went to school. My phone's been stolen so I couldn't call you –'

'It has not been stolen.'

'It flipping well has been! Why would I lie?'

'Same reason you lie about everything. What were you doing yesterday in Dorset Street? As if I have to ask.'

'What are you talking about? What would I go there for?'

'You went to shake Giles down. You. Are. Despicable.'

'I did no such thing. I –'

'And you're back with Blue. Of all the miserable, low down things you've ever done in your life, this beats it all. Don't you have any loyalty? Self-respect?'

'Don't you speak to me about loyalty. Not after what you did with my boyfriend. And is it self-respecting to throw your cat at married men? Your married man, by the way, is in a tiny spot of bother.'

'What d'you mean?'

'I reported him, didn't I?'

'You didn't.'

'I fucking did. You'll have to go down the cop shop on Marylebone Road. They want to interview you. I'll go with you. You have to be with an adult. And it doesn't matter what you say to defend him. You are fifteen. Which makes him a rapist. End of.'

Is she bluffing? She wouldn't put it past Marie to lay a trap for her. She takes a good hard look at her mother, before she sweeps up her things and reaches for her coat.

'Well? Aren't you going to say anything?'

'There's nothing to say.'

Marie calls after her down the stairwell. 'You're gonna have to talk to them sooner or later, you know. They're gonna be all over him like a rash. And serve him right, the filthy wank –' The door to the outside slams shut, blocking out the rest of her tirade.

ELAINE

Elaine's neighbour, Ed, calls her on her mobile.

'Elaine, I think you'd better come home.'

'What's going on?'

'Your house has been defaced with red paint. I would have stopped them, but there were three of them.' Ed's eighty-three. 'I'm sorry, love. I called the cops.'

'Oh my God! When will it stop? Thanks for telling me, Ed. But I can't come home before my shift ends.'

'There's a disgusting message painted on your front door.'

'What is it?'

'It says *Rapist Scum.*'

SERENA

'Hello darling. Did it go okay?' asks Giles.

'It was fine,' says Serena. She'd had one snide comment: 'You giving away popcorn with the free movies?' and she had the feeling there was some sniggering behind her back. She can live with that. It's the teachers who are seriously bugging her. They're killing her with kindness. Asking her how she's doing, is she okay, does she want to talk, does she need time out? She just wants to be left alone. She dumps her backpack in the hall.

'Where's Mum?'

'Pottering somewhere. There's a letter for you.'

She gets stuff in the post from time to time: birthday cards, postcards, official letters from places like Pony Club and the Duke of Edinburgh Awards, and she gets statements from her child savings account which her parents started for her when she was tiny, but she seldom receives handwritten letters. The writing is uneven, a mix of lower and upper-case letters. It's got to be from Billy.

'Is it from him?'

'Yeah, it is. I'll take it upstairs.'

'I'll put the kettle on. When you're ready, come down for a cup of tea.'

Serena opens the letter in her room.

Dear Serena

I'm a total twat. The video should of been something private and special for you and me. No one else. I swear I didn't post it. You have to believe me. I love you, babe.

Please don't ghost me no more. Please. I need you, babes.

Love from Billy

She slumps on the bed and reads it again. He's right. He's a twat. A semi-literate twat. But he doesn't try to excuse himself or blame anyone. She wonders if he's been interviewed by the police yet. Tears prickle her eyelids. She can't help crying. He has so royally fucked up both their lives.

MARIE

'So I was having a fag outside and I tried to stub it out in one of them wall ashtrays – you know the ones – and a bit of the ash fell on the floor, and then all of a sudden this huge security guy collared me and dragged me inside and, told me off like I was at school, right in front of all these people who were all staring at me, and he was, like, really aggressive and –'

Her phone rings. It's the police.

'You're in luck, Miss Ryan. Terence Ford has decided not to press charges.'

'Oh, thank God.'

'Yeah. He was worried your daughter may be taken into care if you're prosecuted. Do yourself and everyone round you a favour, Marie, and don't shoot your mouth off in future.'

Marie is dying to ask this jumped up little shit if he's getting off on his power trip. Instead, she swallows her bitterness and says, 'Yeah, I will.'

'We need you to bring your daughter in to make a statement about Mr. Hawthorne. Sooner it's done, the sooner we can investigate.'

'Yeah, ok. Thanks for ringing. 'Bye.' She ends the call. 'So, as

I was saying, he was, like seriously aggressive, and I was sooooo humiliated, then next thing I knew...'

NEVEAH

'Livvy, hi. It's Neveah. You know, Jackie's daughter.'

'Gaaaah! Nevaaaaaay! How you doing, sweets?'

'I hope you don't mind me calling –'

''Course I don't. I heard you had, like, a major bust-up with your mum. Your dad said you've nicked his spot at your Granny's,' she cackles. 'Not that I mind, I like him right here where I can keep my beady little eye on him. We was gonna shack up sooner or later anyway. I think he misses her cooking, to be honest, and I'm not much cop at laundry, but I got other talents if you know what I mean. Not only that, I fix a mean cocktail. You should come round. I can do you a mojito or a sea breeze and we can get, like, the most amazing grub from this brilliant Afghan restaurant across the road from me. Abdul, the guy who runs the place, fucking loves me, and he always gives me these free garlic breads, they are so yummy they're like, to die for ... he never does takeaway for anyone else but me, and only 'cos I've been his best customer since forever. Anyway, you never rang to hear me banging on. What's up? You okay?'

'Yeah. I need your help with something.'

'Ooh, my giddy auntie, what is it? Whatever it is, I'm game.'

'I need you to do my nails for me. Can you give me, you know, proper long ones that look like the real deal?'

Livvy laughs. 'Yeah, 'course I can. I'm so chuffed you asked, 'cos I don't mind telling you I noticed you got some seriously fleabitten digits, darling. I don't often see them so bad, but don't you fret, 'cos there's nothing I can't fix. I can do gel for you. I got some real funky colours. I got a purple which is rocking, and I'm digging this peacock green I'm wearing right now, and –'

'I need something old school. Sophisticated.'

'OMG. Look. No. Further. We can do, like, any shade of red, a deep plum, how about aubergine? Maybe oxblood? Seriously, sweets. Come see for yourself. There's, like, no shortage of colours, darling. When were you thinking?'

'Like, now?'

MARCH

GILES

It's been a couple of weeks since Giles was taken in for questioning, and he, Christine and Serena are curdling in the house together like a bad cocktail. Serena won't look him in the eye. She's monosyllabic, evasive, withdrawn. He can't stand it.

When he'd been arrested, the temptation to talk to the cops, to explain his very unique situation had been overwhelming, but he hadn't said a word until Richard Fox had turned up. Thank God he has Foxy on the case, but even so, he's living in a horrible kind of limbo. A process is underway, a relentless, unstoppable process, and there's nothing he can do to influence it or speed it along.

The sound of Serena crying when he'd been arrested still lingers in his ears. Christine's attempts to comfort her had made him feel infinitely worse. Anxiety and uncertainty are taking a terrible toll on all of them. It's like seeing a preview of Christine as an old woman. And it's all his fault. His stupid, blind, libidinous, cock-led, penis-wielding fault.

He can't see a decent way out for any of them. Even if he's not charged, this kind of stain is never completely erased. Christine and Serena have done nothing to deserve it.

And if he goes down for it? It hardly bears thinking about. He doesn't fancy his chances in prison. Not as a middle-class nonce. What in God's name will Christine do? They have some savings, true, and she earns some money from her translations, but if he's banged up, she'll have to get a proper paying job. With her agoraphobia … God, how is she going to cope? She'll have to sell the house. Move to somewhere smaller, cheaper. Just as Serena's about to do her GCSEs. The least of their worries now, he supposes, in the grand scheme of things.

He's astonished how quickly a life can spiral out of control. One day you're a successful, solvent family man merrily swanning around town with a gorgeous young girlfriend, the next you're a broken pariah, who can't provide for your loved ones.

Looking on the bright side … well. It's a struggle.

He knocks on Serena's door.

'Yeah?' she calls.

He opens the door and pops his head round. She's lying on the bed with her headphones in.

'Mind if I come in?'

She sits up and takes her headphones out. She doesn't answer and visibly suffers him entering her room. He sits at the foot of the bed. She curls into herself, shrinking from him as if he's diseased.

'Serena, I want to talk. To explain.'

She sits up. 'What exactly do you want to explain? The cheating on Mum bit? Or the paedophile bit?'

He winces. 'I realise it must seem –'

'Get out of my room.'

'Serena, seriously, we can't carry on –'

'GET OUT OF MY FUCKING ROOM.'

CHRISTINE

From downstairs, Christine hears Serena yell at Giles. A savage burst of satisfaction blooms in her chest but it withers within moments, leaving behind only a sludge of sadness.

SWEETMAN

Laura's cooking dinner and Sweetman's playing Labyrinth with their daughter, Petra, at the kitchen table. Their son is at a play date. Lady Gaga is playing on the radio.

Sweetman's phone rings. The caller's ID is withheld, but he always takes these calls, as they could mean prospective new clients or gigs. 'Hello?' Pause. 'Yeah.' Pause. 'One second,' he says, and leaves the room. Laura looks at him quizzically.

He returns a few minutes later.

'Who was that?'

'The cops.'

'Have you done anything wrong, Daddy?' Petra asks.

'No, my lovely. They just want to ask me some questions.'

'Oh my God! What about?' asks Laura.

'About Neveah. They want me to come in and make a statement.'

Petra's eyes widen. 'Has Vay done something bad?'

'No, sweetheart. They want something cleared up, that's all.'

A song, *Feel (Your Body)*, starts playing on the radio. Petra jumps up. 'I love this song! Mummy, can you turn it up?' Laura whacks the volume up, and the child starts singing along and dancing.

While Petra's distracted, Sweetman murmurs to Laura: 'They want to ask about her and that Giles guy.'

Laura nods significantly. 'Wow. I wonder how they found out.'

'No idea,' he says. 'But the guy is, like –' he pauses. 'I wouldn't want to be in his shoes.'

Her face hardens. 'Serve him right, the – Petra! Stop that!' she yells above the music.

The little girl ignores her, and turns her back on her parents, then throws her head over her shoulder, lowers her chin and arches an eyebrow as she sings: *'I wanna feel (your body), I need to feel (your body), I gotta feel (your body)…'* She has a small knowing smile on her face, and she's swaying her bottom suggestively from side to side.

'Petra! Stop it!' says Laura, and with a wooden spoon still in her hand, she marches over to her daughter, who giggles and runs up to her father, grabbing his hands and pulling him towards her, then she twists away from him and sings – she's word perfect – with her arms in the air, waggling her backside from side to side, then she bends to put her hands on her knees, pushes her bum out and starts twerking like a pro.

Laura looks helplessly at her husband, who is shocked but is trying not to laugh, then back at her daughter. 'You are seven years old, Petra! It's completely inappropriate for you to dance like that, I mean, where did you even learn …'

CHRISTINE

'Fred? How are you? It's Chrissie.'

'Chrissie! Oh my holy Good God, how the devil are you?'

He sounds as if she's been off the planet for decades, but they're in regular contact, either by phone or email.

'Oh, I'm fine, thanks,' she says in a deliberately false, perky voice. 'Yeah, just peachy in fact. For someone who has a husband on bail for statutory rape.'

Silence. 'You're pulling my rather chubby leg.'

'Sadly, I'm not. The last month has been a nightmare. I feel like we're living in a Kafka novel.' She fills him in on the details.

'OMG. I'm literally fumbling for words here. So…' he lets the question hang.

'So what?'

'Are you going to stay with him?'

'I don't know.' She sighs heavily. 'But Fred, that's not the worst of it…' and she tells him about Serena's misadventures.

'Oh God, Chrissie, your gorgeous girl. I'm so very sorry. Is there anything I can do?'

'Yes. There is. You can help me get my job back.'

GILES

'Giles, is that you? Terrible line. Ah, that's better. Sorry to hear about your drama.'

'I wondered if you'd heard.' Giles waits for Bruce to say something like, *I knew you were shagging her,* but he doesn't.

'How are you holding up?'

'Taking it one day at a time. The process is glacially slow, but that's not necessarily all bad. It gives me some time to mend fences with Chrissie and Serena.'

'How are they?'

'As well as can be expected. I'm not exactly flavour of the month, but Chrissie's focused on Serena, as she should be. You heard what happened to her?'

'I did, yes. What a nightmare. And you?'

'I'm okay. It's not certain the CPS will prosecute. Neveah apparently gave a statement fully corroborating mine. She turned up at the cop shop dressed to kill and gave her business cards and her diary entries as evidence that meetings took place during school hours and repeated the line she'd fed me about dropping out of college.'

'Bloody hell. How do you know?'

'She texted me all the details.'

'You're not still …'

'God, no. Apart from that, there's been no contact. I don't expect I'll ever see her again.' He says it flatly, then takes in a breath. 'Listen, Bruce, I'm glad you called, as I have a huge favour to ask.'

'Go on.'

'I'd like you to hire Neveah to help you with your book. The website and Insta and Pinterest and all that whatnot.'

'You're kidding me, right?'

'I'm deadly serious. She's bright. Really bright, and she deserves a chance. Her parents are both deadbeats and she doesn't have the opportunities that our kids do. You could really help her get a foot on the ladder. If she went to uni and got herself some decent contacts, there'd be no stopping her. Obviously, it's not appropriate for me to do anything on her behalf, but you, on the other hand …'

There's a long silence.

'I'll think about it,' says Bruce.

APRIL

ELAINE

Billy's mum, Elaine, is walking home from the bus stop. The clocks have changed, and the light's stretching further every day. Normally, she loves this time of year, the sense that summer's around the corner, sap rising everywhere, even in patches of the pavement, but now she appreciates the light for a different reason: she can keep an eye out for who's coming. Once someone has spat in your face, you never want the experience repeated.

She's a creature of habit. She used to come home from work, kick her shoes off, put her slippers on, make a cuppa and unwind in front of the telly while thinking about what to cook for Billy's tea. Or she'd make herself something easy if he was going out. Beans on toast is a proper feast if you do it right. You just have to have the right mindset. Nowadays, she never knows what horrors she'll come home to. Sometimes there's nothing for days, then as she starts to breathe again, it starts up anew.

The problem with dog shit is there's an endless supply of it. No sooner does she clean it up, or wash off the paint and dismantle the effigies, than some bright spark with nothing better to do comes up with some new way of messing with her head. She feels bad for thinking it, but if they channelled the same kind of dedication and energy into finding a job, they'd conquer the sodding world, she has no doubt about it. Short of putting someone outside her door twenty-four-seven, the cops can't do anything. And even when she's within her own four walls, she gets no peace, wondering what's going to be chucked at the window or slipped through the letterbox. She feels bad for old Ed next door. He's collateral damage, but what can she do?

As for Billy … she's worried sick about him. He hasn't left the house for weeks, not even to go on a bike ride. On a good day, he sits and vegetates in front of the telly. The rest of the time, he doesn't even bother getting out of bed. He's lost his job, and while he should look for another one, realistically, he's in no state to even go to the shops by himself, let alone go through with an interview. Nothing's going to change until the trial's over, and if he's put inside, she may look back on this time when her boy's home as a golden age. It's so unjust. Makes her want to spit. Whatever happened to *innocent until proven guilty*? Her boy's no rapist, of that she's certain. But he's made a terrible mistake. Which he's paying a heavy price for, day after pitiless day.

As she gets closer to home, she sees there's something taped to her front door. Anxiety, now so familiar to her, mounts in her chest. When she's close enough, she reads:

Mum, the doors bolted from the inside. Dont come in. Call the cops. I love you.

Fear seizes her, and she shivers. He's never told her he loves her before. Even as her chest cavity hollows and the blood drains to her feet, it registers dimly that her boy still has no idea what an apostrophe is for. She runs around to the back of the house to break in, fumbling at the same time for her phone.

JULY

SERENA

The glorious summer weather has suddenly changed and the skies have clouded over. Serena breaks out in goose bumps. She'd left the house in blazing sunshine that morning, so hadn't bothered with a jacket. She checks to make sure she's got the right house. She knocks on the door. Her chest flutters. She doesn't know what kind of reception she's going to get.

She's made a detour on her way home from work. She's got a summer job as an office dogsbody in a legal firm for a month before she goes to Spain for a couple of weeks with Georgie and her family. She'll start at sixth form college when the new term begins. She's looking forward to a completely new chapter. Georgie is upset they won't be at the same school, but that can't be helped.

Things are slowly getting back to normal at home. As normal as they can be, considering they've got a huge shadow looming over them.

'How can you stay with him after what he did?' she'd asked her mother in a fury.

'Who says I'm going to?' Christine had retorted, before immediately backing down. 'God, I'm sorry, darling. I don't want to drag you into our mess.'

Sometimes her parents barely speak to each other. Other times, they act as if nothing's happened. It's fucking annoying, and she can't wait for Spain.

Her mum starts her new job in September and has taken fitness to

224

the extremes. She doesn't seem to be able to do anything by halves. Serena's still furious with her dad, but she's stopped giving him the silent treatment. He's been brilliant in lots of ways. He'd wangled the job for her. Had supported her in her college applications when Christine had been so set against her leaving her school. He's helped her through her guilt over Billy. They've talked about it a lot, and it's largely due to him that she's here, standing on the doorstep on a street of ex-council houses in West London, knocking on Billy's mother's door.

There's no sign of life inside the house. She tries again. Nothing.

A wizened old man sticks his head out from the next door property. He glares at her, giving him the look of a suspicious tortoise. 'What are you after?' he growls.

'I've come to see Elaine Watson.'

'She doesn't deserve to be pestered. She works night and day in that hospital. Where would we be without people like her, that's what I want to know, and you come here –'

'I really need to see her.' Serena interrupts. 'Do you know when she'll be back?'

The old man gives her a searching look and realisation dawns. 'She'll be home in a while. You can come in for a cup of tea, if you like.'

NEVEAH

Neveah takes a selfie of her and Hugo next to the Wall Street sign and sends it to Sharna.

She and Sharna have made up. She and Marie have not.

She's in New York for the summer holidays, staying with Bruce and Hugo in their fabulous Upper East Side apartment. She's building their website and working on their social media account. The book isn't out yet, but they want all their ducks in a row well in advance of the launch. She's working hard but has plenty of time during the day to go sightseeing or hang out with Hugo while Bruce is at work. Hugo's free for the summer before he starts at Duke University.

In the evenings, when they don't eat out, Bruce and Hugo take it in turns to cook, and it's her job to make the salad. They rib her constantly, especially about her very conservative tastes, but perhaps because of the drastic change in environment, she has become more adventurous with food. She has strayed from the safety of iceberg lettuce and become a demon at making salad dressings. She's even started to have a small glass of wine with dinner.

She loves this city. She's been here for two weeks and has the rest of the summer before she has to go back to school. Next week, they're decamping to the house in the Hamptons, as it'll be too hot to stay in town. Already, the pavement sticks to her flip flops when she goes out to the grocery store or to Bruce's club. Bruce has got her a temporary membership. She loves the outdoor rooftop pool.

She had been beyond gobsmacked when Bruce called to offer her the job.

'I can't take it,' she'd said in a flat tone. 'You'll find this hard to believe, but –'

'Don't worry, I know. You're still at school. You're fifteen years old. Sixteen in May. Is that right?'

'Yeah,' she'd croaked.

'Giles suggested I go ahead and hire you regardless. He said you're a worker bee, that it'll be a win-win all round. You'll get to broaden your horizons, and we'll have someone dedicated to the book and the website.'

Her eyes had smarted that Giles would do that for her, after the shitstorm she'd shoved him into. 'How is he?'

'Oh, you know. Hanging in there. I hear you gave quite the statement at the cop shop,' he'd laughed. 'So ... do you need some time to think about it? Look, if you're worried about hanging out with two blokes ... I'm at work all day, and Hugo's a seriously nice kid ... I know he's my son, so I'm biased, but he'd love another youngster to hang out with for the summer. He's fresh out of boarding school and doesn't know anyone in New York. He's shy, a bit –'

'What?'

'Well, a little socially awkward. You'd be great company for him.'

'I'll do it.'

'Brilliant. You got a passport?'

'No. I've never even been out of the country.' It was an amazing feeling not having to lie.

'You get yourself sorted then. Do it soon so I can organise your flights. And you'll need parental permission to travel alone, I'd imagine.'

'My dad will do it.'

'Great.'

A few weeks after she'd moved in with Granny South, she got a call from Granny North.

'Your mother and that fella Blue have split. I had a feeling about it,' Granny had said, as if she had special powers of clairvoyance. 'I can't say I'm crying about it. How she chooses 'em ... mind you, I wasn't much better, but she's gone from bad to worse. Your father ...' Neveah rolls her eyes, waiting for a derogatory remark about his womanising, his lack of a steady job, his skin colour ... 'was never a nasty, evil little gobshite. Not like that Blue. Soon as I clapped eyes on him I thought 'uh-oh.' Do you know he's only gone and done the dirty on her with some piece she works with in that club.'

'Peaches?'

'Tha's the one. Anyways, he should never ha' come between the two of youse. But, darling, you can go back home now. You should, you know. A girl needs her mother.'

Not that kind of mother, she'd wanted to shout. She'd resisted the temptation to spell out exactly how badly Marie had let her down.

'What kind of life can it be for a young girl to be livin' wit' *her*,' Granny had said, meaning Granny South. 'One foot in the grave ... she shouldn't be buying green bananas, so she shouldn't.'

Neveah had laughed. Granny North was a good ten years the senior. 'It's fine, Gran. She'll outlive us all.'

'Why not stop here for a spell?'

'It's too far from school,' she'd said, diplomatically.

'Aye, true enough. But promise me you'll be going back to your mother. Soon as you come back from America. She needs you, darlin' so she does.'

Neveah is only beginning to understand that the bond she has with Marie isn't one she'll ever be free of. But whenever she's tempted to weaken, she forces herself to remember how low she ranks in her mother's priorities, how little regard Marie has for her, how willing she is to elevate scumbags like Blue over her own child.

How can she explain this to Marie's own mother? She's not nasty enough to spell out exactly what Marie has done. Her Granny's old. Real old, and that kind of knowledge would poison whatever time she has left.

SERENA

Serena's sitting in Elaine's kitchen. The kettle's boiling. She's already had a cup of tea at Ed's, and she really needs a wee, but it seems rude to ask for the loo when she's only just got there.

Billy's been dead three months. There had been a small write-up in most of the papers, but a big splash in the *Mirror* and on *The Biscuit*. They'd shown a picture of Elaine at Billy's funeral. *'He didn't deserve to die. My boy made a terrible mistake, and he couldn't live with it. He was sorry enough to kill himself. Isn't that enough?'*

Yes, it was enough. Enough for Serena.

Billy's death and the picture of Elaine has haunted Serena ever since she set eyes on it. Gaunt, haggard, hounded ... losing her only child to suicide ... spending the rest of her life burdened by dark thoughts about the son she'd loved so much. Serena couldn't bear the thought. So here she is.

'I want to show you something,' says Serena, picking up her phone. 'I don't know if you ever watched the video. I really hope you didn't. But look at this. You don't have to see the nasty bit. Just this.'

Elaine sits down heavily, and Serena shows her the footage of her hugging Billy, kissing his temple. 'Whoever posted the video cut it off before this bit was shown. Billy loved me. I know that. I really want you to know it too.'

Elaine stares at the video and replays it. Her eyes fill with tears. She grips Serena's hand and sobs. 'Oh, my Billy,' she says. 'Thank you, sweetheart. You don't know what this means to me. Can you forward it to me? It'll mean the world to my mum and my sister.'

Serena's flustered. She'd wanted to comfort Billy's grieving mum and hadn't considered this would be anything other than a private revelation between them. But she reminds herself that she's alive and Billy's dead. He wasn't bad, only stupid. No more stupid than she was. His mother does not deserve to spend the rest of her days in a living hell.

'Yeah,' says Serena. ''Course I will. You show it to whoever you need to.'

NEVEAH

Neveah's stuffed to the gills with Bruce's delicious lasagne which he made from scratch, and it's her turn to stack the dishwasher, while Bruce and Hugo are clearing the table for a game of gin rummy. Her phone rings. It's Sharna.

'Okay, sister, so kill me. Tell me 'bout the cool places you been and the hip folks you been doin' while I been stuck with a bunch of retard kids and their seriously caffeine addicted parents.' Sharna has a holiday job in the café at a giant indoor soft play facility in West London.

Neveah laughs. 'So today was rough. Like, seriously hard. We had scrambled eggs on toast on the balcony, then I went to the pool with Hugo, then this afternoon he took me to the Met, then we went for ice cream in Central Park ... I'm suffering, babe. It's, like, torture.'

'Bitch.'

'This place is like... hot. Boiling. You know, Sharn, my shoes stick to the pavement when I go out.'

'Well boo hoo. I'm just crying into my coffee for you.' Sharna's voice drops to a whisper. 'So tell me. Has Hugo ... you know? Has he ...'

'Has he what?'

'You know … has he made a move yet?'

Neveah laughs. 'Nah, you numpty. He's like –' she's about to say 'like family', but she stops herself, knowing Sharn will take the piss.

'Oh, come on. Cute little white boy… Wassa matter with him? He gay or something?'

Neveah clamps her phone to her ear while she finishes stacking the plates and glances over at Hugo and Bruce who are laughing at something while they wait for her to join them at the table, and she wonders at her friend, she really does. How long has Sharna known her? She loves Hugo. Okay, so she's only known him for a few weeks, but they've been together day after day during that time, and the very nature of the project they're engaged in means they're connected on a deeply personal level. Ever since she's arrived, he's welcomed her like a sister.

But Sharna's way off base, as per usual.

'No way's he gay,' she whispers. 'But he ain't the one for me.'

She steals a moment to stare at Bruce, who's horsing around with Hugo. He's whipped his tie off and has his shirtsleeves rolled up.

He is so gorgeous.

'I gotta go. I'll call you tomorrow, yeah?' she says to Sharna.

She presses the button on the dishwasher and firmly closes the door, listening out for the click and the trickle of water that tells her the cycle's begun, then she struts to the table.

'You two bitches ready to lose your shirts?' she says.

'Fighting talk,' says Bruce. He narrows his eyes Clint Eastwood style while he shuffles the cards, a menacing smirk playing round his lips. 'Time to separate the men from the boys.'

And once again, Neveah has to stop herself from leaning down to kiss him.

ACKNOWLEDGEMENTS

To the girl on the bus: I don't know anything about you, but your glorious poise and self-possession provided the spark for this story. To David Llewellyn, to Justine Solomons and her team at Byte the Book, to the Chippy Theatre writers and to the Collier Street Fiction Group: huge thanks to you all, especially Bruno Noble, whose writing career weirdly mirrors my own. A big thanks to Jodie Evans, for her very thorough early editing. I also owe thanks to Damien Mosley at Indie Novella. Special thanks to Stephanie Francis and Charlotte Murphy, who provided such sensitive feedback on highly emotive topics. I'm very grateful to you both. I'm also grateful to Gregg Dawe for being so generous with his advice, based on his vast inside knowledge of modern policing. Any errors are entirely my own.

To Jurcell and Rachelle Virginia, for making the process of writing and producing books so much fun. To Thea Toocheck, who has transformed Inkspot Publishing from a tiny crackpot idea existing in my own head to a small but serious thing of beauty. To the supremely talented Sarah Bowers, who has voiced the audio book to an incredibly high standard, giving each character their own distinctive voice.

Special thanks to Miles Poynton and Matt Haslum, who have both been so generous with their advice and time.

To the Inkspot authors: Lela Burbridge, Rita Carter, Mus Coombes, Annie Dawid, Sarah Hutchinson Jarman, Hideo Muramatsu, Bruno Noble, Richard Vaughan Davies and Jurcell Virginia, who have all made my transition into publishing so worthwhile. May your books sell in the gazillions.

Mum, you're great. I don't know why the mothers in my books are always so ghastly. Kitty, Ollie, Helena and Romilly: for the constant entertainment and never-ending supply of new ideas. Last but not least: my lovely Ricardo. No matter how many dragons he has to slay, he's always happy to give me a hand in dispatching mine.